# GHOSTDANCER

Ben Zeller

Strategic Book Publishing and Rights Co.

Strategic Book Publishing and Rights Co.
12620 FM 1960, Suite A4-507
Houston, TX 77065
www.sbpra.com

ISBN: 978-1-62516-559-6

Book Design: Suzanne Kelly

*Ghostdancer is dedicated to:*

Tom Cade Ph.D.
Founding Chairman and Director
The Peregrine Fund
Conserving Birds of Prey Worldwide.
www.peregrinefund.org

The author also wishes to thank:

Wendy Gray, who edited the first drafts
of the novel, *Ghostdancer.*

Bonny Arnold, associate producer of *Dances With Wolves*
and Producer of many other films.
Bonnie read the screenplay version of *Ghostdancer.*
and encouraged me to build on it.

Above all, I wish to thank my wife, Ev,
who listens to my endless story telling
without complaint.
Ev mixes a damn fine martini!

And here's to Old Taylor, an ultimate inspiration.

# CHAPTER ONE

# "The Dream"

The year is 1969
The dream is 1905

In the late sixties Jack Parnell Mackenzie, a dropout from medical school, a would-be cowboy fulfilling a childhood dream, arrived in Rainbow, New Mexico. His pot of gold turned out to be rich in dreams only, negative dreams, streaming a fear of flying . . . not on dope. Other than booze, dope bored him. These were the sixties. He'd done enough peyote, refined LSD, pot and poppy seeds to know it didn't work with him. Nor was his nightmare fear of a plane malfunctioning in flight; crash-landing in no man's land. Jack Parnell had no destination. Rainbow, a ranching community, filled his childhood fantasies. He was comfortable here, or had been, until this terror crept into his sleep—into his dreams—dark dreams, in empty colorless space – in no man's land. In sleep, something propelled him; clutched him, forced him through a blackened atmosphere; swung him high, then swept him close to earth, through trees and brush at tremendous speed. Pushed him into gray light and shadows—through feathers of silent mist, and always toward a blur of orange burning through the haze.

Flames rose in the stillness. Violin strings screamed in silence, sweeping him into a sea of fire. Everything went out of focus as he tumbled, helpless, in the blinding heat to explode with flying timbers and shards of blasted glass beyond. There, still blistering, still in the heat, he stopped—was stopped—suspended.

On the steaming earth beneath, a scorched man writhed in agony, a bearded image of himself.

The man on the ground, like Parnell, was in his mid thirties, sporting a somewhat singed, but trim Van Dike. The man's clothes, smoldering and torn, were a snappy nineteen hundred's cut: sports coat, vest, polished, square-toed boots and tapered pinstriped trousers. His vest and jacket were ripped across the right shoulder blade where blood oozed freely from a deep cut wound. Jack Parnell stared in wonder. He knew this man.

Rolling on his back, the man glared up at Parnell. The dreamer watched him kick backwards away from the heat. Scrambling to a half crouch he raced to escape the image hovering above him. He stumbled toward a barn and corrals, where a horse drawn buggy stood.

Parnell, again in flight, was sucked helplessly toward the retreating figure—. Metamorphosed—he became one with him—and as one now, they ran wildly from the flames toward the horse-drawn rig in the open barn door.

A lantern hung, bright, beneath the hayloft. A scythe leaned against the wall. A wooden man-drawn hay rake and horse-drawn plow made the place a museum in Parnell's dreaming mind; a picture blazing from the turning century; a farm scene flashing from a sepia photograph snapped years before the Great Depression.

The burning house behind them, roared in orange heat, lighting it all grotesquely—frighteningly absurd.

In his dream—in his new person—a sheet of blazing refuse flew past Parnell Mackenzie. It landed in loose hay. New birth— new fire. New flames raced with rapid fingers across the barn floor, flashed up a cobwebbed ladder to lick around the oil-bright base of the lantern.

The fiddle music screamed. With it, Parnell heard the frenzied whinny of a trapped mare thrashing wildly in her heavy, plank-framed box stall. Parnell groped through the heat. He grabbed a saddle slung across the top rail of the stall, and a bridle hanging from a hammered spike. He hurled the leather tack from the enflamed barn. They floated, lazy, butterflies in flame, through the torpid roiling atmosphere. The air, thick with heat and swirling smoke, bled Parnell's exhausted body of speed and purpose.

He skinned off the torn jacket to cover the eyes of the terrified mare. He threw a cotton rope about her neck. Blinded, he brought the animal from her stall to lead her from the barn. With a roar the lantern shattered in the heat. Dust-dry hay in the loft exploded. Rearing, shaking free of Parnell's jacket, the mare lunged. For a moment Jack Parnell hung on, his fear reflected in her eyes. Blood from the shoulder wound streamed down Parnell's chest.

Breaking free, the mare wheeled back into her stall of death by living flame. Giving up, Parnell plunged through the raging fire toward safety and the open door.

* * *

1969

In the town of Rainbow, New Mexico, a plastic clock radio on a bureau in front of a cracked mirror read 1:40 AM. A black and white TV filled the cheap hotel room with gray-blue flickering shadows. An open bottle of Old Crow was reflected in the light. There was no glass beside it. Parnell's roughly handsome clean-shaven face, bathed in perspiration, expressed stark fear. In his dream-sleep he twisted beneath thin blankets. Kate, lying beside him, had been awake some time. She watched, not daring to disturb his tortured body. Fearfully she rolled from the bed and stood back. She flicked on the bare light bulb screwed into a porcelain fixture on the wall.

Kate, in her early thirties, was a lively looking lady with a slightly battered past. She had brought Parnell home to his hotel apartment from Lake Nine, where she tended bar two nights a week. Five days she worked breakfast and the noon shift at Delmonico's Restaurant across the Colorado border. Her body, trim and hard,—she hadn't had the time to let it get sloppy,—she stood naked in the sudden white light. The barely discernable

3

stretch marks from the birth of her two children, the boy, sixteen, living and working on a ranch during the summer months, the girl five, spending nights with Kate's mother when Kate worked the bar, were barely visible. There would be no more children. She'd had her tubes tied when the youngest was born. The fathers of both her children were losers and long gone. This man, thrashing in the sweat-soaked blanket, was a loser, too, she guessed. Rainbow, the little New Mexico town she lived in, a town she should have left years ago, was a holding pen for losers. *Some knight in shinning armor, this one.* She shook her head and threw up her arms in hopeless surrender.

Kate was pretty … at least some people thought so. She had her doubts, but tried to put them down.

Rainbow was situated on the edge of a fantastic range of mountains riddled by failed coalmines and long dry oil wells. An old opera house, built at the turn of the century, featured the high school play and an occasional touring production. To the east, the town faced millions of acres of parched farms and mediocre cattle country. Weathered ranchers, their wives, cowboys and unemployed miners made up Rainbow's dwindling population. Kate's choices hadn't been great and she had been too young. Like most of Rainbow's unmarried mothers, Kate first got pregnant in high school. Not sure who the father was, she had married no one. The baby crushed Kate's plans for college. She took a job as a waitress in a fast food truck stop on I - 25 and worked her way up to manager by the time she was nineteen. She married a truck driver who gave her the second child. When his rig jackknifed on an icebound road in upstate New York, he was killed. He never saw his daughter. Kate put the meager life insurance payoff in a savings account, which she hoped would pull her son and daughter through college. She added to it when she could. Following that tragic episode in her life she had abstained from sex entirely. It had been a long dry spell. There was no one—until Parnell.

Kate developed a sharp sense of humor to cope with the difficult life she'd been forced to live—was still living. She looked down at the terrified man twisting in his tortured sleep, if sleep it could be called. Was this man to be the next joke played on her life?

* * *

Parnell, more of a rodeo cowboy than a real one, had drifted into Rainbow New Mexico, six months earlier. He had met Kate at Delmonico's, where she served him a plate of hot chili and over-easy eggs on two corn tortillas. He ordered a beer but they didn't serve beer. He drank three cups of black coffee and worked his way slowly through two slices of apple pie a-la homemade ice cream. By that time the breakfast crowd had thinned down to no one but him.

The man left with Kate was good looking in a worn way. He had been in the sun, but when he took his hat off, which he did when he sat down (an unknown act in these parts), he didn't have that white Stetson sun-blocked line across his forehead like all the local cowmen. He definitely was not a local. *Maybe this one is a live one,* she thought.

"I been down in old Mexico," he said. Other than ordering enough food to fill a mineshaft that was Parnell's opening line to Kate. "Practicing my roping there. I'm a fair roper, but those vaqueros are geniuses. They can roll a loop along the top log of a corral and drop it over a wild steer's horns at sixty feet. Hell, in this country we only have forty-foot ropes," he said. He tipped back his third cup of black coffee and drained it.

"We got some good ropers here," Kate said and filled his cup for the forth time. She wasn't eager to see him leave. That surprised her.

"You work cattle?" he asked. "Some women are very good at it."

"I can sit a horse, but I'm no roper," she said. "I do better punching eggs and coffee. There's no money in punching cows—cowgirling." She turned on a winning smile and added with a laugh, "or cowboying."

"You can say that again." He sipped the hot black coffee. "You live here?" He asked the question quietly, looking out the cracked and duck taped plate glass window into the empty street.

"You kidding?" Kate sat on the edge of the low counter a few feet across from him. "Would I live in a half horse town like this? I come from the big city of Rainbow, New Mexico." He grinned, and nodded as if he knew it well. "You been there?" she said.

"Passed through it," he said, distracted, his eyes still searching the empty street. "Got a strange feeling I should go back there and settle for a spell." He grinned and looked straight at her. "Is it a dangerous town?"

His smile was contagious. "Hardly," she said and laughed. She shook her head and let the flood of rich auburn hair, tied up in a knot until now, fall about her shoulders. *Was she flirting?* She hadn't flirted with anyone in a long time. It was kind of fun. "There is no crock of gold in Rainbow, Cowboy. You'll just find the crock."

"I don't know about Rainbow, but you have lovely hair," he said.

"My Irish heritage," she said. At the compliment, she felt the blood rise and turned away. *I haven't blushed in years,* she thought. "My grandfather came across the water to mine coal. It was a mistake." She busied herself behind the counter. Thankfully, he changed the subject.

"I think it's a dangerous town," he said. "I nearly got lost in the tangle of streets in that metropolis. And almost run down by the Rainbow school bus." Kate looked up. His grin was genuine. Kate liked him. He certainly was a fresh face. Rainbow needed a fresh face. Not that he would turn around and go back, let alone stay there.

"In Rainbow you can get kicked in the head by a wild horse," she said, "or a mule." Kate found herself smiling openly for the first time in weeks. "What will you do there, Cowboy? Buy a ranch?"

"Maybe work on one. I drove round and round in that town before crossing the state border and finding my reason to go back. Now I'm sure my intuition was right."

"You're taking a big chance …"

"Your name's Kate. I can see that by the sign you got pinned on you. I'm Parnell Mackenzie. Jack Parnell Mackenzie." He grinned sheepishly. "Rainbow? Right, Kate?"

"Yeah, right." She rolled her eyes up to the ceiling then back to him. "The name's a bit contrary, but that's the town I come from."

"If the clouds build up to wet, and the sun shines," he said, "I'm looking forward to meeting you again … at the end of the rainbow."

"You're a dreamer," Kate laughed. "And, I think you got a bit of the blarney in you, as well."

"You have, too, Kate. And I think you're a beautiful dreamer." He said it quietly. "See you around." He dropped a twenty on the counter and headed for the door.

"You can't buy me," she called after him.

"I don't plan to," he said and stepped out onto the street.

Before she made change and pocketed the lavish tip she moved around the counter and followed him with her eyes. Parnell walked up the street and got into an old Chevy half-ton pickup with tarps tied down over his gear stacked in the back. He was towing a one-horse trailer. *So he has a horse,* she thought. Parnell pulled a U-turn, and tipped his hat as he passed Delmonico's.

Parnell Mackenzie was on his way back to Rainbow. Kate had stepped out of sight but she knew he knew she was watching.

\* \* \*

That was six months ago. Now the same happy-go-lucky rhinestone cowboy was in a fever of sleeping madness. It was as if the town of Rainbow had claimed his soul. It couldn't be her that disturbed his sleeping hours. She wasn't responsible for his dreams. In Rainbow they had seen each other often. It was nice. Kate really liked him. It seemed inevitable they would become lovers. They had been sleeping together now for over three months. Both Kate's son and daughter liked Parnell. But lately,

7

something strange and disquieting had twisted his thinking. He was no longer the free, loving man she had met in Delmonico's. The town of Rainbow, or the surrealistic countryside that surrounded it, had sparked a cancer in him. He had cow-boyed on a number of ranches helping with roundups, calving and the branding. He was good with a rope, the braided rawhide rope he brought back from Mexico. He was never short of cash. He had some kind of a monthly check that came through the mail to general delivery. Kate never questioned him about it. It was none of her business. No one questioned him—except—Kate had fallen in love with him ... She had fallen in love with the man she had met in Delmonico's. But now, who was this enigma screaming silently in his sleep, wrapped in a sweat in the bed beside her? *Who was Jack Parnell Mackenzie? And what was tormenting him?*

Kate's face was damp with the summer heat of the room, and with the fear building in her heart. She looked down at the tortured Parnell. Over the past two or three weeks the dreamer had awakened her in this state a number of times. Each awakening was worse. Without disturbing him, Kate reached for a large paper fan. She moved it back and forth above his face, stirring the hot still air over him. Beneath the sweeping fan, the nightmare went on.

\* \* \*

Something unreal moved in the flames of his dream; a bird in flight, or a dancer in vaporous costume; her arms, like feathered wings, sensuously fanning the heat with growing intensity; a female creature of prey, hovering, searching for just that—her prey. The flaming wings beat a hypnotizing rhythm as they drew closer.

Parnell snapped to a sitting position in the bed. He struck wildly at the fan, knocking Kate to the floor. His eyes flashed white and wild. A sudden hot breath of air billowed the cheap lace curtains into the room. Parnell raced for the open window, tearing at the old lace drapes. Gulping air he leaned out into the night. Kate struggled to her feet. Afraid he would fall she made a grab for him, and wrapped her arms about his trim naked waist.

"I'm sorry, Parnell," she cried. "You'll fall. You're dreaming again."

Parnell, his face drained of color, stopped struggling. He stared into the star-filled New Mexico sky. "Kate?" Reality was coming back to him. "I'm sorry too, Kate." He tried to shake the unknown images from his mind. "I don't know where the hell I was. He pulled back in the window and faced the woman trying to help him. He shook his head in dismay, "What the hell is the matter with me?" He surveyed the room. Kate dropped to her knees to gather the torn curtains. "What the hell did I do, Kate?" Parnell staggered to the bed and picked up the whisky bottle. "What the hell was I dreaming? Did I drink too much of this?" He took a healthy slug and swished it around in his mouth before swallowing. "I didn't wake up until I was half out the window, Kate. You grabbed me or I might have kept flying." He stared at the bottle in his hand and considered another drink. "I was flying?" He took the drink.

Kate dropped the torn curtains on a chair and sat beside him, waiting to hear more if he wished to tell her more. Their naked thighs pressed together. She put a hand on the bright jagged birthmark on his right shoulder. "Flying, Parnell? Kept flying? … What kind of dreams have you been having Parnell. They scare the shit out of me, and they are not even my dreams."

"I wish I knew." He considered the whisky level in the bottle and decided against another drink. He found the cap on the bed table and screwed it back in place thoughtfully. "Maybe they have something to do with what's in this bottle," he said.

Kate gave him a sidelong look. "It was you that said it Mister Mackenzie. Not me."

Parnell smiled at her. She looked away, a grin on her face. One of the things he admired about Kate was the fact that she was never judgmental. She never criticized. *She would make a fantastic wife for some good man*, he thought. Parnell never let himself consider marriage. He considered himself a responsible person, and as such, marriage was out of the question. The bonds of that responsibility terrified him. An affair was as far as he would let it go. He enjoyed affairs. He was beginning to depend on this one. That was scary. Parnell looked down at his hands. They were no longer trembling and his breathing was back to normal. "I'm supposed to be at Sully's at dawn to help with the branding. I need to get some sleep. But I'm afraid to." He lay back on the damp blankets and stretched full length across the old double bed.

I can think of things to do that will give us both sweeter dreams than alcohol," Kate said softly.

"If I'm an alcoholic, Kate, at least I'm a functioning alcoholic."

Kate looked down at the man she was, despite his madness, falling in love with ... had fallen in love with ... was in love with. "At least you function, Parnell. She turned toward him and lifted her knee over his shins. Leaning back, her butt cradled against his feet, she ran her firm hands and fingers up his hard thighs. Parnell felt himself stir to life. "At least you function," she repeated.

Kate's long hair brushed up his legs and across the taut muscles of his belly. If this was a dream, it was beautiful and would be one to remember. He let himself flow with it. When he awoke before dawn, his mind was free and clear. He was himself again and glad to be there. He covered Kate with the thin blanket, kissed her softly and slipped out the door. She opened one eye to watch him go, and smiled to herself. She didn't know how long it would last, but she would hang on to it as long as she could. Other than her children, and an almost forgotten dead truck driver, Parnell was better than anything she had ever had.

\* \* \*

CHAPTER TWO

# The Falcon

The white hot morning sun cut Tinaja's volcanic plug with a razor's edge, forcing the morning's chill down onto the mesas below and into the deep surrounding canyons. The day held its breath. No sound. No movement. Dry wisps of last years grass sheltered the new green pushing up through it, sucking desperately at the light dew forming in the change of temperature. The fiery edge of the sun, cresting the ancient, long dead volcano to the east, burned life into the day; drove the sharp point of new moon into the Sangre de Cristo range of the Rocky Mountain peaks to the west.

In the stillness on Tinaja's flat rim-rock peak the peregrine falcon eyed her vast hunting grounds. Gracefully she extended her four-foot wingspan and with a piercing cry of warning, dropped off the pinnacle. The cool down draft carried her steeply into the shadows. In flight the dry music of the wind husked through the bird's feathers. Beneath her the topography was painted in incongruous images. Colors of gold, subdued red and washed out yellows in varying intensities blurred in the speed of her flight. Mesas jutted out of the primal earth, their upper planes cut flat as wood smoke of a freezing morning. Tinaja's peak had defied the continuing blasts of nature. Being born of fire and thrust into the atmosphere with Nature's full violence, Tinaja refused to give way. She cooled; she crystallized and plugged the flow of molten lava for eternity—perhaps.

Her feathers singing, the falcon cut through canyons. She cruised just above the flat, cactus-studded surface of a giant mesa and over the rim where the land dropped in a clean hundred foot cut to the wide valley below. Pinion trees, crouched at the base of the rim rock, gave way to an open meadow browned by lack of rain and the unrelenting sun. In the center of the valley, a dusty ranch road led from a narrow cut at the south end and twisted up through rocks and trees on the west perimeter. Midway through the valley the road split. The east fork led to the Sullivan ranch headquarters, a ramshackle collection of gray weathered corrals and outbuildings. A rambling adobe stood a hundred yards to the north. Farm machinery, junked cars and battered pickups were scattered about a muddy, dust rimmed stock pond centered in the dry meadow.

Beneath the falcon's flight path and the cutting swath of sunlight, the old corrals were filled with action; rolling dust, smoke, men, horses and bellowing cattle. Unseen, the falcon dipped her tail feathers, threw her chest forward and braked with her mighty wings to light on the canyon's rim. She studied the scene below; her eyes iced diamonds of clarity.

A mile to the south, out of the steep narrow cut leading into the meadow, an unlikely vehicle shrouded in a moving cloud of dust pushed into view. The aged touring bus, towing a twenty-four foot box trailer, crept into the valley at a slow pace. The bus needed a paint job as well as a good overhaul. The dull chipped logo on the side read:

**CATHERINE REXWROTH'S ACTORS ENSEMBLE**
"WE PLAY THE WORLD"

Inside the vehicle an assortment of bored actors lived with the fact that they must have taken the wrong turn, if not in life, at least in this bus. Some were asleep, or trying to get some troubled rest. With one exception, those awake could care less about the surrounding countryside. The exception was Catherine, the fiery leader of this band of itinerant actors. Her attention riveted on the world surrounding her, The Cat, as she was known by those who worked with her, stood in the open door well clutching the warn brass handrail. The wild landscape intrigued her. It was breath taking.

Toad, Catherine's squat begrudging stage manager, in a state of agitation, hunched over the wheel. Turning at the fork in the road, he jammed the bus into a lower gear to start up the steep rise out of the valley. The sudden motion jerked Catherine almost out the door. The bus stalled. Without looking to the lady, Toad grumped: "You got us on the wrong road, Cat."

Catherine, back in balance and concentrating on the view, was unconcerned by the accusation. "I know, Toad. It was a lucky turn." Toad rolled his large bloodshot eyes and set the brake for what it was worth. He knew there was plenty of gas. He hit the starter and prayed. The motor coughed into life.

"This thing needs an overhaul, Cat," Toad groused.

Catherine paid no attention to him. Toad was an indispensable part of her company and needed to be humored at times, but not now. In her standard dress: white shirt, faded jeans and tennis shoes, she got a new grip on the old brass rail. Close to forty, she didn't look it. Catherine had the lithe build of a dancer: an athlete. "Look at that rim rock, Toad," she cried. "It's a beautiful face. I'd love to climb it. It's not as challenging as the Alps, or the Rockies, but it would be a great workout. I'd love it."

"It's grotesque." Toad had the bus moving again, but wouldn't get out of low gear until they reached the crest.

"Look at the corrals, Toad," she cried, "and the ranch buildings. I think they're branding."

"I've been driving all night. It is too early right now to be doing anything, let alone burning cows."

Cat wasn't listening. Her attention was directed to the ranch buildings and the activity surrounding them: horses, cattle, smoke and dust billowing up. It all looked strangely familiar. Deja vu? A troubling thought. She dismissed it. "It's fascinating, Toad. The views, the action, it's unreal. It's beautiful." She leaned further out of the slow moving bus to get a better look.

From the heights above, with a killing shriek meant to paralyze her prey, the peregrine falcon swooped down, accelerating over a hundred miles per hour. In a blur of feathers, she stooped to within inches of Catherine hanging from the open door. The lady ducked back with a start. The bus stalled to a jerking stop.

Recovering quickly from the shock, Catherine leaned forward in awe, watching the graceful bird as it soared vertically into the blue. "Unbelievable," she whispered. "Bloody unbelievable. It's a peregrine, Toad. The breed is vanishing, I understand." Her eyes followed the bird, circling above them in the sky. It looked the size of a sparrow now, but maintained, still, the grace of a conquering queen. Toad stepped on the brake and threw his hands in the air.

"What next Catherine? What next, dear lady?" he croaked. But Catherine's eyes were on the falcon in the sky.

Toad turned the key and pressed the engine back into choking action.

\* \* \*

In the Sullivan's corrals, Parnell was mounted on his mare, Diana, among the calves and mother cows milling in the riled dust. He spun his braided leather lariat, building a small loop. It shot out like a snake. The stiff loop's upper edge hit the raised hind leg of a fleeing calf. The lower curve of leather swung up and around the animal's hoof. Parnell jerked the line tight. "Heeled", the calf dropped in the dust. Parnell smiled to himself with the accomplishment. He was good. He was goddamned good. He knew it, and he knew he was sitting a great roping horse. His mare settled and dragged the bawling animal to the branding fire. Sully and his older brother released the preceding calf, a steer now, castrated, inoculated and marked with Sully's brand, a double XX. Sully set Parnell's rope free and lashed the new calf's front and back legs together with the "pigging" rope. His older brother, Tom, sat on the calf's front quarters to keep it from kicking free.

Coiling his rope, Parnell jogged to the edge of the corral. His mount, a beautifully built and well-cared for bay mare he'd named Diana, or Di, after the Greek huntress, was covered with dust and starting to break a sweat. Parnell petted her front shoulder then raised his arm to clear the first drops of sweat from his eyebrows. The sun had just touched the canyon floor. Already the day promised to blister his skin. Pushing his hat back, he noticed the out-of-place bus at the forks in the ranch road. One fork was basically the driveway into Sully's ranch headquarters. The other completed a 28-mile circle in and out of the town of Rainbow. He studied the bus with curiosity.

"Where the hell did that come from, Sully?" Sully didn't hear Parnell's soft-spoken question. It hadn't truly been directed to the rancher. It was more a murmur, or a thought. Parnell didn't reach out for an answer. He tried to read the logo on the side of the dusty bus. It was out of range. *The bus stopped. If they're lost why don't they ask directions?* The bus just sat there at the forks. Someone was standing in the open door well and looking up. Parnell searched the sky but saw nothing.

Parnell's handsome, weathered countenance was a study of troubled intelligence. He was dressed with more flash and glitter than his friend, Sully, but the glitter was tired and warn. The faded jeans he pressed himself were tucked into patched, at one time fancy, boots. His shirt and vest sported fake pearl snaps instead of buttons. Kate had marveled at his neatness. She offered to wash his clothes, but he shrugged the offer off. He had allowed himself to use her washing machine a time or two. Usually he did his laundry in the hotel sink or in the old claw-footed bathtub down the hall from his room. "It's my penance, Kate," he told her. "Don't ask me what for—for dreaming maybe." He laughed. He'd told her that before the bad dreams started flying in his sleep. *What about this bus?* Right now his mind was floating.

Parnell's absent thoughts were sharply interrupted by the frantic bawl of a tortured calf. He winced and looked back into the work being done. The fire-hot branding iron burned into hair and flesh. A thick oily cloud of smoke rose from the scorched young animal. Tom Sullivan, in his late seventies or early eighties, a scruffy looking old man of slight build (he shaved each morning but never quite finished the job) was kneeling on the calf's neck and shoulder grinning. The old man held a large hypodermic syringe with which to inoculate the calf. His younger brother Sully, in his early fifties, held the hot iron firmly in place until his double XX was set.

The iron was too cool. Three others were cradled in the gas-blasting heater. They glowed red in the flame. While his brother reached for a fresh iron, Tom thrust the needle home and injected a measure of vaccine into the young heifer. She had given up the struggle.

The bus started moving. Parnell watched it crest the hill, oil-rich smoke belching from the rust-laced tailpipe. *Maybe it did belong on this ranch road,* he thought with a grin. *It fits in with the other pieces of junk.* The bus appeared again for a moment on the flat west mesa between the evergreens and then disappeared as if it knew where it was going. Parnell shook his head and reached for the bottle balanced on a corral post. He tipped it back to drink. Looking up through the swirling glass and amber whisky he spotted the falcon circling high over the ranch buildings and corrals. As he lowered the bottle to watch, she folded her wings and went into a hunting dive, or stoop.

Dropping straight toward the corral, the tiny spot grew larger as she gathered speed. *What did she see?* Speechless, Parnell watched her plummet toward earth like the remnant of a star dislodged from the solar system. At any moment he expected her to burst into flame.

At the branding fire the calf bawled again as Sully applied a fresh iron to polish his double XX signature. The mother cow, in the adjoining corral, took issue. She charged the gate that separated them. At that instant the screaming falcon stooped into the dust and smoke. Her sharp claws extended for the kill. Her great wings flashed out as she pulled up like a jet out of a power dive. Heading straight for Parnell, she swept inches above the already spooked cattle. Parnell Mackenzie froze, unbelieving.

The wild-eyed mother cows panicked. With a swell of action, they burst through the inner barrier of the old brittle post and pole-constructed corral, knocking over the roaring gas heater in the melee. Branding irons, cherry red in the heat, went flying. Sully and Tom backed off yelling, trying to restore order; trying to keep from being trampled. Spellbound, Parnell's eyes locked on the bird. The falcon, breast out, claws unsheathed, wings breaking the air like silent thunder, came at him. Inches from Parnell she filled the frame of his imagination. Against a backdrop of smoke, dust and the bucking shadows of panicked cattle, she glared at Parnell.

"No... No. God damn!" Parnell screamed, burning in his dream. His mare, reared in fright. Smoke and dust swirled darkly around them blinding all vision except the bird. Then the falcon dissolved into dust before his eyes. "God damn," Parnell cried. "Where'd she go?"

Clutching the giant needle, old Tom clung to the corral rails where he sought refuge from the stampeding cattle. For no apparent reason the old man was giggling. "Get along little doggies..." he howled, staring at Parnell. "God damn what, Jack? I know! God damn what?" He yelled, his face twisted in a distorted grin.

"Shut up, Tom. I didn't say a thing. Where's Sully? He okay?" Parnell was back to reality for a brief second. Then his attention was drawn to a swirling vision before him.

The cattle sensed it. In lock step, they pulled back and were silent ... eyes wild ... deathly still. Sully Sullivan rose up among them. Rough looking his beard twisted in the settling dust and smoke stink of burning hair he gazed about in wonder. Abstractly he pulled up the still blazing branding furnace and closed the valve on the propane tank. "Shit," he grunted. "What started that bullshit?" It was going to take time to get things back together. At least the gas hadn't exploded. "Tom?" he cried, worried. He turned to find Parnell staring, speechless, into the thick, lingering pall of smoke and dust drifting to the south.

Parnell was stricken—hypnotized by something in the smoke. "Look at her, Sully. Look!" He cried.

"Look at what? Who?" Sully turned toward the heavy cloud rolling in the slow breeze. "It's just dirt in the air, Parnell. Adobe dirt, dust. It rises. What the hell spooked these damn mother cows? Where's Tom?" Then he spotted his brother clinging to the rails of the corral. Tom's attention was curiously riveted on the roiling dust too. Parnell, still sitting the uneasy mare, pointed angrily. `

"She's right there, damn it! Right where you're looking, Sully." The mare began to crow-hop. Tom broke his concentration and looked past Parnell at his brother.

"If there is a woman there, I'd see her." Old Tom giggled. A mother cow lowed a mournful cry. Terrified, her calf pulled in under her.

"To hell with this bullshit." Sully angrily started picking up branding irons. He'd had enough. His corral was down and needed to be fixed. What the hell had happened to the cattle? What had spooked them? He looked again at Parnell. Parnell was out in left field. *Christ, had he been drinking all night? He was fine when he arrived.* Sully had seen some pretty weird things in his life. He didn't want to see any more. His brother, Tom, was enough to cope with.

Sully was saddled with Tom. He was a full time caretaker for his crazy brother. Sully loved his brother, but his brother, years ago as a boy, had suffered some kind of bad shit that Sully didn't understand: didn't want to understand: didn't want to know about. His parents had never fully explained, except to insist that Thomas had been through some terrible experience that twisted his life.

"Your brother's mind is fragile," his mother told Sully. Your father's gone, and when I am gone, Thomas will be your responsibility. She had told Sully this on her deathbed and God knows she remained on her deathbed long enough. Sully had heard it for years. She had taken to that bed the day of his father's funeral and only left it when they carried her out to be buried next to him. Sully's father had once opened up to Sully about what happened to sink his oldest son into his "abyss" as Tom's problem was referred to by Sully's parents.

Sully's father was drunk the one time he spilled the crazy story to his youngest son. Sully didn't want to believe what he heard. It would have been hard to believe coming from a sober stranger. Things had been said, but it was impossible to make sense of them. Perhaps neither of his parents knew the whole truth. In any case, Sully tried to lock uncertainty out of his mind. He took his responsibility for his older brother seriously. And he had prevailed. Tom was alive and well—physically. His brother hadn't had a drink in eight years now. In his drinking days, Tom was accused of physically "bothering" a young teacher in Rainbow. Your brother touched her in secret places, the sheriff had explained to Sully. Tom had spent time in the county jail, but had never gone to the state penitentiary—or the state hospital. It had cost Sully in lawyer's fees, but he prevailed.

Sully had married, but there were no children. He and his wife, Iona, were fearful that his brother's malady was hereditary. They were very careful. It was a tricky situation until the "pill" came along and was proven to be safe, *if you could believe the USDA, or whatever the hell the initials were.* Sully was sure the letters chosen were the wrong ones. So what? In any case, Iona died of cancer. *Hell, everybody died of cancer.* She sure didn't die of childbirth, and she had plenty of time for that blessed event to have taken place. Iona was thirty-seven when she passed.

Sully never remarried. He had been alone fifteen years now. Not that he had been completely celibate during those years. He had even had one serious affair five years after Iona's death. But when he brought the lady to the ranch, and she met Tom, that hope went out the window. It was the way she met his brother, Sully reasoned.

Sully and the lady lay naked in the summer heat, heat that had spurred their passion into action. Tom, very drunk, lurched over the foot of the bed and fell upon them puking his guts out and screaming incoherently about some fucking bird. The lady, who had come to town for a summer job at a dude ranch in the hills above Rainbow, left that hot afternoon for the rest of her life. Sully had her address, but could never bring himself to write. *Write what?* Life had its fuckups. Sully tried to make the best of it.

The next time his brother was arrested by the local Sheriff for drunk and disorderly behavior, and "bothering" a girl much younger than himself, (they didn't call it child molestation then) Sully was sorely tempted to leave him to his fate; to be rid of the albatross, the bird tied around his neck. The fucking bird again. He left Tom in the county jail until the new sheriff, Sully's friend and neighbor for years, Julio Romero, called to say he was no longer seeing weird creatures crawling the walls. "I'll drop the charges, Sully," he said. "You know, bothering the girl. She wasn't really hurt Sully, just scared a little. Nothing serious," he said. "If you will just lock your crazy brother up on the ranch, and for Christ sake keep him there, I'll bring him out to you."

Sully agreed to try. The sheriff brought Tom out and turned him over to Sully. There were few words spoken. Tom said nothing. Like a begging hound dog he tried to get back in the sheriff's car for a ride back to Rainbow. Sully held him while his friend drove off, then in anger and frustration; he beat the shit out of his older brother. Tom never lifted a hand to protect himself.

After several minutes of blind fury Sully caught his breath and swore to his brother that if Tom ever drank again he would kill him and dump the body in the canyon beyond the mesa. It was the threat of the canyon drop that brought about Tom's reaction. Sully's brother curled up, trembling in fear. He whimpered he would do anything his brother wanted. *Anything.* In the end, Sully held him in his arms and, tears streaming down his face, begged forgiveness. Tom wouldn't, or wasn't able to answer. Sully put his brother to bed. Tom didn't speak again for months: not a word.

Sully was stricken with guilt. He had lost control. Tom wouldn't even move from the bed. Sully had to carry him to the bathroom and set him on the pot and scrub him clean. Then he changed the sheets and put him back to bed. The younger man fed his brother like a baby. With three weeks gone and no change, he bundled Tom up and drove him through a winter storm to a doctor in Las Vegas, New Mexico. The psychiatrist wanted to keep Tom for observation at the state mental hospital there. Sully refused. The man shrugged indifferently and prescribed a renewable prescription, —nut pills of some kind. Sully filled that order many times.

It was a year before Tom started to show signs of wanting to live at all. It was four years before he reached the state he was in now. Although Sully couldn't understand his brother's mental condition, he never stopped loving him. It was all in the family and Tom was family: Sully's brother Tomas was Sully's responsibility.

* * *

Sully Sullivan turned to his brother:"Most of what Parnell sees comes out of that bottle, Tom," he said. "It gives the world a sort of amber look—like when you were drinking. You remember?"

Tom looked away guilty. He didn't want to be reminded. Sully shifted his gaze back to Parnell. "Jack," he said, I don't know what the hell you're seeing. But then sometimes I don't know how the hell you see at all, with all the bourbon you drink?"

Parnell, still shaken, was not listening. "Did you see the bird?" He said flatly.

"What bird?"

"The one that spooked the cows—the hawk."

"Chicken Hawk? Red tail? What?" Sully looked at his disturbed friend and shook his head. "Maybe if I had enough of that whisky, I'd see fairies too. Give me a hit, Parnell." Sully didn't like this mention of birds. Tom had always babbled about a bird when he was drunk. Sully forced a laugh. "I'll look again." He gazed into the distance, shook his head and cut his glance back to Parnell.

Intensely Parnell's eyes followed the fading pall of dust and smoke. He dismounted and, still staring after it, walked dumbly to the warped gray planks of the outer corral. The whisky bottle dangled from his fingers. Old Tom followed him. In Thomas' deranged mind, he saw something too. For a moment there was a startled, almost frightening expression of recognition in his usually vacant eyes. He turned away, confused. Violently the old man struck his head with the palm of his hand to clear the vision. Sully watched, picking up on his brother's confusion. He didn't like it, but tried to make light of it.

"I said, deaf man," he called out to Parnell, "I would take a hit off that jug. You usually hear when somebody talks about drinking whisky."

Like a sleepwalker awakened in mid stride, Parnell shook out of the trance. After a moment of orientation, he turned back to Sully and held out the bottle. "Forgive me, friend." Then vaguely reaching in his memory: "Forgive me, Sully." He looked around at the high rim rock surrounding the valley. "How many times have I been to your place in the past months?"

"Too many, evidently." Sully took the near empty bottle and studied it in mock sincerity. "It's a good thing Tom don't drink any more. There ain't enough left here for a parched frog." He glanced at his brother for his reaction. Tom's mind, what there was of it, was again intrigued by the vanishing smoke and dust. He shuddered, and turned away. When he caught his brother watching him, he actually blushed. He spun around, did a dizzy dance step and broke into a giggle.

"I'd take up drinking again if I was sure I'd see dancing ladies," he laughed, "'stead of snakes." Tom snorted. "Never cared much for snakes."

At Old Tom's words, Parnell turned back. He studied Tom seriously for a moment. "Dancing ladies, Tom?"

Sully looked at his brother, then drained the bottle. "Women can be bad for you too, Thomas. Don't forget that."

"Only bad women are bad for you, Sully," Old Tom said seriously. "Iona was a good woman. I liked Iona. I'm sorry she died. She was a good wife for you. She was good to me too. She told me there were good women in the world." Tears started running down the old man's face. "She said even some dancin' women were good." Thomas collapsed on one of the fallen corral logs and sobbed quietly. He didn't cover his face. He just let it happen. Tears poured from his troubled eyes. "She was good to me, Sully." He turned to Parnell who was watching closely. It was the first time Parnell had seen Old Tom break down like this.

"Sully's wife was a good woman but she's dead! Iona's dead, Parnell." Tom cried out to the dust surrounding him. The uncontrolled tears coursed down the rivers of his weathered face. Sully ran to his brother, dropped to his knees and threw his arms about him. He held the old man close, patting his back and rocking him as one would a crying baby.

"It's alright, Tommy," he said soothingly. "We all know Iona was a good woman. God knows I do." He threw a quick look to Parnell. There was no shame in his eyes. "Now just calm down, Tom," he added firmly, but gently. "I'll get your medicine for you. Don't get yourself all worked up." Murmuring about how it was going to be all right, the big rancher pulled the silk bandana from around his heavy neck and wiped the tears from his brother's face.

Parnell was visibly shaken by Tom's reaction to everything, as well as by the crazy things he saw in the smoke and dust. They couldn't be real. It all made no sense, no more than his nightmare made sense. And he didn't even know what his nightmare was about—other than the terrifying feeling of uncontrolled flight. *It is all damn near enough to make a man quit drinking.* Parnell considered this rash thought and hastily reconsidered … *but not quite.* He crossed to his mount and pulled a pewter flask from the saddlebags. He walked back to the brothers and handed it to Sully. "Sorry about the empty bottle."

Old Tom seemed to be coming out of his crying jag. The old man was utterly wasted, his body loose as a half filled feed sack. There was no spark of fun there now. The silly grin had been replaced with emptiness—nothing. The eyes were blank. Parnell put his hand on Tom's stooped shoulder: "You saw the hawk, Tom, didn't you?" He asked quietly.

Sully looked up sharply and waved Parnell to silence. "My brother saw nothing. We'll leave it that way. He's distressed." Sully thought a moment, studying his brother. "He didn't take his medicine this morning. I never checked. I thought he was over it. I'm goin' to have to start watchin' him again." Then to his brother: "You forget to take your medicine this morning, Tomas?"

"I saw the bird." Old Tom stated in a monotone. "I saw her dance." His eyes stared vacantly into the distance. "She's back. Why would she come down here? There's nothing for her down here. She belongs on the mesa and in the canyon."

"Who you talking about, Tom?" Parnell pushed the question. "Who wouldn't come down here?"

"Don't get him started, Parnell." Sully looked up sadly. "The poor bastard only got half a mind as it is. I don't want to get that half fried too." Old Tom staggered to his feet and started a disoriented dance step. It was amazingly light and airy for its abstract moves. Sully tried to grab him, but his brother quickly sidestepped. He started singing in a frail light voice:

"I only see ladies and Sully says
The ones I latch onto are bad …
I only latch onto the bad ones
But boy, I latch on to 'um good."

He continued the dance step humming quietly to himself. He was off in a world of his own. Parnell watched him. "At least he's not crying any more, Sully. I think you better have a drink." Sully waved off the flask.

"Not now." He got his arm around his brother and led him toward the house. "He needs his medication. I thought this was all over. This is the first time he has broken down in over a year." He opened the main gate of the outer corral and looped the loose chain back through the slats to keep it shut behind him. "I'd be beholdin' to you, Parnell, if you'd push those cows back into place and shake out a bale or two of hay for them. I'll be back to help you fix the rails. We can haywire them up temporary."

"You got it Sully," Parnell said. "I'm happy to do it." He paused, looking at Old Tom. "Will your brother be all right?" he said.

"He'll be fine." Sully and his brother moved slowly toward the old adobe homestead built by their father's father in the early eighteen-hundreds. Old Tom was still floating to some rhythm or other. Parnell turned into the tack shed to find baling wire to lash up the broken poles. Before going in he searched the sky for sign of a bird the size of an eagle with the claws of a Sphinx.

It certainly was a riddle twisting in his mind, and it was one he couldn't even try to answer. Not now. On the horizon there was nothing but blue sky fringed by rim-rock and the green of pinion scrabbled along the rock edge. He put the flask back in the saddlebags before starting on the repairs. He guessed they would finish branding tomorrow.

Parnell stripped the heavy saddle from his mare to cool her, and flung it over the top rail of the outer corral. It had already been a long day. *The Sphinx be damned*. Parnell knew, somehow Tom had seen the same shadowy image he had seen in the smoke and dust. *What the hell was it? What the hell did we see? And, (an even bigger question), why the hell did the two of us see it, and not Sully?* The riddle had yet to be answered. He hoped he was allowed time to figure it out—or the blessing to forget it. Jack Parnell Mackenzie was worried.

* * *

It was an hour before Sully returned to the site of the cattle madness. Parnell had the hay opened and spread for the thirty or so cows. The calves were with them, nursing, or laid back. All was quiet. He had started repair on the broken corral. He looked questioningly to Sully.

Sully shook his head in dismay. "Tom has got to stay away from thoughts of wild women and whisky. I don't know what the fuck got him started this morning." He looked sidewise at Parnell. "I don't know what the fuck got you started either?" He said it under his breath but meaning for Parnell to hear it. He paused for a moment. Parnell said nothing. "And then that crazy wind that came up, and you talkin' about birds—and my poor damn brother starts seeing dancing women in the smoke… "

"Nothing wrong, him thinking of women, Sully." Parnell laughed uneasily. "They are on my mind all the time, even when I'm swinging a rope. A woman is a thing of beauty. Why look at a reproduction of the Mona Lisa when you can look at the real thing? They all have that grin of secret knowledge – superiority—whatever you want to call it. I believe they are the superior of the sexes, too," he went on. "We all live in a matriarchy. We should just give up and accept it, Sully. Women rule."

"Okay, they do. I will have to accept your judgment on that one. I have no choice."

"I love them," Parnell said.

"That's 'cause you only eat the frosting. Once the sweet's gone, you drop the cake. I took one woman to last me a lifetime, and Godamit if she didn't die. Iona only lasted <u>her</u> lifetime." Sully gave himself a moment of quiet sorrow. "I got no woman to lead the way any more. I got to forge ahead for myself. I don't like it, but I make it work." Sully grabbed a corral pole. "I got a chain around my neck, Parnell. That chain is my brother. But Godamit, it's a chain I love. I'm committed to it. I can't burn it off. I can't cut it. It was left me by my mother and tended by my wife, who understood a lot more than I do about Thomas. That poor son-of-a-bitch... I use the word lightly, Parnell. My mother was a saint, albeit a suffering saint. So was my wife, but it was a different kind of suffering. It is just that Iona cut out early. She didn't mean to." He looked darkly up to the heavens. "It's just that that fucker up there took her." Angrily he threw a middle finger to the sky. "It left me with no answers." Sully slammed down the corral pole he was lifting into place. "You still got that flask, Parnell? Is there anything left in it?"

"It's full, Sully." Parnell crossed to the outer corral rail where he had left his gear and pulled the flask from the saddle-bags. "We going to brand any more today?"

"No."

"What about tomorrow?" Parnell said, returning with the flask. "If Tom's not up to it, we can find someone else, or do it without him."

"Ya, Parnell, tomorrow I can use a hand. Thanks. I'm short, about five head. Half wild. They got their calves hid up in one of those canyons somewhere. It's a lot of country to ride for one man." Sully looked toward the house. Tom was on his way back. Sully let his eyes roll up toward the heavens again.

"What the fuck have I done wrong, God?" he cried softly. "My whole life is taking care of my idiot brother and this ranch which hardly supports that care." He grabbed a length of baling wire and started lashing his end of the final rail to the post. It was a makeshift repair, but it would have to do. "Ya, I need help, Parnell. Thanks for offerin'. One man and a idiot can't do it." He looked to his brother, now hanging with a grin over the top rail of the corral. "You up to branding the rest of these critters, Thomas?"

Old Tom giggled, and looked to Parnell. Then to Sully: "We got some of them marked. Sully, we can finish. The corral looks good." He cut his eyes back to Parnell. "That dude's pretty good with that leather rope of his. Heat up the irons."

Parnell cinched the saddle back on the mare. *Whatever pill Sully had given his brother sure had worked.* Parnell wished he had one.

"Let's get it done, Sully," Parnell said swinging into the saddle, "then we'll go to town. I think you need a little night out. Tom will hold down the homestead." He looked to the old man. "How about it Tom? We finish the branding, you rub down my mare and feed her, and I'll take your brother Sully to town to do a little fishing at Lake Nine. Okay?"

Tom smiled a big open grin. "You take my brother to Lake Nine, but don't get him drownded. There is a pretty wild tide on the shores of that lake." He punched his brother playfully on the shoulder. "He might get carried away by a couple of mermaids."

"He might." Parnell was grinning now. "You're alright, Tom, and you're right about Lake Nine. It is a dangerous piece of surf to navigate; a dangerous place to dip your line."

"Are we going to get these Godamn calves cut and branded?" Sully snapped, a bit short. "Or are you two going to spend the day bullshittin'?" *The pills still work*, he thought. It had been a year since Tom had broken down like he did this morning. Sully hoped all was back in place; his brother's mind was back to numb. It was just a short breakdown. *I can handle it if Tommy can.* He struck a spark on the striker. The propane brand furnace roared to life. He put the irons in the fire. Parnell pulled his mare into line and shook out a loop. They were back in business.

# CHAPTER THREE

# LAKE NINE

A faded wooden sign reading "LAKE NINE" swung in the dim light of the street lamps. From inside the bar a country-western band was shit-kicking music out into the street. Sully and Parnell pulled Parnell's battered Chevy pickup into the turmoil. Always ready for a quick get-away, Parnell backed up to the curb. Emerging from the passenger side door, Sully took the last hit from Parnell's flask. He regarded the empty soulfully, shrugged and tossed it in the back of the truck. Parnell slammed the driver door and circled back to the tailgate where they could both study the sign. In their slightly drunken state, they silently agreed that this was the place to be. Lake Nine, the hotspot of Rainbow, New Mexico.

A poster taped inside the bar window caught Parnell's attention:

RAINBOW'S CONCERT ASSOCIATION PROUDLY
PRESENTS
*CATHERINE*
R E X W R O T H
FROM ENID, OKLAHOMA
Miss Rexwroth
AND HER NATIONALLY ACCLAIMED
TROOP OF ACTORS, SINGERS AND DANCERS
PRESENT
A TRUE THEATRICAL
MUSICAL & BALLET
EXPERIENCE.

## *THE LADY LIVES FOREVE*R
## FOR TWO NIGHTS ONLY
## EXCLUSIVELY AT THE RAINBOW OPERA HOUSE
Tickets available at the door.

Sully scratching his beard, studied the poster for a moment. "Culture comes to Rainbow, New Mexico," he said, still reading. "Enid, Oklahoma? Catherine the Great, no doubt. Parnell, You ever heard of Enid, Oklahoma?" Parnell studied the poster. Sully continued: "I passed through there once on a cattle buyin' trip." He turned to his companion seriously. "There is something suspicious here, Parnell. What in the hell could possible come from Enid, Oklahoma but dancin' cows? Maybe some sheep." He studied the advert again. "Ballet?" he scoffed. "Bullshit."

Parnell turned to his friend seriously. "Don't knock it if you if you haven't done the steps. They get some beautiful women dancing this shit, Sully. You might like it."

"I hear they get some very pretty men doin' it too." He gave Parnell a sidelong glance.

"I've known some cowboys a bit light in the heels, Sully. It takes all kinds." Parnell checked the time on the sign. "Too late to catch them tonight, amigo. You're safe. Or you will be until they swarm over here after the show." Parnell's eyes were drawn back to the poster. Something in it hooked his mind. He started reading the sign aloud. Sully had had enough. He grabbed Parnell and pulled him toward the door.

"Maybe tomorrow, Parnell." He indicated the dimly lit sign above them. "We are on the shores of Lake Nine. It's time to go fishin'."

"Catherine Rexwroth?" Parnell mused, holding back. "Wasn't that the name on the bus that stalled out by your ranch this morning, Sully?"

"They probably took the shortcut from Enid and got lost." Sully faced his friend squarely. "Forget about it, Parnell. I have. I don't want to remember this mornin'—or the rest of the day neither. I came in town to forget it. I plan to exhaust myself in this kettle of fish where I might even find a member of the opposite sex lusting after my body." Sully considered his last statement. "Parnell, I haven't had a woman in two and a half years. Iona was a good woman. Her spirit will forgive my wishful thinkin'. She might even encourage me." He made another grab for Parnell and shoved him toward the Lake. "Come on. You're the one talked me into comin' to town."

In the eyes of Sully and Parnell, and every other honest drinking miner and cowman in Coal County, New Mexico, Lake Nine was one of the state's finest watering holes. In truth, it opened in the depressing years of prohibition—as a watering hole. The water of Lake Nine had been touted as the finest alcohol purified spring water in the county. The "cover" in those dry years had been candy, ice-cream, moxie and a questionable brand of homemade sarsaparilla. They also dispensed a surprising quantity of Lydia Pinkhan's vegetable compound, a recognized legal medical wonder distilled to sixty-nine percent alcohol content by volume. Singing of Lydia's healing powers, those of both sexes in ill health, or good, scarfed it down with a sarsaparilla chaser. It was a big seller. In 1933, however, when prohibition was squelched, the ice-cream coolers were filled with beer and there was a marked improvement in the quality of spring water served to reveling customers.

* * *

Inside the bar, Lake Nine was shrouded in a pall of tobacco smoke. Green metal shaded bare light bulbs hung on twisted, cloth-bound electric cords from the high pressed-tin ceiling. The place was ablaze with activity. Parnell and Sully adjusted to the pleasant atmosphere. Behind the bar, in front of a cracked mirror, hung a huge, stuffed, worm-eaten northern pike. Crossed fishing poles hung above it. A number of frogs, a plastic mermaid (mailed by a previous patron from Las Vegas, Navada), and a stuffed beaver added to the atmosphere. Beneath the pike, "Lake Nine" was scrawled in painted letters on the back bar mirror. Under that: "We serve the finest drinking water in Coal County."

Mondo Vallucci, the owner and bartender, recognized Sully and Parnell. "Thought you must have left town Sully," he said. "And now I find you in this company. What is your excuse? A man of your culture and high tone upbringing should be at the opera house tonight."

Sully did a little pirouette, which nearly dropped two customers and himself. "Sorry folks," he apologized. "I'm dancin' for my drinks."

"You keep that up," Parnell cut in, "they won't even serve you Alka Seltzer."

"You're the doctor, Parnell," the bartender laughed. "I know it's not her night to work, but I thought Kate might drop in to help me take care of you."

"No nurse tonight, Moe. I'm doctor enough to prescribe Old Taylor and soda for the both of us."

"And two Kamikazes." Sully looked in mock wonder to Parnell. "Doctor? Shit, Parnell, you were a dumb rhinestone cowboy and drunk, and broke, when that beat-up Chevy of yours collapsed in this town... and, you're still dumb."

"And still broke." The bartender added with a raised eyebrow, "regardless of the monthly remittance."

"And still drunk!" Sully added.

"And you're getting that way, Sully," Parnell said.

"Once a month I get drunk in a hurry." Sully Sullivan said with great dignity. "The next day I'm fine and ready to get over it. It takes you all day to get drunk, Parnell. And you do it every day. At least you have recently. Shit, what you got to hide from?"

"I got no skeletons in my closet, Sully. My background is clean."

Sully strutted indignantly. "You won't find no bones in Sully's closet, Doctor Parnell. I take them with me wherever I go." He paused, standing back from the bar like a politician preparing to stake the world on his reputation. "Just like I'm takin' you, Parnell."

"I'm the one brought you, remember?"

"And I'm the one buyin'." Sully expansively slammed a twenty on the bar. With that rash move, he looked quizzically into his old worn wallet. It was the last twenty. More importantly, it was the last of his greenbacks. He quickly folded the wallet and slid it into his frayed hip pocket. Some things were best out of sight, out of mind. Turning to his partner, he changed the subject. "A Philadelphia lawyer, Parnell?" He bellowed. "That where you dropped out of law school, Parnell? Philadelphia? I know damn well you're a dropout."

Kate had come into the bar. She stepped quietly up behind the two men and stood listening to their conversation. She hadn't expected Parnell to come looking for her, but it would have been a nice perk. Kate left her youngest with her mother and in turn went looking for her new charge, Parnell Mackenzie. It had not been that she wanted to track him down, or to let him know that she wanted to be with him, or needed him. Something pushed her, and it wasn't a totally subconscious nudge. Over the past weeks Parnell had taken up a permanent stool at Lake Nine. If she wanted to spend the night with him, this was the place to find him. And, kicking herself, she did want to spend the night with him. She wanted to spend more than the night with this strange, irresponsible man. She wanted to understand him. She wanted to help. Parnell needed help. She wondered how far she would go.

For the first few weeks she and Parnell had been together the atmosphere had been warm and comfortable. He stopped by the house, the old swaybacked house on Folsom Street Kate inherited from her grandfather. Kate's mother still lived in the home she shared with her second husband. Parnell had helped Kate repaint her porch and the kitchen. Parnell was handy with his hands in more ways than one. He even helped with the cooking, creating some completely new dishes for her taste buds. Her children became accustomed to him; even liked him. To date, however, Parnell had never spent the night in her home. *Too much of a commitment?* After the relationship warmed to an almost family situation, she suggested it. Parnell backed off. When they became that intimate, she went to the room he rented above the long closed Corner Bar—the room with the fire escape entrance. The room she had been in last night, and the one she wanted to join him in tonight, the nightmare room. Jack Parnell had never had his bad dreams two nights in a row.

Tonight Parnell was more detached then usual. She could feel it. Their relationship was definitely changing. *Am I clinging? Or does he really need me?* She admitted to herself a fear of losing him. Had she pumped her hopes too high? *The third strike and out?* All she could do was swing the bat and hope for the best.

In Parnell she felt a fear of unseen chains binding him— pulling him astray. She wasn't sure which. Kate did not want to "tie him down", if such were the words to use. She wanted him to be himself, but not the tortured self he had become since the dream started. She tried to remember the date of the first disturbing nightmare. He had awakened confused and in a sweat, but not screaming as he had last night. He never remembered what he dreamed. Last night was the first time he had mentioned flying. The recurring experience, a fright mare, she called it, was getting seriously intense. As it did, Parnell started drinking more heavily. He had always had a bottle in his room. She kept one for him at her place. They shared a cocktail or a couple of cold beers in the evenings, or a few more on a Sunday afternoon. Parnell was a heavy drinker, but he had never let it get in the way as it was now. What had he called himself—"a functioning alcoholic"?

When they graduated to a sexual commitment (something he never pushed), it was beautiful. It was easy for both of them. Even if their relationship had not been a long one, it was pleasant and relaxed. *I could love this man,* Kate thought. In her heart she knew she already did. It was dangerous for her to admit it, even to herself. She didn't want him to know how strongly she felt about him for fear he would leave her. Kate didn't ask for a commitment. Even in her dreams she didn't ask for a commitment. She would stand on the edge and take what kindness, what touches that passed as love, perhaps, what passion, (there was a sweet abundance of that) came her way. Sexually, she had never felt anything to match Parnell's strength, gentleness and consideration. He always reached to please her, to leave her fulfilled, satisfied. Kate didn't have to reach to please Parnell. She just knew that sexually she did please him. It was a good knowledge. In bed they were great together. She wished she knew she pleased him in other fields. She thought she did – she hoped so.

But what happened? What demons had invaded his life without his knowing it? What had turned him over? What had made him now, in so short a time, frighteningly dependent on her at one moment and wanting to be independently free of her in another? With Parnell, she felt it wasn't just the male thing. He was different. His changes came without warning. Asleep, he held her desperately in his arms making it, at times, impossible for her to get any sleep. In his dreams, thrashing about with her strapped in his arms, the experience could be brutal. He frightened her at those times. She clung to the hope life would resolve itself in him, although she was helpless to do anything but be there for him. Was that enough? She could only hang on and hope. Why?

* * *

Kate had known Sully for years. She had introduced Parnell to him three or four months back. At the time Sully was working cattle on a high mesa he leased north of Rainbow. It was miles from the small ranch he owned, the ranch he and his brother Tom grew up on. He and Tom had a shack on the mesa by the summer corrals. The weather was too fierce to run cattle on the high mesa in the winter months. In the summer it was a wonderland of green. When Parnell was helping the brothers out Kate had gone up with him for a few days. She and Parnell camped out under the stars that clung to the sky fat and thick as grapes at harvest time. The sky was so close and the stars so large and plentiful the two of them had stayed awake for hours "drinking the wine of life", he said. It was one of their happiest times together.

About three weeks ago Parnell had volunteered to go to Sully's ranch headquarters in Tinaja where a heavy summer hail had torn up the roof. With the help of Old Tom, Parnell laid down rolls of thirty pound roofing felt and mopped on tar to cover the damage. The adobe walls of the old ranch house had been laid in the seventeen hundreds by a cantankerous old Mexican. That was in the days when New Mexico was still Old Mexico. Sully's grandparents homesteaded the original one hundred and sixty acres after New Mexico became a US territory in the eighteen hundreds.

The Sullivans bought up the headquarters building and, some adjoining property, owned by the grandson of the original Mexican bandito, a diminutive man, as the story goes, with a big gun. He and Sully's grandfather didn't get along. About nineteen hundred, the bandito sold a few more acres on the mesa above the Sullivan house to a gringo from the east. The buyer left the home site after some kind of scandal a few years later. What the scandal was, or why? Kate didn't know. She did know there had been trouble of some kind between this man and Sully's father. She heard that place had burned to the ground. Old Tom, then a boy, had been involved somehow. There was a dark mystery about it. She had once mentioned it to Sully. It upset him. "It happened before I was born," Sully said. "It's a God damned ghost story." He didn't want to talk about it. Kate shrugged it off. It was not her business.

She heard stories about Old Tom, too. The whole town knew how he had been a crazy drunk, off and on, for years. She knew that was true. When she was in high school she had seen him that way. But then, there were a lot of drunks in Rainbow. Sully and his wife, Iona, had a hard time taking care of Tom. Kate didn't push Sully for more information. After the fire, the acres on the mesa reverted to the Sullivan family. If this was by default or chicanery, Sully, if he knew, wouldn't say. Kate knew there had been bad blood between his family and the new owners from the east. "Real bad blood," it was said.

Old Tom Sullivan was a case Kate couldn't comprehend. Unlike others in the town, she left it alone. She only knew, according to her father, at some point in Thomas' childhood he had flipped out, crazy. Iona and Sully had saved him from completely destroying himself.

Tom, born in eighteen ninety-two, was nineteen years older than Sully. There had been no children in between. According to Sully, his birth was a mistake of passion. His mother had been in her active forties when Sully was born. His father delivered his unexpected son at the ranch and tied the cord himself. His father died when Sully was twelve. Both his parents were dead by the time he was seventeen. Sully, "Brian", Sullivan, had never gone by any other name than Sully.

* * *.

Listening to Parnell and Sully banter at the bar, Kate stood unnoticed behind the two men for some time. She knew they were well on their way and must have had a number of drinks before they reached Lake Nine.

"I dropped out of medical school, Sully," Parnell said with agitation. "I never planned to be a Godamned lawyer. I was going to cut the livers out of people, not the hearts."

"Medical school?"

"In Philadelphia where, God help us, lawyers breed like rabbits, Sully. But I never wanted to be a lawyer or a doctor. That road was my parents' plan. What I only really ever wanted to be was a cowboy." He downed his drink. "And here I am—a success. The American dream come true."

"Bullshit."

Kate bumped her knees in the back of Parnell's, knocking him off balance. "You're an American dream, all right, Parnell—a wet one," she said. "Come on, let's dance."

Caught off balance in more ways than one, Parnell sulked back to his drink. "Not tonight, sweetheart. I'm waiting for wonder woman to make her moves on me." He straightened up to the bar.

"Wonder woman?"

"He wonders where she'll come from," Sully interjected. "So do I. He's been wondering all day. I'm beginning to wonder about him myself." Sully was beginning to slur his words.

Parnell felt it was his turn to take offense. "When she comes through that door," he pointed without turning his head from studying the images in the back bar mirror, "in that direction." He shook his finger at the door, "through the front door of this fine establishment. When she does, you will see me dance on the walls."

"And fall on your ass," Sully concluded with finality." He bowed graciously to the surrounding company and came up in front of Kate. "Kate, my wonder woman, allow me to assist you onto the dance floor. Let me float you through the ether mists of my wonder world. I am at your disposal. A ballet master, gay as a goose, to lift you eternally into heaven, the haven of my bliss."

"You are a cowboy poet, Mr. Sullivan," Kate said rolling her eyes. It will be my pleasure to dance with you."

The resident country western band, back from their break, struck up a two-step tune. It was a little after ten thirty.

"And, Sully," Kate added. "You are full of bullshit, too." She gave Parnell's tight buns a not unkind slap, and let Sully lead her onto the sawdust-covered expanse of dance floor. Parnell turned back to the bar and ordered another double.

* * *

Still in makeup from her final scene, Catherine Rexwroth, stormed out the stage door of Rainbow's Old Opera House. A number of the crew standing there on smoke break quickly made room for her. The star of her show, Catherine was pissed. They knew it. Before she arrived on the dock it had been their topic of conversation. Catherine had changed from her nineteen-O- five wardrobe to tight-fitting jeans and a man's white shirt seductively open at the neckline. The jeans were tucked into high western boots. It was a fresh copy of what she had been wearing that morning when the bus passed Sully's ranch. Her stylistic make-up, touched up after dressing, accentuated her magnificent eyes with sequins, dark lashes and brows. The over-all effect was witch-like in a wild and provocative sense.

The steam of The Cat's anger had built to a dangerous level as she changed from her costume. It was time to give it vent. Toad, her stage manager and the butt of her fury, followed at a safe distance. He was stooped even lower than he had been over the wheel of the company bus that morning. Wolf Zimmerman, the company's manager, orchestra leader, and Catherine's sometime lover, in his early forties, and Teddy, the leading actor/dancer, a gay Sylvester Stallone, were among those on the dock as Catherine, in full voice, swooped out into the open air.

"What do you mean, it won't happen again, Toad." Cat cried. "It happened, Toad. I am supposed to be engulfed in flames."

Finding himself surrounded by an audience, Toad pushed forward defiantly, his head tilted up from his stooped shoulders. Assuming a pose at the edge of the dock, his hands clasped behind his wide back, he stared out into nothingness. It was a lot easier than meeting The Cat's fiery eyes. "Smoke, Catherine," he cried in his flat tenor voice, "smoke is what the script calls for—that and the smell of brimstone. What ever the hell that is."

"And flames. I added the fire effect yesterday to sharpen the scene." She grabbed Toad by the stoop of his left shoulder and forced him around to look at her. "You told me it was in the bag! What kind of bag did you mean, asshole? You can't stage manage shit!"

Under heavy fire, the embattled stage manager tried to inject a bit of reason into his defense. "There is always a chance," he stammered, "that a complicated technical effect, put together in a rush situation, can go awry, Catherine."

"There is always a chance that someone as inadequate as you, Toad, can be fired." She glanced at the members of her company standing by. There were a few shrugs. As difficult as Catherine was, jobs in the theatre were not easy to come by. They waited for Toad to break. He didn't. Catherine went on: "Wolf held the orchestra interminably," she took a deep breath, holding for effect—"while I, the star of this questionable attraction balanced, forever—waiting—waiting for the fire to engulf me. And the only flaming thing around was," her eyes flashed to Teddy, "this faggot holding me by the crotch. I felt as stupid as Joan of Arc in a rain storm."

Toad threw up his arms in resignation. "What can I say, Cat, you called it."

Few in the company dared call the star "Cat." Catherine reacted to Toad's call and moved in for a kill. Wolf stepped quickly between them. He almost laid hands on her, but not quite. Not even Wolf dared touch Catherine when she was in this sort of mood. The orchestra leader tried to speak diplomatically.

"Catherine, true enough," he said. "A mistake may have been made, a miscalculation, maybe. But the audience never realized it. Toad brought up the red lights to cover. The audience burst into spontaneous applause. You and Teddy were a magnificent picture, truly professional."

"Wolf, I thank you," Toad said quietly. "It is kind of you to come to my defense. However…"

"I thank you as well, Wolf." Teddy broke in. "If I do say so myself, I think we <u>were</u> quite magnificent, Catherine. They loved us. The only drawback for me was having to hold you by the crotch for so long." He sighed dramatically. "But then, what an artist won't do for the sake of his craft."

Catherine glared at the posturing Teddy. She would not lower herself to a retort. The star turned her attention back to the stage manager. "Put out an early call for tomorrow, Toad! I want to rehearse that scene so we—so you don't muck it up again. Understood?"

Toad nodded ascent. "Yes, madam. Is there anything else, madam?"

Catherine was finished with him. She turned to Wolf. "Let's go get a drink. I desperately need a change of scenery." She took his arm leading him down the rickety steps of the old loading dock and up the alley toward the bright lights of Rainbow, New Mexico. The cast, relieved to have her gone, moved back into the theatre. Toad was left under the lone light over the stage door. His dark hooded eyes followed his employer until she and Wolf turned the corner.

"You will have brimstone tomorrow, madam, and the devil's fire, if I have to soak your bleeding costume in gasoline." He stood a moment contemplating the imagined result of his orchestrated pyrotechnics. The picture pleased him. Back to work, Toad turned into the old opera house. It was time to bring down the house lights and close the building with the local custodian. In two days they would be back on the road, but he would be God damned if he would ever turn off the paved road again, as he had this morning—not for Catherine—not for anyone.

\* \* \*

In Lake Nine, the band was taking another break. Sully and Kate were back beside Parnell at the bar. Parnell, still in a dark mood, was not a part of their conversation. He studied his reflection lurking beneath the stuffed pike in the back bar mirror. Parnell Mackenzie was not in a festive mood. The bartender set up another round for the three of them. He counted out the change on the bar. They were short. He looked from Parnell to Sully. "You want me to start a tab, gentlemen?" Sully downed the fresh kamikaze.

"Good advice, Moe. I should never be allowed to spend money when I am in my cups." Parnell made no comment. Mondo spread the bills and change back on the bar before them.

"You are a crazy Irishman, Sully." Kate said, raising her glass to him. "And you drink like an Irishman too." Sully grinned in satisfaction.

"I'm wonderful too, Kate." Sully announced.

Parnell watched them in the mirror. "He is certainly not modest," he said. Sully raised his eyes to Parnell's image.

"I'll not be squelched by a sourpuss who didn't have the intelligence to graduate from a mediocre medical school. Parnell, you may have the family name of one of Ireland's heroes, but you don't have his class."

"Intelligence had nothing to do with it. I quit medical school."

"Quit medical school?" Kate looked from the man on her right to Parnell. "You, enrolled in medical school, and you quit?" This was a part of Parnell she hadn't known.

Parnell shrugged and turned away. "I stuck it out three years and that was three years too much." *I should never have let that bit of information drop,* he thought. *My past is going to haunt me.*

"Forget the good Doctor Parnell," Sully exclaimed, expansively. "Forget him, my darling Kate. Let you and I adjourn to your humble abode and writhe beneath the scented sheets of ecstasy. I am awash with love."

"And about to drown," Parnell grunted. He had to break a grin. Sully Sullivan was getting into his Irish heritage.

Kate laughed, glad that Parnell was finally loosening up. "I told you Sully was a poet, Parnell."

"Another skeleton exposed Mister Sullivan?" Parnell turned to the booze-faced, bearded rancher with a pseudo-skeptical look. "In what dark anthologies have you been penned? Or are you only published in your cups?" Kate, laughing openly, turned to Parnell. Past him something caught her eye. Her expression changed to one of amazement. The babble of voices in the bar reduced to hushed mumblings. Sully turned to see what the attraction was.

"Well, I'll be damned, Parnell," he said. "There is your wonder woman." Parnell stood to look. The bar had gone completely silent. Catherine Rexwroth, The Cat, Wolf over her shoulder, posed in the open door of Lake Nine.

Parnell was stunned.

Her timing perfect in the silence she created, Catherine smiled triumphantly. She had made her entrance. In any town, even without her makeup, The Cat created a resounding presence. In the small cow town of Rainbow she knocked them out. The star enjoyed the moment, milking it for what it was worth before speaking with regal modesty. "Thank you. Thank you kindly." She bowed slightly then looked about the room expectantly. In the embarrassed silence there was a general move to make a passage for her and her companion.

Although eighty percent of the patrons of Lake Nine would never go to a live theatre presentation, there was no doubt in their minds who this dominating presence was. Catherine continued her entrance graciously. A different person than the one standing on the loading dock a few moments earlier, she played the role she loved: the star being admired. Catherine, the actress, moved toward the rear of the long, high, pressed-tin ceiling room. Those at the bar pushed back between the stools making room for her to pass.

As she moved toward them Parnell stared, transfixed. "I know her, Kate—from where, Kate?—Where do I know her from?" Kate studied Parnell and then looked back to Catherine.

"From Philadelphia, perhaps?" She arched a dark eyebrow skeptically.

"Or Enid, Oklahoma." Sully muttered. He hadn't taken his eyes off the striking apparition now about to squeeze past them.

Catherine moved smoothly until her eyes locked with Parnell's. The moment broke her confident stride. Her defenses dropped. Shocked by a questioning recognition, she stared blankly back at Parnell. The moment was not lost on Kate. Wolf's eyes caught the sharp interchange as well. A positive/negative charge surged between The Cat and Parnell. It sparked and held. Wolf nervously nudged Catherine forward. His glance flashed from Kate to Parnell—to Catherine. He nudged The Cat again. She pulled herself together. With exaggerated cynicism the actress gave the rhinestone cowboy a controlled once over look—from head to foot. Parnell wilted. Catherine was back in control.

Kate nudged Sully. "That witch is from somewhere, Sully, but it sure ain't Enid, Oklahoma."

Catherine crossed eyes with Kate: a flash of flint and steel. Then she beckoned Wolf to follow and moved toward the smoke filled back of the room and dance floor. Patrons were settling down again to their tables and drinks. The country Western band, taking a break, quickly stood to make room for the star and Wolf. Catherine, in full Mae West fashion, responded. "Thanks, fellers. Now why don't you strike up the music? We are here to shake it out."

Something forced her to cut a look back to Parnell. He was staring. He had not taken his eyes off her. Wolf had seen her put her claws into other men. She was not above a one-night stand for her amusement, but this strange and strained connection was beyond a recreational engagement. Although Wolf was jealous of her "sporting pleasure", as she referred to her brief sexual encounters, she always returned to him. But not with a passion he would have liked. Her sexual encounters with him were more of a release for her, a pill to put her to sleep. Wolf settled for the fact that she needed him, if only to orchestrate her traveling show and be a sounding board for her countless hours of bitching. *One day, one time ... she will really need me,* he consoled himself, stirring his thoughts in bitterness. In the meantime he would be there, her suffering, silent caretaker.

Wolf glanced toward a darkly frustrated Parnell. The cowboy was speaking to the big bearded man at his side. The lady with them was watching Catherine. Wolf noted the frustration in her glance. She must be the cowboy's lover, he reasoned. They had something in common he could identify with. There was a little consolation in that thought. A half smile parted the thin lips beneath his pencil thin mustache before he turned away. He washed the cowboy from his mind—or tried to.

Somewhere, in the nether regions of Wolf's past there was an irritating itch of recognition. Had he known this man? Wolf forced his attention back to the present. The itch lingered beneath the skin. *What the hell were they doing playing this cow town, anyway? Where had Catherine led them this time? Why?*

\* \* \*

"Where the hell do I know that woman from, Sully?"

"Your dreams, cowboy." Sully answered flatly. He turned back to the bar for his Kamikaze.

Parnell considered his unknown dream for a troubling moment before dismissing the thought. If the woman he watched brought on his nightmares, he would remember her. "In my dreams? Bullshit, Sully."

"I wasn't being serious. Hell, I don't dare dream about a woman like that." Sully looked back toward the table where Catherine and Wolf had settled in. "I would awaken in a pitiful state, forced to start life over as a eunuch." Sully watched Wolf give an order to Maggie, the stout waitress. She gave the trim stranger a questioning look. After ordering, he ignored her. With a shrug, Maggie headed back to her station. Mondo was waiting.

"They want wine," she told him. "A bottle of white wine on ice and they want it in a bottle—with a cork, Moe. Can you believe it? None of this screw off gallon stuff. That's what the weird duck said." The bartender grinned. "We got that shit, Moe?"

"You'll have to hang on a minute, Maggie. It's in the cellar. A bottle of that "shit" as you refer to it, hasn't been decanted since my old man, Mondo the first, had it smuggled in from Italy during Prohibition. Mother buried the balance of the red with the old man when he died. She saved the white." Moe raised a trap door behind the bar and dropped through into the darkness. Sully leaned over the bar and watched in anticipation until the bartender returned cradling a dust covered green bottle. He washed it under the tap. What was left of the label went with the dust.

Parnell was amazed to see Mondo produce a corkscrew. He'd never seen one before in Lake Nine. The cork was sound. Moe sniffed it and nodded in appreciation. He noticed Parnell and Sully watching. "There been six of these bottles lying down there in the dirt since Mama died. When I was a kid there used to be cases of it. Ma drank a bottle every Sunday until she passed on. Only one customer used to buy it. I guess he left before it was all gone." Parnell nodded, half listening. He was concentrating on The Cat.

Mondo filled a galvanized bucket with ice and screwed the tall bottle down into it. "Here, Maggie." He slid a tray onto the bar. "Tell the lady we got no stem ware. She'll have to drink it out of a rock glass." He put two heavy pieces of non-crystal onto the tray with the wine.

"Stem ware?"

"Never mind, Maggie, just tell her. And tell her it's on the house." Maggie did a double take.

"On the house?" She shook her head in wonder, hefted the heavy tray and headed back into the fray.

Sully had done a double take as well. He turned to face Mondo. "On the house?" He mouthed the words with exaggeration. They were words seldom heard in Lake Nine. "I hope that

44

woman becomes a steady customer," Sully said. "I liked the sound of that, Moe."

"I won't let it become a habit, Sully." Moe glanced about. All eyes were on the star. "But one time for you and Parnell while nobody is watching. Kamikaze?"

"A double, amigo." Moe winced.

Catherine and the band members were in a deep discussion. Ill at ease, Wolf sat by in silence. Catherine indicated her escort. "He's a great fiddle player. Go on, Wolf, sit in with them."

Wolf, studying Parnell again, brushed aside her comment. "Where do we know that man from, Catherine? That cowboy at the bar?" Catherine cocked a skeptical eye at him.

"We? … You too?" She cast a quick glance toward the bar. "Don't include me in your past escapades, maestro." Knowing Wolf despised country music, she gave him a nudge under the table with the sharp toe of her cowboy boot. "Tighten your G string, Wolfie, and play with these fine musicians. Here is a chance to express your versatility." She was rewarded. The muscles of Wolfgang's tight Russian jaw line bulged, exhibiting marbles of discontent an inch beneath each ear. He knew he'd been had. Catherine was slyly pleased.

"It's not my kind of music, Catherine. I don't know the "licks". Let it be." But she was not about to let it rest. Turning imploringly to the be-spangled bandleader, surreptitiously spitting his cud of spearmint-flavored Copenhagen into a coke bottle, she said:

"Wolf is shy. It's his Romanian heritage." Wolf flinched at being called a Romanian. "But, despite his birthright, he has a real country flourish when he gets a fiddle under that pointed red chin of his."

"I am a Russian," Wolf growled almost under his breath. He was used to this game. Why did he let Cat get under his skin? "I am not from the swamps of Romania."

"Ah, yes, he's a Red, folks. But then, Russians can be musical, too. Come on, Wolfie. Show them." She gave him another nudge with her booted toe.

The bandleader, on his feet now, fingered out the remainder of his Copenhagen. He was free to speak. "Hell yes," he said. "You can't be that bad. We'll try to foller ya." Other members of the band were in general agreement. With Catherine egging him on, Wolf had no choice.

The regular fiddler crossed quickly to his stand. He grabbed his prized instrument and presented it to the frustrated Russian. "We're open minded here, man," he said. "Red, white or blue, we don't care where you're from as long as you can make music. Play her. She's a jewel. My grandpa brought her from Italy."

Amidst scattered applause Wolf was urged onto the improvised platform where he grudgingly tuned the strings. Although it was not the quality instrument he would prefer, he was inwardly surprised to find it quite resonant. *From Italy? An Italian cowboy?* He took the piece of rosin he carried for his own instrument, and rosined the bow.

The regular fiddle player watched, impressed. He leaned in to Catherine. "That friend of yours is a true professional."

"He's been around a few times," she answered. Highly amused, Catherine grinned at Wolf's displeasure. Underneath her surface reactions she had a purpose. The bottle of wine, iced in the galvanized bucket was placed on her table. The country fiddle player, proudly showing his knowledge of worldly ways, poured a taste for her. Catherine swirled it in the highball glass, and sniffed. She was pleasantly surprised. "Italian wine too?" She raised an eyebrow to the country fiddler. He shrugged. Maggie stood by.

"Moe says it's I-talian." She stressed the "I" in Italian, a local custom. "Not only that, it's on the house." The waitress looked back to the bar for confirmation. A free drink was definitely something special in Lake Nine. Moe grinned with a nod. Maggie went on: "Mondo's mama used to drink it, so Mondo says. It's I-talian like she was—the wine that is. She was I-talian, too, Mrs. Mondo. Mrs. Mondo they used to call her. I met her. My old man used to bring me in here, until he died, while I was in high school. I dropped out my freshman year because of it." Maggie shrugged. "Who am I? Me, I don't know?"

Catherine was trying to ignore the waitress, but Maggie persisted. In the hazy back of Maggie's mind she thought she might get a tip out of this one. Here, it didn't happen often. In Lake Nine, the best Maggie could hope for was to get laid. She wasn't into women, but maybe the fiddle player, the regular one. She didn't want to get laid by a Russian, a "Red?" *No way.* Giovanni, the regular fiddle player, had taken her to a motel in Trinidad once—last year?—or was it the year before? She looked at him. He was looking the other way, his prick attention totally on the "STAR". Maggie shrugged again. *You win one you lose ten.* "We don't have no stem ware." She blurted the line out louder than she meant to. It hooked Giovanni. He looked up at her. She would give him the impression she was knowledgeable in the realms of stemware. "Mondo sends his apologies." Maggie smirked at the fiddle player. Catherine pushed a crumpled bill into her wet hand. The waitress checked to see if it was a one or a five. It was a five. She broke into a victorious grin. She'd take a fiver over Giovanni any night.

"Who's the fading rhinestone at the bar?" Catherine asked with feigned nonchalance. "The guy who can't take his eye off us?" Maggie double-checked the "five" on the edge of the green bill. She knew who the lady was talking about. She didn't have to look. She'd had a wet spot between her legs for Parnell since he came to town. But Parnell was in Kate's corner. Maggie knew she didn't have a pink chance against that one. Kate was here tonight, standing right behind Parnell. Maggie was suddenly intrigued. *Was this weird one, guzzling I-talian wine, going to cross with Kate? It would serve that uppity bitch right.* Maggie did not like waiting tables the nights Kate bartended. Kate made her feel inferior.

"I don't know", she said, answering Catherine's question. " ... Parnell, I think"

The fiddle player looked sharply up. He didn't like Parnell. Men who met Parnell either liked him instantly or were jealous of his easy winning ways with women. The fiddle player was one of the latter.

"He's here every Saturday night," Giovanni broke into the conversation. "Every other night too I guess." He topped off Catherine's glass with the chilled wine. "He's a Godamn alcoholic."

"Really?" Catherine ignored Giovanni. She smiled up at Maggie. "Does he dance?"

"He dances good, lady." Maggie had had the tail end of a dance with Parnell one night. "He can move to any kind of music." Maggie looked over to Parnell, remembering. She turned back to Catherine. "He does it real good!"

Catherine dismissed her with a nod of her head. Maggie stepped back, remembering that one dance.

The fiddle player tasted the white wine. To him, dry was sour. He didn't like it, but hid the fact. Catherine attention was on Parnell. He didn't like that either. "That cowboy is too drunk to dance," he said. Gathering his courage, he stood and offered his hand to Catherine. "Would you do me the honor?" He nodded toward the band. "Your friend is pretty fair on the strings." Catherine wasn't listening. Parnell had hooked her. From the corner of his glance, Giovanni saw Maggie watching the interchange. He knew his moves wouldn't work. So did Maggie. She grinned. There was a long beat of frustrating silence. "But, maybe you're too tired, Miss Catherine," he offered lamely, "dancing on the stage and all." Catherine wasn't listening. The fiddler gave Parnell a cold look and took his seat. He signaled Maggie to bring him a beer. *The fat waitress might have to do tonight,* he thought. *She's a bit heavy, but responsive,* he calculated, recalling vaguely the night he had taken her to the motel. *A thank you girl.* "Thank you, thank you," said the fat and ugly ones. That was as far down the charity lane as the Italian fiddler would go.

But Maggie's mind was in a negative mode. *I'll fetch his Budweiser for no tip, but I'll be no second fiddle tonight. Hard to get, that's me.* Who was she kidding? Maggie turned to get the beer. From the corner of her eye she spotted a new comer to the festive atmosphere of Lake Nine. This one was something else, and being something else, conceivably a tip. She hoped he would find a table and not stop at the bar.

* * *

Teddy Lungran, Catherine's lead male dancer, caused little fuss as he moved along the crowded bar. He was playing the "macho" role he used on stage and when he was cruising a new hunting ground. His eyes roved the tight denim covered cowboy butts along the bar, marking in his mind the younger ones:—*a smorgasbord.* A sudden change in the music's pace from the platform diverted his attention. He stopped behind Parnell. *What the hell is Wolf doing with this poor-boy country band?* Then he realized. *Cat must have put him up to it.* Teddy pulled the black Stetson down close to his eyes. He spread his legs and crossed his arms. *This would be a show. The Cat was here somewhere.* He spotted her at the table with the fiddler.

"Can I find you a chair at a table in the back?" Teddy looked down at the stout pretty waitress standing before him. He smiled.

*Keep them fooled.* "No thanks, Ma'am," Teddy said, assuming his Gary Cooper façade. "I'm a-goin' to find a tight slot here at the bar."

From two steps behind him, Kate watched this new addition to the company. She picked up on the phony speech and moves. *Another actor wasted in a great body.* The muscles were for show. *This man did no work.* Parnell, surprisingly sober, rose from the stool and turned to face Teddy. Intent on his goal, he pushed the bigger man aside. Brushing past Kate, Parnell started for the dance floor. Bewildered, Kate watched him go. Then she understood. *What has this witch from Enid got?* She thought. *What curse has she put on Parnell?* Parnell was not acting on his own. *He's under a spell.* Kate pushed Teddy onto the stool left vacant by Parnell and stepped out where she could get a better view.

Walking among the tables, Parnell pointedly ignored Catherine, the Star. He stopped to exchange a few words with a friend, patting the lady sitting with him familiarly on the shoulder. Thinking the intriguing Parnell Mackenzie was asking her to dance, she got up, happy to accept. About to move into the unusual blues rhythm of the music she found herself confronted by Catherine's back. The Cat lady had stepped between them.

At the end of the bar, her back against the wall, Kate watched with curiosity and a flush of jealousy.

Catherine moved with the slow heavy country blues beat drawing Parnell after her by some taut invisible cord. Parnell's body swung tightly with the music. By contrast, Catherine flowed, her body loose and easy. As the rhythm changed subtly, her moves and sexual aura taunted the man following her, drawing him closer; cutting him back. Holding him at a stiletto point: honing the edge, letting him feel the steel, skin close, then giving him space he didn't want.

Led by Wolf, who knew what he was doing, the beat became staccato, changed rhythms, plowed ahead in a different key. The music stopped in mid stride, stumbled momentarily, as the musicians tried to sync with Wolf's lead. He directed them into it, and they picked up the pace on cue. Wolf had the music by the gonads—Cat had Parnell by the balls. Cat took a strong lead. Other dancers, confused by anything more than a country two-step cleared the floor.

Grinning, Wolf switched to a comic beat leaving Parnell acting like a fool, fumbling to catch up. Catherine grinned and clapped her hands overhead, flamenco fashion, hammering her steel-capped heels into the hard pine floor. She flew into the Spanish dance, bringing a new thrust of music from Wolf's frantic strings. The crowd cheered, howling at Parnell's desperate effort to keep up. Catherine acknowledged the reaction with a sweeping bow. With no warning she grabbed her stumbling partner and pulled him close. Biting the lobe of his ear, drawing blood, she led him now into an exaggerated tango step. Wolf followed her lead, snapping the desperate country western band from one step of Spain to another. The Russian's playing was in a different class but they were into it now. They loved it, hanging on, kicking out the best they could. Confused, excited by the challenge, their eyes followed Wolf's lead. The guitar, keyboard, bass and banjo, first dominant were dominated now by the fiddle. The band added to the dissonant fire and the tempo built. Wolf eyed the dancers. Darkly, he changed the pace and mode on The Cat's instinctive command. Wolf knew these "licks".

Somewhere in his subconscious Parnell heard the violin scream from his dreams. He gathered strength. He fought back, struggling to the surface, reaching for the air. Gulping down life's breath he seized the seductive Cat's snake-hard waist, and forced her into an improvisational wild country-come-jazz number that built with the wild tempo and intensity of Wolf's mad playing. For the moment Parnell's unorthodox moves forced Catherine to the edge—but not over it.

The dance was a savage duel: a contest of one mind and body against the other. For this moment, Parnell's moment, the players were evenly matched, raw and sexual, verging on violence. Around the floor and at the bar, the bewitched observers, caught up in the barbarous heat of the rhythm, reacted with a true human blood lust. Crying out, they clapped and stomped their booted feet in cadence with the insane beat. Catherine played her audience throughout. The actress in her gave her an added rush, a second breath she desperately needed. She and Parnell may be alone on the floor, but they were snared in the coils of swirling fate. The coils were contracting.

Parnell grinned. Heroically hiding his fatigue, he hung on. "Go Parnell!" Sully yelled from the sidelines, encouraging his friend, fading in the arms of Wonder Woman. His words were lost in the tumult.

Parnell was not one to give in easily but he was out-danced and outclassed here. He was in deep shit, to put it succinctly. Sully could see it. So did they all. Kate, as if a witness to an execution, couldn't turn away. She was mute, deaf to Sully's cry of false encouragement. The dance stormed like a prairie fire in a hot New Mexico wind. With steel heels, Catherine beat out the cadence. She had her second wind, now. It carried her like a ghost before the ground-hugging furry of the flames. In her wake, singed earth and ash.

The Cat, knew the end was at hand. She looked to Wolf, giving him the nod. The musician, swinging through darkness, drove the tempo even faster. Reaching for a killing climax, screaming in the fire, the fiddle blazed. Parnell made a last valiant effort to prevail. It was in vain. His tangled feet, driven to a frenzied blur, no longer could articulate. His equilibrium lost, he dizzily collapsed. Wolf took the music out with a flourish. Decibels in Lake Nine dropped to zero. It was over.

Catherine struck a pose, meeting the crescendo on the final beat before the silence. In triumph, she towered over the dropped Parnell. Exulting in her conquest, The Cat stepped gracefully upon a table and bowed grandly to her audience. They stood in awe. Tempered by guilt, having screamed for blood and seen it flow, they now shifted in uneasy silence. The applause faded. They had seen a man destroyed. He lay before them, a testament to sacrifice. It took some minutes to realize the man wasn't dead.

Parnell, his head in his arms, gasped for breath. His was the only sound heard in Lake Nine. The fallen dancer struggled to look up at Catherine. "What do you want, woman?" He barely got the words out. "What in Christ's name do you want?"

"You, Parnell! You owe me. On a platter. I want you."

"So—Bring me the head of John the Baptist?" He said in defeat. Parnell's head sank back into his arms, back between his knees. He had had it. "Shit." His words hushed around the stunned patrons of Lake Nine.

Then, there was a guilty snicker from the crowd followed by an empty scattering of applause. Slowly it grew in volume. Even Sully joined in. *No one was dead,* he reasoned. *No blood was spilled. No harm done, except perhaps to Parnell's ego, and that could stand a few blows.* Sully looked about him. Kate was staring blindly at the wall. Teddy, the big man who had taken Parnell's seat was strangely silent. Sully questioned his reason. *Maybe blood had run in the sawdust.*

The applause, joined by hoots and yells, gained momentum. Sully looked from the stranger back to Kate. Kate stared poison at the woman who had danced her man into the dust. The eyes of the two women locked. In the background Sully saw someone help his fallen friend to a chair at the table upon which Catherine posed. The witch lady broke eye contact with Kate. She withdrew the savage stare like a blade from flesh. There would be no more applause from Sully. Something had gone down here tonight that was not exactly human: something vicious: *perhaps all too human,* he thought. Lust for blood was a very human quality: a feeding frenzy. Sully wondered if he should go to Parnell.

Catherine stepped from the tabletop to the floor via Parnell's lap. He didn't wince. Sully did. Without a backward look, The Cat collected Wolf. They headed for the exit. Sully and Kate made room for them to pass. It was a narrow channel mined with electricity. Parnell, unmoving, gathered enough strength to look after them. When Catherine passed Kate neither woman drew a dagger Sully heaved a sigh of pent up relief and went to Parnell.

"What's your pleasure, Dancin' Man?" He cocked an eye down at the destroyed Mackenzie. "Or have you had all the pleasure one man can stand in a restricted lifetime?"

"Bring me a double Kamikaze, Sully. I'll never again accuse you of drinking poison."

# CHAPTER FOUR

# After the Ball

Wolf and Catherine stood under the muted street lamps in front of the Santa Fe Railroad station. Over the hoods and windshields of scattered cars and ranch trucks in the parking lot, the lights of Lake Nine gleamed in the distance. Catherine, leaning against the building, was watching the front of the bar. "We will wait here for developments, Wolf." Wolf was not a happy fiddler.

"Why, Catherine?" he cried pacing back and forth, his eyes flashing from Cat, to the lights of Lake Nine. "What developments? What the hell are we doing playing this provincial cow town?" Catherine made no move to answer. "Why here, Cat?"

"It was an open date, Wolf. Better play for half price than not play at all. As you say, 'play to pay'. We got to pay the company, Wolf. You know the business." The few people who had followed them out of the bar with curiosity had drifted back inside. No one was in the street. Nor were there any new sounds from the Country Western band. Catherine kept her furtive attention on the distant entrance of Lake Nine.

"I know the business, Catherine," Wolf continued, cutting a quick glance at Lake Nine, "and I have seen the books. I went over them this afternoon. It seems our date in Denver has been canceled. I made a call to verify my fears. You might have mentioned that fact. That was a big date, Cat. We needed it." In agitation, Wolf produced a silver cigar case. He slid a slim dark panatela between his even teeth and clamped down on it. "Look at me, Catherine." Catherine took her attention away from Lake Nine for a moment to meet Wolf's gaze. Trying to keep her attention, he cried out in frustration. "Forget about that damn cowboy, Cat. You've done him enough damage. You tore him up. Why? I don't know." She stared at him blankly. "So be it." He sighed and popped the cigar case closed. Wolf struck a match angrily. "Instead of Denver, we end up with this gig. Rainbow is a ghost town, Cat. This is nowhere. To lead us further astray, you gave Toad the wrong directions and we drive in clouds of dust over dried mud ruts for forty miles to get here." Catherine made no move to answer. Wolf puffed fiercely on the panatela, shrouding them in smoke. "What the hell is going on, Cat?" He cried.

No response.

In the silence of Wolf's frustration he looked south. His gaze followed the railroad tracks rounding the bend past a row of coal bins. "I wish we traveled by train," he sighed, the anger gone for a moment. "That's the way it used to be done. It would be an easy trip to Santa Fe." He paused a moment, then looked back at her. "We do still have that gig don't we? ... the Santa Fe gig?"

"You didn't call to check?" Catherine pushed from the adobe wall and moved only far enough to lean against a cast iron lamp-post at the rear door of the closed Santa Fe station. Her eyes had drifted back to Lake Nine. She spoke laconically. "How close did you look at that dream book, Wolfie?"

"Dream book?" Wolf shrugged. "I looked close enough," he said, " to surmise that the Santa Fe date is the only solid date in the near future."

Catherine reached out and took the cigar from Wolf's mouth. She drew deeply and inhaled, holding the heavy smoke in her lungs. "Tomorrow night may be our swan song, Maestro. You better prepare to pawn your strings." The words went up in smoke.

Wolf glanced pointedly at the sign on the railroad station. The station, the sign existed. What else was real? "Damnit it, Cat, we do play Santa Fe next week. —Don't we? We still got that date?— Don't we?" he repeated with vanishing hope. She looked at him, raising a brow sarcastically. Her gaze drifted back to Lake Nine. "We don't still have that date, Cat?" he paused. —"Do we?" Wolf knew the answer by now. Catherine clarified it.

"It's like looking at the Sears Roebuck catalogue when I was a kid," she said quietly. "It's the dream book of Enid Oklahoma,' Aunt Lucy used to say. Uncle Joe ordered enough seeds and farm tools to keep the book coming each year. Aunt Lucy ordered cardboard boots and long johns to be passed down from my big brother to me and on down three times from there. No one ever got the lace panties the boys used to look at when the book made its ultimate way to the outhouse. Uncle Joe and Aunt Lucy Wiggins ran an orphan farm, Wolf. Thirteen state supported orphans passed through their hands before I reached the age of fifteen and fled." She looked back at the fiddle player. "No, Wolf, the dream book just <u>says</u> we play Santa Fe. Just like it said we were to play Denver."

Wolf stepped fruitlessly below the Santa Fe sign and looked up. Catherine sucked in another lung full of cigar smoke and held it. "It's all wishful thinking, Wolf," she said. "It's fantasy, Wolf. Just like the theatre. We live and sell fantasies." She finally exhaled. "Fantasies go up in smoke."

"For Christ sake, Catherine. You've told no one?"

"You, Maestro, are the first to know." Through the shifting cigar smoke, The Cat saw nothing change under the lights of Lake Nine. "Consider yourself lucky," she said absently. "You have an extra twenty-four hours to prepare for unemployment." Wolf wheeled about and marched angrily back to confront her. Cat shoved the cigar butt in his mouth. "Thanks for the stogie." She turned back toward the bar. Wolf choked.

"Actors are resilient, Wolf," Catherine went on in a maddeningly calm voice. "Don't worry, Wolfy. Actors can't fantasize failure. They have no self, but what they portray on stage, wherever that stage might be. Actors live in another world, to coin a phrase. We live and die on cue."

"But why here, Catherine? Why come here to end it all? Nobody needs a rehearsal to die. You do it right the first time. Death is one act you don't fuck up, lady. You don't forget the lines." Wolf stalked back under the Santa Fe Railroad sign and looked up at it as if it were pointing the way to heaven. *Railroad to heaven: steel tracks, a skid-way, The Death Special.* Beneath his troubled thoughts of a failed career, there was something more frightening. The fiddler felt a heavy undertow. Something was sucking him into the quicksand beneath the clouded water, suffocating him. He looked down to Catherine. She looked very unlike The Cat. She looked afraid—terrified. "Cat," he said quietly, "What's the mater?"

"I know this place, Wolf. I've been here. That's why I was brought back here." Her voice was off center and off stage. "Wolf, I played this town before. When? I have no idea. I mean it's crazy, but I played this town—and I came back—I was pulled back to play this town again." She twisted her mouth up and raised an eyebrow. "A fantasy, right, maestro? A dream? No, I think not. This second time is the final curtain. No third chance."

"You're crazy, Cat." Wolf was decidedly uneasy. Despite his denial he felt the draw, too. He was in a land of ghosts. "What the hell are you talking about, Cat?"

"You feel it too?"

"Not me, Cat," Wolf denied. "I got no feelings. I've worked for you too long to have any feelings left."

"We feel it." She said it as a fact that needed no further explanation. "We." She nodded thoughtfully. "This 'we' is very interesting."

Wolf shook his head vigorously. "I've never been here Catherine. I can't even imagine I am here now. Never!" He studied the woman he worked with. He had never seen her like this. Her face was pale, her hands trembling. For the first time in their ten years of working together, The Cat was frightened.

"Cat," he said softly, changing the subject, trying to buck her up. "We can get the show back together, add a few new scenes. We can rewrite the whole god damned thing if you want. Or better yet, do something completely new. I mean we are running around in an old shoe. Let's do some really new stuff, give it some fresh licks ... slightly absurd … Theatre of the Absurd, Oh Dad, Poor Dad—Becket?" *This whole thing is absurd,* he thought. *This is like Waiting For Godot.* But he went on, desperately trying to convince Catherine to make a break from the past and get on with the show. "We could do something like that crazy dance you did tonight with your drunk cowboy, something unreal. Cat, lets get on the road with stuff kids like; pump in some of this rock music—country, if you want—anything to get us back on track." The Cat was unmoved. Wolf wondered if she even heard him.

"Never," she said absently, her mind in another world— another life. Inwardly Wolf collapsed, drained.

Thunder cut through the blue night heat of the high New Mexican desert. With it came a blast of Country Western music. The Lake Nine band was back in action. Live bodies burst from the entrance of the bar. Suddenly alert, Catherine sprang from the support of the iron light pole. Wolf sank to the steps beneath the Santa Fe Railroad sign. Win or lose, Catherine was on a roll. Live or die, he was hooked. He would have to stay with her.

Years ago Wolf had put his career—his life on the line to boost her into her first leading role. He had escaped a legitimate murder charge but it had cost him. Now he was dependent upon her. She was his meal ticket in more ways than one. He was stuck with her. Or was he just too weak to strike the needed blow and walk away? *Why? Habit? Loyalty? Masochism?* He cursed silently and hurled the cold cigar butt out into the parking lot.

* * *

In the burst of Country music, Sully and Teddy lurched through the swinging doors of Lake Nine. One at each end, they carried a muddled Parnell between them. Kate followed. She crossed quickly to Parnell's truck and rolled down the bedroll she had shared with him, on a number of less troubled evenings. Kate spread it out on the rusting floor of the pickup. "Easy with him," she cried, the nurse leading the dying into the emergency room. Sully and Teddy, not exactly concerned with the plight of her patient, swung Parnell roughly back and forth, gathering momentum. "On the count of three," Sully cried, hanging on to Parnell's booted ankles. Teddy had him by the wrists. They were both very drunk.

"Easy!" Kate cried again. Her words went unheard. On the count of three, Parnell took flight.

"One Kamikaze coming up." Teddy cried. He lurched against the fender of the Chevy and regained his balance.

"I said, be careful," Kate cried. Too late. Parnell's limp body crashed heavily against a bale of hay and slid into the nest she was trying to make for him. It was not ready. Beneath the bedroll lay a heavy wagon jack and a couple of spare tires. It made little difference where Parnell landed. He felt no pain.

Satisfied with the placing of their charge, Sully pulled a new bought pint from his hip pocket and raising it heavenward, proposed a solemn toast. "Here's to the new and undisputed Kamikaze king of Rainbow, New Mexico." He glanced at the supine Parnell and took a heavy belt before passing the bottle over to Teddy. Teddy took a guarded sip.

*Why the hell am I doing this,* Kate wondered, as she pulled out the jack and tried to arrange the heavy tires. *The man's a fool and a looser. What's my connection here? Why do I care?* Undeterred by her reasoning, she tucked her inert lover into his makeshift bedroll.

Sully took the bottle back. He wiped his mustache and beard. "Never saw Parnell pass out before, Theodore," he said to the dancer leaning over the edge of the pickup bed. "Of course, I never seen him act like he did tonight either. And him a God damned Doctor, an MD. You know that, Teddy?" But Teddy was now contemplating the fact that a middle-aged Parnell would be better than no boy at all. "Theodore?" Sully gave the dancer a sideways look. *There might be a problem here.*

Teddy calculated his possible moves. "This boy just didn't know when to quit, Sully, that's all," he said. "He must have downed twenty of those suckers." Teddy started to hoist himself over the tailgate. "You drive, Sully. I'll see that he's taken care of." Kate got a grip on Teddy's sturdy but unsteady body and jerked him back.

"I'll take care of him Teddy," she said. "I think you better go home to bed so you're ready for tomorrow's performance."

"But," Teddy interjected, crestfallen; then with a sudden rush, the determined would-be lover flopped over the tailgate and sprawled among the assorted junk at Parnell's feet. The stars twinkled above. "The boy didn't know when to quit, that's all," he cried. "I'll watch out for him. He'll be alright." He stroked Parnell's unfeeling thigh. "This man needs someone to take good loving care of him."

Kate pulled at the dancer, trying to drag him back. "I said, Teddy, I'd take care of Parnell. I doubt if he needs your loving care."

Don't worry, Teddy." Sully was now a bit concerned. "Kate can take care of him, Teddy. She's in love with him. He's used to her." Sully moved in beside Kate. "Theodore!" he cried out.

Kate slammed the dancer with her shoulder purse, "I'll take care of Parnell!"

Sully got a loose grip on the dancer's boots and started pulling. "She'll take care of him, Teddy," he yelled. "Just ease up."

Teddy gave up and lay back. He looked at the stars twinkling above and sighed. It was definitely a night for romance. *Must it be unrequited?*

The Cat's voice materialized out of the darkness. "They'll take care of him, Teddy bear." "You better go get some rest." Catherine stepped from the shadows and looked at the wilted Parnell. "My, my, down for the count. That makes twice in one evening."

"You put him there," Kate hissed between clenched teeth.

"And again and again, my dear, and once more again. It is so written." Catherine turned dramatically to the chagrined Teddy. "Go home, Teddy bear, like the lady said. Go to bed. Sleep it off. You need your beauty sleep."

Kate spotted Wolf lurking in the background. Her eyes cut back to Catherine. "Just who the hell are you anyway?" She said. "And where do you come from?"

"She comes from Enid, Oklahoma." Teddy said matter-of-factly, lifting his head over the tailgate of the pickup. "She is the orphan of Enid. That's where she comes from. As to who she really is? —That's a good question."

The Cat beckoned to Teddy sternly. "Come on, little bear. This is out of your league." Teddy crawled from the truck and leaned against the wall of Lake Nine. Catherine glanced down at the apparently defunct Parnell. "Your friend looks dead."

"If Parnell is dead," Kate replied with a chill, "and he drank enough to die, he will come back to haunt you, lady, like he did before. He'll dance you into Hell." The remark unsettled Cat. She stepped back, tripping on the curb. Wolf moved quickly forward to support her.

"Come on, Catherine. This just isn't worth it." He collected Teddy on the way. The three of them melted into the darkness.

Kate and Sully watched in silence until they were out of sight, but not out of mind. Sully opened the driver door of the truck. He reached in to start the engine then thought better of it. He turned back to Kate. "You comin' with us?" He was thinking maybe it would be safer if she drove.

"No. It's time this kid either died or grew up. It won't be the fresh air blowing by the bed of this truck that kills him." She reached in one last time and tucked the sleeping bag in around him. "Take the body with you, Sully." She checked Parnell's pulse. "Something is pumping through his veins," she said. "He'll live. I'm going home." She hitched her purse over her shoulder with determination and struck out in the direction the three thespians hadn't taken. Sully shrugged and lurched in behind the wheel. The keys were still in the ignition. He snugged his battered Stetson down close to his eyes and drove, very carefully, out of town. In 1969, Rainbow's police department curled up early. If he didn't run into a lamppost, or drive through a plate glass window of the local meat market, they wouldn't uncoil. In his troubled mind, Sully determined it would be some time before he returned to Lake Nine.

# CHAPTER FIVE

# THE MORNING AFTER

The morning sun revealed Parnell's old Chevy crosswise of the cattle guard leading into the Sullivan ranch headquarters. Sully was wedged behind the wheel in a deep alcoholic coma. In his pickup bed, Parnell had not moved. Old Tom considered them for a while. He had been relieved to find them still breathing. He went back into the ranch kitchen and started a large pot of cowboy coffee: "one heaping tablespoon of grounds to one cup of water. When it comes to a boil," he muttered. Sully didn't like his brother talking to himself – but Sully wasn't there. Tom sliced potatoes and started thick strips of slab bacon frying over the middle lid of the Majestic wood-burning range. The blazing heat of the pitch-rich pinion had the front burners too hot for anything but boiling water for the coffee. He would slide the potatoes into the bubbling bacon fat when the time came then dry the fat out of them on paper towels used later to start the next fire.

Tom Sullivan was a fair ranch cook. Sully's wife, Iona, had taught him the ranch menus. His specialties were all basic but tasty meat and potato dishes. Old Tom liked to cook and retained the recipes surprisingly well in his shaken mind. He even invented variations of his own. His salads were a thing of wonder Parnell had told him. Although there were things about Parnell that stirred his troubled mind, Old Tom liked Parnell for saying that. Sully got used to his brother's salads: watercress, wild asparagus, lambs quarters; various fresh and dried herbs went into the making. Parnell knew about lambs quarters, or pigweed it was called, back in the east. Parnell had never heard of it being eaten. "It's delicious, something like spinach." That was the closest comparison Parnell could come up with. "Lamb's quarters is a kinder name than pig weed, Tom," he said.

When cooking, or gathering herbs, or "weeds", as Sully called them, Tom's mind was at rest in a world of his own making. He enjoyed the comfort and freedom of creation it gave him. In fruit season he baked pies. He tended and carefully pruned the two gnarled apple trees and the cherry and apricot that grew behind the ranch house. He made great jam although it was a bit tart for Parnell who had a sweet tooth. Tom treated growing plants tenderly and got the most out of them. Tom Sullivan understood plants better than people.

As Tom finished slicing the morning potatoes, he watched through the window for signs of life in the lopsided truck. Nothing. The stove was very hot, the front lids beginning to glow a soft red color in the heat. He paid no attention to it as he slid raised sourdough biscuits into the oven. He stared back toward the truck. Still no sign of life. He shook his head and muttered some platitude learned from his brother about the evils of drink. Sully, thought endless repetition, had drilled it into Tommy's unreceptive mind. "The evil of drink makes your life stink." Tom repeated it now, again and again, thinking maybe he should teach it back to his brother.

From the cupboard over the sink he pulled out a fifth of Old Taylor bourbon and two double shot glasses. Tom hadn't taken a drink in eight years. He was not about to start now, but from past experience he knew about the recuperative powers of "a hair of the dog". Satisfied, he sat at the round oak table where he could watch both the stove and the truck. He figured rightly that breakfast would be ready before his patients were. —"Patients?" he snapped vehemently, starting to his feet and staring angrily at the glowing Great Majestic kitchen stove that had been there since he was a boy. Smoke rose from the frying bacon. In a flash it burst into flame. "I am no God Damned Doctor!" Tom screamed, sloshing coffee from the pot into the flaming grease. Smoke, fire and steam exploded, rising in a flash to the rough beamed ceiling. Tom stood, unfeeling, holding the blackened coffee pot fiercely as the smoke and steam clouded around him. "I am no God Damned doctor!" He repeated the words with quiet intensity. The fire died out. Tom rinsed the pot and set fresh water to boil.

Tom didn't like moments of unexpected clarity like this. For almost eight years, after coming out of his last alcohol induced slump, and after his brother brought him around, or back to the semi-living, his habit actions had been exactly the same every morning. Today was an exception. Exceptions bothered Tom. His troubled night's sleep had been an exception too. He dreamed of the smoke and the bird he and Parnell saw diving through it. "It was the bird that spooked the cattle." Tommy knew that. Tom hadn't dreamed the bird in years. He knew Sully was afraid of it too. He didn't know what the wild bird meant, but it was not a good dream. "It is not good to have that bird dream in my head." Tom repeated that twice, ducking to look through the window to study the sky—to make sure the falcon wasn't there now.

When Old Tom woke that morning, he found he had fallen asleep in his clothes. He hadn't crawled under the covers either. He was cold and stiff—stiffer than usual. Sully had not looked in on him. Sully always looked in on him, even when he came in late, which he did on occasion. His brother would have got him undressed and under the covers. Maybe he had been waiting for Sully to do that. Sully always did that. "Sully always looks in on me. Sully always takes care of me," Tom spoke aloud. Tom didn't mind going to bed in the empty house because he knew, like the child he was, that sometime during the night his brother would look in on him. Last night, Sully had not looked in on him and he had had bad dreams.

Right now, half of Tom was acting on habit control. The other half was on the edge. Maybe it wasn't quite fifty-fifty. *Should he take his medicine? Had he taken it?* Tom didn't know. Taking his medicine was a part of his morning routine, but he had eased off on it the past year. Things had been good. But Sully gave him some yesterday. This morning he didn't know if he should take it or not—or if he had taken it. Yesterday he might have taken it twice. He wasn't sure. Sully had given medicine to him after the bird had swooped down, scaring the cattle. "That was twice in one day. Maybe?" He never took it twice in one day.

*Things are different with Parnell here,* he thought. W*hy?* "Maybe I should walk up onto the mesa", he said aloud. "Maybe? —Maybe that was not a good idea. Sully will be angry. Sully hates me to go to the mesa. I won't tell Sully. Should I go now?" He shook his head. "I'm talking to myself. It is not good."

The coffee water started to boil again. The sounds of the bubbling hot water brought Tom from his seat. He jumped up and looked around. —coffee. He was supposed to make coffee. He smelled the bacon and moved it back on the stove. It was over crisp. That was not good either. *Sully would be in from doing the chores and would need breakfast.* He looked out the window. *Sully would not be in from doing chores.* Tom tried to reason. Something was wrong. Sully was not moving in the truck. He would take Sully coffee in the truck—in Parnell's truck. *Was Parnell in the truck?* "I don't know." He couldn't remember going out to check.

Old Tom spooned eight tablespoons of coffee grounds from the battered coffee tin into the boiling water. It swirled up and boiled over on the stove. Quickly Tom pulled the pot back to the rear of the stove where it was cooler. The coffee settled down. "Bring it to a boil three times," he muttered. He could remember Iona saying that. "Where is Iona?" he said aloud. Sully is in the truck, but where is Iona?" Tom asked the questions. There was no one there to answer them. He didn't know the answers this morning. The coffee boiled over again. He remembered the cold-water treatment Iona had shown him. "Pour cold water over the boiling grounds and they will settle," he repeated what she had told him every morning. He would take coffee to his brother and his brother's friend—"If Parnell is in the truck. Parnell?" He was giving voice to all his thoughts. "That Parnell? The new Parnell?" The Parnell name jogged a lost thought in his twisted mind. "Parnell," he repeated. "Parnell knows the bird. Parnell saw the bird just like I see the bird. Sully never sees the bird."

Tom knew he mustn't tell Sully he saw the bird. "Sully hates it when I see the bird. But <u>the bird was in the smoke. I saw it.</u>"

Old Tom walked absently into the bathroom with the flush toilet and the claw-footed bathtub and oak cabinets where Iona had kept her things. He opened the cabinet where he and Sully put their razors. There were extra bars of soap and a squeezed tube of toothpaste. On top of the cabinet were extra rolls of toilet paper. There was a green can of Bag-Balm for cuts and soars. He reached in and took out a bottle of large yellow pills. He shut the cabinet door and looked at himself in the cracked mirror on the front of it. The old beveled mirror was clean. There were no smudges on it—just the crack. The bathroom was clean. Old Tom cleaned it every day like Sully liked it. He would clean it again later today. Old Tom walked back into the kitchen. He opened the old wood stove lid. The fire had gone down. He threw the bottle of pills into the coals. They were hot enough to melt the glass. Tom forgot about it. He scraped the burned bacon into the fire with the pills and laid fresh slabs in the cast iron fry pan. Beyond the stove, he saw the truck. "Sully?" he said, wondering what the truck was doing off the road.

The old man turned back to breakfast again. He had work to do. He poured cold water over the coffee and set the pot on the table to settle. He saw the whiskey and poured the two shot glasses full. He set the bottle and the shot glasses on the bread-board. He would use the breadboard as a tray. Then he poured two big thick China cups full of the black coffee. He liked sugar in his. Sully didn't. He didn't know about Parnell, so he didn't put sugar in either cup. He put the coffee cups on the breadboard tray and lifted it gingerly. He pushed open the front door with his toe. He had forgot to put his boots on, but that didn't matter. His feet were tough. He seldom even felt the stubble when he walked barefoot. At night he walked barefoot a lot. Sometime he woke up walking barefoot, with just his long johns on—or in the summer, sometimes nothing. He woke up sometimes walking at night – sometimes he would be way up on the mesa, a mile above the ranch house, where he wasn't supposed to go. He never knew how or why he got there. He never told Sully. Sully would be upset. He made himself come home, took a pill and crawled back into bed.

* * *

No one in the truck moved. Tom started singing a tune he learned as a child. One of the songs his mother sang when she was alive. He knew four or five of her tunes. The words were unclear in his mind. He knew other tunes, as well, but couldn't remember where he had learned them. He never sang these words to Sully. It made no difference. He made up words any-way—any words that he felt like singing. Tom tapped on the windshield and sang the words again in his frail high voice:

"Good morning to you.
Good morning to you.
Your horses are saddled.
You ought to be paddled.
What more can I say?
To brighten your day?

Behind the wheel Sully shook himself to almost life. He opened one bloodshot eye. Steam was rising from the thick China cups on the breadboard tray. Sully presumed it was cof-fee, hot coffee. "Just hand me the bloody cup, Tom," he grunted, "and shut up your mouth."

Old Tom giggled. "You got the doors locked, Brother Sully, and the windows up," he said. "Just who are you lockin' out … or lockin' in?" He giggled again.

Sully shook is head violently to clear it. Immediately he regretted the move. Inside his vibrating skull, the brainpan rattled loosely. He steadied himself, gained control and opened the door. "What about the body in the back, Tom? Is Parnell still there?"

"Here and ready to go," came the remarkably strong voice of last night's victim. Tom held out the breadboard tray. In hor-ror, Sully watched in the rearview mirror as Parnell reached out and took one of the shot glasses. He tipped his head back and drained it. Parnell smacked his lips. "Better than Alka-Seltzer, Sully. No plop-plop fizz-fizz. You should shoot the other one."

Sully shuddered. "I have contemplated shooting myself, Parnell. I don't know why you're alive this morning, let alone happy. You sure looked dead last night."

"I don't remember. It's a second coming, Sully. Best not to remember the first." He vaulted out of the pickup bed and regarded the second double shot. "Your brother Tom knows how to treat a drunk," he said. Sully crawled from the truck, gagging.

"Jesus Christ, Parnell. In my condition, seeing you drink that booze is more sickening than watching you pick your nose."

"You not well, Sully?" Parnell asked. He lifted the second shot of whiskey. "Somebody got to do it," he said. . "Brother Tom was good enough to bring the right medicine. If you're not going to take it, I shall." He drained the second shot. "Thanks, Tom. Now I shall pass judgment on your coffee." It had cooled a bit on the trip from the ranch kitchen and went down easily. "And thanks again, Tom." Parnell looked at Sully leaning over the fender of the truck as if he were about to upchuck. "Still not well, Sully?"

"Sick… And it's your damn fault, Parnell. You and the company you keep."

"You were the company I kept. I went to bed early. You stayed up all night. Parnell helped himself to another generous shot from the bottle Tom had been thoughtful enough to bring along balanced on the breadboard. Parnell offered the bottle to Sully.

"God, no. Help yourself, but do it out of my sight." Sully had a gray pallor, which didn't go well with the morning sun cresting Tinaja. Parnell turned to Tom.

"What's for breakfast besides the juice of whisky kindness you have fetched us here"?

"I got limp bacon, heating up, the way Sully likes it, and grease warmed eggs a-waitin' in the house."

"Enough! That's it," Sully cried. "That's it. Leave the truck where she is. We'll deal with her later. Let's mount up and ride out of here… get some fresh air. I been suffocatin' on my own farts in that sealed up cab too long. I need air."

Old Tom burst into a gale of giggles. Parnell put the bottle back on the tray. "Thanks anyway, Tom. We'll eat later when Sully is feeling healthy. The night on the town was too much for your brother."

"Speak for yourself, O King of the Kamikazes." Sully heaved a heavy sigh, snorted up a head-full of alcohol-induced phlegm and spat. He wiped beads of sweat off his furrowed brow. "Let's get these caballos saddled and ride into the hills. See if we can find any strays. I got to do something to ease my guilt." He took a sip of the coffee and held it down. "Drinkin' with you, Parnell, I feel worse than Christ crawling out of his tomb three days later."

"And you don't have half the problems to face that poor bugger did." Parnell grinned. "All we got to do is find some strayed cattle."

"Well, roll the rock aside and let's get on with it. I'm on the devil's own road as it is." Sully made a determined path toward the corral and the horses. Parnell shrugged and followed.

* * *

Old Tom watched them saddle up and swing on board. He fought off a strong desire to taste the whisky filling his nose with memories. He didn't touch it, but it had been the first time in years he wanted to. He wondered about that. What was happening? His mood changed quickly, as it often did. He giggled to himself and let it build into a loud, harsh cackling laugh that made Sully, even in his present condition, look at him sternly. Tom shut up. He glanced again at the whisky bottle. He shook his head and turned back to the ranch house.

"Keep the grease and eggs warm, Tom," Parnell called after him. "Sully will want them for lunch."

"Just shut up, Parnell." Sully pulled his gelding around and tried to think. "I'll ride the lower canyon, Parnell. You check the high ground on the mesa. We better come up with some cattle. I got a feeling I got a bar tab to pay. If you see any new calves, brand them where they are and keep the count." Both men had a branding iron shoved into the rifle boot lashed under the saddle skirt.

"You should never have tried to drive home, Sully. In your condition you might have ended up in jail. Me, I would have slept in the truck."

"You did sleep in the truck." A very sick Sully grumped and pushed his mount off into the trees. Then he remembered the chores and turned back. "I got chores," he called after Parnell. "And I want to check again on Tom. I'll catch up." Parnell waved him off and headed up the steep trail to the mesa.

"Thank God I did sleep in the truck," he mumbled to himself. Now that the act of acting as if he were healthy was over, he slumped over the roping horn of his saddle and let the fresh whisky settle him. He was glad Tom brought it out. He was glad too that he was going to be alone for a spell. He had fresh bourbon in him, now all he needed was time—a few hours of forgiving time.

\* \* \*

When Parnell broke out on top of the mesa the dry, hot, east wind hit him head on. He turned a quarter into it. The sun was already high enough to raise curls of heat waves off the black volcanic rocks that studded the brown grass and cactus. Ducking down into a swale he startled a crusty old cow and her unbranded calf. The calf at her heels, the cow lumbered up onto the flat at an awkward gallop. Parnell's mare automatically swung in behind them. Parnell pulled her in. There was no rush. He'd walk them along until he spotted some scraps of wood to make a fire to heat the branding iron.

On the mesa's east rim the cow turned toward the charred ruins of a small fire-gutted adobe home. The ruins had been left to the ravages of northern New Mexico weather for years. Tufts of gamma grass and cactus grew within the low, dissolving mud walls. Two vigas, or log rafters, sagged from the highest remaining northeast corner wall. A small section of sod roof clung to the old hand-hewn beams. Beneath the high end of the rafters was a typical beehive fireplace. The chimney was of adobe mud and stacked shale rock, which weathered better than the adobe and held the timbers up. Sections of wall facing east and north from the chimney had also survived. In the east wall was a small four-light window, the glass and mullion long gone. The window's opening framed Mt. Tinaja's striking volcanic plug. The plug, the final thrust of molten rock to rise from the heaving bowels of the earth cooled, holding its shape, and plugged the volcano's core. A mile in the distance it raised to the height of eight thousand feet.

In the same adobe wall, south of the window, stood the blackened remains of a doorframe. The charred plank door sagged from one hinge. The old feral cow turned in through the door and kept going, easily leaping the low adobe wall to the west. The calf followed but was pulled up as Parnell's braided leather Mexican rope snaked out circling the calf's heels. The heifer hit the ground, squalling. The old cow whipped around. Parnell was already on the ground. His trained mare backed automatically, taking up the slack in the rope. In seconds Parnell had the calf's hind and fore legs lashed together with a short length of "pigging" rope. He tossed the loop of the lariat aside. The mother cow charged back as far as the low adobe wall where she skidded to a stop and bellowed her rage.

"Don't worry, cow, we're not going to hurt your baby. Just burn her a bit with the same brand you been marked with. Didn't seem to slow you down any." He left the little heifer and coiled his rope back to the mare and tied it to the saddle. He slid out the branding iron and stepped back into the ruins. "Lots of wood scraps here, old cow. Your baby is no bull calf so we won't have to cut her. Be thankful for that. She can grow up to enjoy sex." He scuffed scraps of wood in front of the fireplace hearth. One piece looked vaguely familiar. He picked it up and wiped away the dry adobe stuck to it. It was the blackened neck of a violin. The ebony pegs were still in place, the delicate neck and fret board, charred but very recognizable. Parnell studied it in silence. Something snapped.

The alcoholic fog shrouding the memory of last night cleared. The music came back. The dark tan on his face turned an ashen gray beneath the sun color. Clutching the fiddle neck, he staggered to the fireplace, sliding back into his haunting dream of two nights past. Only this time he was awake.

Parnell panicked. Smoke lifted from the ancient walls and rafters. The window and door were in place and shut. Trapped in the dream-blaze he struggled to force the door. It wouldn't budge. Something was wedged against it from the outside. Desperately, he groped through the smoke for the corner window. Leaping head first, he smashed through the glass, hitting the ground and rolling free of the flames that roared after him, that clung, with fire-orange fingers to his clothes. Blood streamed from his shoulder. Screaming in pain on the open dirt and rock he rolled about to extinguish the flames. Frantically he leaped to his feet. His imagination blazing, pursued by his dream, Parnell Mackenzie spun in circles of bright sunlight.

* * *

Sully, dogged by his hangover, but determined, followed a cow with one unbranded calf and a yearling bull, also unbranded, up through a cut in the northwest end of the mesa. The bull, her calf of last season, she had kept hidden in the sulfur canyon. Sully wouldn't ride that canyon. It was too rough and tangled with brush. Not many cattle would venture into it, but this old cow was a loaner and meaner than shit. Her yearling bull had avoided the brand, and the knife. He still had balls and was unbranded. Sully was pleased to have caught the rebel cow and her two offspring in the open. He could brand the heifer calf and the bull wouldn't get away this time. He topped out with the livestock onto the open flat of the mesa where he could rope and brand the youngest with no problem. He would need help with the yearling bull. A quarter mile in the distance he saw Parnell's mare standing by the old adobe ruins. *Good. The two of us can drop this young renegade.* He smiled his first smile of the day. But then he heard Parnell screaming. "What the hell?"

In amazement he saw his friend fly through the burned out window of the old ruins and roll about on the rocks and stubble of grass as if chased by demons. *Is the man snake bit? Or am I crazy drunk still?* "Or is he?" In the distance Parnell leapt to a crouching position and started running in circles. Sully rubbed his head, trying to clear the vision. *It's an Irish madness has him possessed,* he thought. "Or the DT's" he said aloud. "It's one and the same." He had seen his brother with the DT's more than once. Tom hadn't acted unlike Parnell in his present state. Sully looked down at the pricked ears of his horse. The animal snorted and crow hopped under him. "You see it too, don't you horse. I'm glad it's not just me. I was beginning to wonder." Sully blinked hard and looked again. "It's got to be Parnell," he reasoned. "He's flipped out, the crazy bastard. He'll fall into the canyon. Kill himself." Forgetting the unbranded bull and calf, Sully spurred his mount forward, thinking: *Maybe a snake did get him."*

Sully watched in fear as Parnell circled closer and closer to the deep canyon wall. *He can't see it, or if he does, he wants to go down,* Sully thought as he pushed his horse harder. The rim rock ledge dropped off a full hundred feet and more. "Go horse." He spurred his mount. "We got to stop the crazy fucker, 'fore he kills his self." The horse, sensing Sully's urgency, dug in.

Parnell, struggling in the bonds of his imagination, turned and raced toward the rim of the drop-off. He tripped over a stone and fell headlong a few feet from the edge, a fortunate mishap. The fall brought him somewhat to his senses. Getting groggily to his feet, he gazed into the yawning abyss. Bewildered and uncertain as to how he got to where he was, he turned back toward the ruins. All was cold and quiet. There was no trace of flame or smoke. *What the shit happened?* He vaguely remembered flames—or a fire. He was sore and bruised, bleeding from the shoulder. "The mare wouldn't throw me. What happened here?" He mumbled in confusion.

From above came a screaming whistle of attack and a rush of wind whipped feathers.. Parnell looked up, his brain a web of queasy fear. It was the bird—the Peregrine Falcon of yesterday. Her wings fully extended, talons clawing space; she was almost upon him. Throwing up his arms instinctively, and stepping back to protect himself, Parnell lost his footing and dropped over the rocky rim. The bird stooped down with him to disappear as Sully, seconds behind the disaster, slid his horse to a gravel slinging stop. Dismounting on the run, the rancher raced forward.

"Jesus Christ, Parnell," he yelled. Terrified of heights, Sully dropped to his knees five feet from the edge and crawled to the sharp drop off. "Parnell!" He cried out. On his belly, he cautiously peeked over the rim.

Ten feet below Parnell, on a narrow shelf, carefully rolled over and looked up. "It's a long way to the bottom, Sully. What the hell happened?"

"You got the DT's or somethin'. I thought maybe a rattler got after you. You was seein' some kind of snakes, Parnell, no lie. Now stay right there and don't move." He crawled back. Sully suffered from severe acrophobia, or to put it in his words, "he was scared shitless of heights." Right now he was terrified. "Don't move, Parnell," he yelled. "I'll get a rope and pull you up." Sully inched back from the edge. He had broken out into a sweat of fear: fear, which he knew he must overcome if he was to save Parnell. The ledge Parnell clung to was, at best, eighteen inches wide. Sully stumbled to his feet and went to his horse for the rope. He uncoiled the lariat. Without getting too close to the drop off, he tossed a loop into the void where he judged Parnell to be. "Just get this under your arms, Parnell and I'll hook it onto the saddle and drag you out of that pit."

"OK, but take it easy," Parnell called up. "That edge is sharp and could cut the rope." Sully twisted his rope to the saddle horn and edged his mount back until he felt weight on the looped end of his lariat.

"You good?" he called.

"I got a grip. Go easy." Sully cinched up the girth of his saddle and pushed his horse slowly back toward the ruins. The well-trained animal didn't panic. The draw was smooth and easy. Sully held his breath. Parnell got a grip on the edge and, with the help of the rope, pulled himself to safety. Sully kept the line snug until Parnell was on his feet and some distance from certain death.

The cowboy was now safe and sober, but shattered. He looked toward the ruins, which minutes before had been in flames. There was no smoke—no fire. He would keep his mouth shut about what happened—what he thought had happened. *What the fuck did happen*? He was shaking visibly, but at a loss to figure out why. *Sully must figure, I'm half crazy. —Maybe I am.*

The calf he had tied down had shaken free of the pigging rope and was standing by her mother a hundred yards in the distance. The animals looked back wonderingly. "I wish cows could talk," Parnell muttered as he walked past Sully. He stopped at the ruins and felt the timbers. They were cold. The door hung askew as it had when he first saw it. There was no sign of smoke. No heat. All was at peace. Nothing wrong. *What the hell happened here?*

"What the hell happened here, Parnell?" Sully said, echoing Parnell Mackenzie's thoughts. Sully was worried. He came closer and studied his friend. "You alright Parnell? You were runnin' crawlin' and rollin' toward that rim as if you had every intention to take the big dive. Then you stood up and took it—backwards." Sully shook his heavy head and scratched his beard. "One body down there is enough, old man."

Parnell snapped out of his dream world. He turned to Sully. "Huh? What did you say?"

"The way you was actin', I thought you'd seen snakes or been bit by one." Sully followed the only line of reason he could imagine – "snakes of one kind or another. It had to be a snake."

"That god damned bird almost got me." Parnell searched the sky. There was no sign of the falcon. "She's a demon, or the devil's mate at any rate."

"What bird?" Sully looked worried. "What god damned bird, Parnell?" he snapped.

"You didn't see the fire either?" Parnell cried in frustration. "Did you?" Sully shook his head in disbelief.

"Fire? What the hell you talkin' about? This place burned down before I was born, Parnell. These coals are long cold and dead. You better get your head together, friend." He looked at Parnell seriously. "They'll be takin' you to the funny house in Las Vegas. That is no place to be entertained, Mr. Mackenzie. Believe me."

Parnell paid no attention. He was looking back toward the canyon. "What body is down there, Sully? You said one body down there is enough." Sully stammered and turned away. He should have never mentioned the body.

"What you talkin' about"? Sully hedged. "What body?"

"A minute ago you said—one body down there is enough." Parnell turned and looked straight at him. "What body down there were you talking about, Sully?"

Sully took his hat off to relieve the pulsating pressure on his throbbing brain. All the activity had not done his retreating hangover any good. "Oh ya. —That body." He gave Parnell a sidelong look. *I should a kept my damn mouth shut.* But he hadn't. Sully mopped his sweating brow with his silk neck bandana. *I might as well get on with it,* he thought, *though I hate to awfully. The Sullivan closet skeleton and I'm lettin' her out.* "Shit," he sighed bitterly. He faced Parnell. "Well you're about three strokes ahead of me, and half a bubble off today, partner." Parnell stared back at him, waiting. "Did I say somethin' about a body, Parnell?" Parnell nodded, pressing for an explanation.

Using his wide brimmed cowboy hat as a face fan, Sully sat on the low wall of the ruins and tried to cool off. There was a long moment of silence. The yearling bull calf bellowed in the distance. Out of curiosity, his mama and the calf were moving closer to the two men and the other cow and calf. The young bull followed behind them.

"I'm waiting." Parnell said.

"I'm not too sharp today." Sully resettled his Stetson and got to his feet. He paused, thinking how to begin the story he didn't want to begin and didn't want to believe in—didn't believe in. He walked slowly toward a dead cedar tree rooted to the canyon

76

rim. Once there he snugged his hat down tighter and clutched a limb of the dead tree for safety. He took a deep breath and forced himself to look into the depths.

Parnell shadowed him as he walked. He stood back a bit from the edge and waited for Sully to speak. Below them the canyon, cradled in black basalt rim rock, stretched a mile and a half to the north where millions of years of fierce weather had gouged it out with torrents of rain, flash floods and snow melt from the freezing winter storms. The narrow north end cut down quickly to a depth of fifty feet where giant Ponderosa pines now towered above the rim. Nature's path grew wider, deeper and wilder as she worked her way toward the open plains a mile to the south. Where they stood, the canyon was a quarter mile wide and varied from a hundred to a hundred and fifty feet in depth. Beneath Parnell and Sully an enormous cedar, small looking in the distance, stood, partially obscuring a crystal green pool of spring water surrounded by boulders, willow brush and thick green moss. From Parnell's point of view he could see to the bottom of the spring where shadows of sharp rock shards gave it a pseudo-foreshortened perspective; eclectic, something out of a Salvador Dali painting. At the east rim, across from where they stood, hundred foot slices of basalt, twenty to thirty feet thick, scattered over the floor of the canyon. A tangle of scrub brush and twisted cedar trees, some dead, some still sprouting, forced their way up between the crags. The sight was awesome. It was a not too miniature Grand Canyon. Parnell studied the view in wonder. His first experience on the edge had given him no time to admire the scenery. He looked to Sully. Sully was experiencing bad vibrations. The depth of this natural wonder had brought Sully Sullivan a rush of unpleasant memories.

"Down there, Sully," Parnell said, breaking the silence, "is no place to be in a flash flood." An early morning mist moved like a ghost above the green pool. "That a hot spring, Sully?" Parnell asked.

"Warm," Sully mumbled, coming out of his dark reverie. "I only was down there a few times. It looks OK from here, but to me, it don't feel comfortable up close. It stinks, too."

"Were you looking for the body?" Parnell pushed. He wanted to get to the root of the story while he had Sully hooked. "I mean, did you help look for the body?"

"Hell no. That was long before my time." He turned slowly to his friend. "Parnell," Sully Sullivan said with sorrowful regret, "I never meant to let the cat out about that crazy bullshit. But now, I might as well skin it. It is an insane goddamn story. It goes back a long ways. I don't even know if it really happened. I don't want to know. You know how ghost stories can grow. If I hadn't heard it from my father, I don't know that I could put any belief into it at all. —Don't know if I believe it anyway. The old man was as full of shit about this canyon as everyone else and he was drunk the time he told me. But right now, with the headache I got this mornin', I'm goin' to pass it on to you. Tellin' it is easier than ridin' that caballo of mine." Sully looked thoughtfully at the ground-hitched horses and the straying cows and calves. The black yearling was standing just beyond the ruins, watching them. Sully took a deep breath, blew it out with a rush, and let his eyes drift back into the canyon. He started talking in a dry monotone.

"The way I heard it, Parnell," he said, "A man named Adolph Alphonso Torez, a little man, Adolphito they called him, claimed this mesa and the canyon in the mid to late eighteen hundreds. My Grandpa and Pop homesteaded ours in the eighteen eight-ies. They started out not getting' along with Adolphito. The bandito, Gramps called him, the little bandit. Gramps wanted this mesa and the canyon because of that spring. Water's always been gold in this country. Well, that godam green spring, below, feeds out onto the level plain." Sully gestured to the south. "Only a goat can get to that sulfur water down there where it comes out of the rocks, but it seeps out, clean, down there in the open. That's where the moisture pays off. The bandito claimed he owned that too." Sully stood, silent, his eyes searching the rough canyon floor. "Adolphito, that means Little Adolph. Hell, Parnell, I don't have to translate for you. You know Mexican. Anyway, Adolph, he was a little man. He never went anywhere without his gun to make up the difference. The damn forty-four weighed as much as he did, Gramps said. The upshot of it was that Little Adolph wouldn't sell to Gramps, let alone share the water. Pop said, Aldlphito and Gramps was always talking about shootin' each other over it. Gramps almost kicked off durin' a shoutin' match with "the Little Bandit". He suffered some kind of a stroke, but he got over it pretty much. Hell, they was both in their nineties and both overdue to die, accordin' to Pop. But they sure wasn't old enough to quit fightin'.

"A week later, two days before the little bandit died, to piss my already pissed off grandpa even more, Aldlphito sold this place to some gringo from the east. Gramps died the next day. That was the end of the feud and the beginning' of the twentieth century. Tom was just a kid. I wasn't here yet. Well one night, a year or so later, the guy who bought the place, a strange duck from…" He looked at Parnell with a quizzical grin …"from Philadelphia, as a matter of fact, unless I got the story twisted—which is possible, I guess. I was told he come from the east somewhere. In any case, my old man said this greenhorn doctor—and he was a doctor of some kind although Pop said he didn't have the medical learnin' to birth a calf—he come racin' down to our place one night and claimed his wife tried to kill him. Locked him in the house, he said, and set fire to it. Then, according to the doctor's story, she set fire to herself and leaped over the edge—into this canyon—'the human torch', Parnell. That's how the story got around." Sully shook his head. "The human torch." Sully looked down into the depths and shuddered. "She must have been a crazy bitch."

Parnell sat down on a protruding rock and stared wonderingly at Sully. This story was more than he had bargained for, more mixed up than his dreams. "She set herself on fire?" He asked in wonderment. Sully nodded.

"So I'm told. I wasn't a witness. Hell, I wasn't born, Parnell."

"And jumped over the edge of this cliff to her flaming, fucking death?" Parnell was incredulous.

"I wasn't here, Parnell, but that's the story I been told. The story my old man told me." It's the story you wanted to hear and the one I didn't want to tell ya."

"Who found her?"

"No one." Sully shook his head, wonderingly. "She never was found. She may have taken flight for all I know Parnell. She may be one of the fuckin' stars we see up there at night... or that bird you keep seein'." Sully let go of the cedar limb he was hanging onto and gazed heavenward. The sun was noon high now, in the steel-blue sky. Sully leaned back, studying the blue before he remembered he was on the brink of death. He stumbled and grabbed for the security of the cedar limb. Sully was trembling. "I fuckin' near fell, Parnell. Did you see that? It was just like I was pushed."

"You didn't come near to falling, Sully. You're just scared of heights. Relax."

"I don't like lookin' down any further than my feet. I can stand looking down from the back of a horse, but that's it." Clinging to the cedar he took one more furtive glance into the canyon. "I don't like this place, Parnell. I love the ranch, but I never liked this part of it. I never come up here unless I have to. It's the edge of death, Parnell. 'The sharp edge of death', Papa called it."

"And nobody found her?" Parnell leaned out over space and looked down. Heights didn't bother Parnell—unless he was flying. "It's pretty thick brush down there pushing through the rocks. Had she survived the fall even, I don't think she could have walked away through that jungle... crawled, maybe."

"Bullshit, Parnell. I mean if she did go down in flames as her doctor husband claimed, she couldn't of landed too healthy. I mean..." Sully leaned fearfully an inch or so further out. "I mean if she sailed off down there in a flamboyant stage, so to speak, the fire wouldn't go out for lack of oxygen. I mean I'm just tellin' you a story as I heard it over the years. The only thing that I will vouch for is the fact that there was plenty of oxygen. It's a bit thin at this altitude, Parnell, but there is still enough to keep a fire goin'." Sully pushed off from the tree he was clinging to and started back to the ruins. Parnell turned and followed him.

"What about the body you said they found down there?"

"Oh yah," Sully said without turning back. "My brother Tom found a body down there the next day, but it sure in hell wasn't a woman's body. No one ever did find her." Sully crossed his stout arms and stared at the ruins and the little group of cows and calves standing beyond it. "We got to gather and brand, Parnell," he said glad to change the subject. Parnell, at this new knowledge, pushed the question.

"Tom found a man's body? Tom found him? Was it the husband?"

"Nope. Pop said it wan't the husband. The husband came to get Pop. Whoever it was down there, was most naked, Pop said." I've heard it from others, too."

"Who was the man they found, then?" Parnell persisted. "And what happened to the husband? —a doctor, was he?"

"You ask too godam many questions and I'm dippin' into a murky soup if I answer 'um. The story's over sixty years old and none of them questions has ever been answered. It bothers me to think about it. Why you want to dredg' it up now for?"

"I have an inquiring mind."

"You have a <u>curious</u> mind, Parnell, curious as in strange."

"It's a curious story, Sully. I want to know." Parnell laughed at his friend's discomfort. "Who was the naked man they found? What happened to the husband, the one that came down saying his wife tried to kill him?"

"My old man had a theory on that one. The older he got, the more he drank and the more he drank he more he talked about it. He always told me not to tell anyone. He didn't want to get involved, he said. Back when it happened, everyone was talkin' it up in the bars—even in church. The story got out of hand long before I come along. Anyway, Pop's theory was, he guessed the man they found was the wife's lover. And it makes sense, Parnell. The doctor comes home early, you know, unexpected, from one of his rounds, chasin' women. Accordin' to Pa's theory. The good doctor traveled about in his surrey practicin' adultery and indiscriminate fornication more than medicine. When he come home and found someone in bed with his young wife, his philosophy took a sudden change. He demanded revenge. He forced the wife's fornicator over Pa's 'sharp edge of death'.

There must have been a fight, Pa figured." Sully was caught up in the story now. The telling of it had got his mind turning anew. Parnell clung to each word. "Somehow," Sully went on, "the house caught fire before he chased the guy over the edge. In any case, Pa said, The doctor got pretty beat up. He come to our house for a patchin' up job. He was bleedin' bad. Then, accordin' to Pa, after Ma patched up his shoulder, Pa lent him a horse to get back home on. Pa saddled another one and rode up to have a look. It was still dark. The fire was most out. No one was there to toast marshmallows. In Pa's speculation, the doctor lashed his unfaithful wife to the back of a horse, the horse the old man lent him, and forced her to flee the scene of the crime with him. In Papa's mind, it was a simple case of the fucked gettin' fucked in return. Mama agreed, but she didn't like the way Pa put it. Pa had a way with words that she didn't like."

"He came to your house, the doctor?"

"I'm told." Sully stooped to gather up scraps of wood for the branding fire. "The doc was cut pretty bad, they said. My mother sewed up a big cut on his shoulder and buttered his burns. Then the son-of-a-bitch borrowed the horse and took off back to the fire, or so they thought. That was the last any one ever saw of him—or the horse—or the wife. When the old man got up on the hill there was nothin' left but smolderin' coals. My brother, Tom, must of followed him." At the mention of Tom, Sully dropped the scraps of wood he had gathered for the branding fire, and sat quietly on the edge of the corner fireplace. "Poor Tommy?" he said quietly—"Except for Tom findin' the body, Pa would have kept his mouth shut. Pa never would have said nothin' to anyone, except that brother Tommy went thrashin' about down there and found the body. Pa felt he had to report that." Sully shrugged off his personal thoughts and gathered up the wood scraps again. "In any case, Parnell," he said, "because Pa did report it, Pa was awarded the deed to the land for the price of the long borrowed caballo the doctor never returned to him. No one ever seen that couple again." Sully scuffed the ground looking for more scraps of wood. "We got work to do. You got a match?" Parnell ignored him.

"You said Tom was here when it happened? He found the body down there, right?"

"I said he found a body. Nobody could figure out whose body it was. It was burned bad. What clothes was on it looked like they come from the east. And, Parnell," Sully turned and looked seriously at his friend, "don't you dare mention it to Tom. It might set him off. He was just a kid when it happened. Don't ever bring him up here. Shit, I think it was the thing—the finding of that body—that mucked up his whole life. Pa knew that too. Tom won't ever talk about it—never has. The old man said somethin' about all that shit makin' an idiot of Tom. Hell, Tom never talked about it since I growed old enough to know him. Pa said Tom never talked about anything after he found the body."

Sully sat in dejection on the washed out wall of the destroyed adobe. "I've said too much, Parnell. Please, just keep it to yourself. I don't' want to think about it anymore. I haven't thought about it for years and I hope it's years before I have to think about it again." Parnell was no longer listening.

Sully bent down and gathered another scrap of wood. He spotted the neck of the fiddle where Parnell had left it on the hearth. He added it to the fire pile. He turned to Parnell looking dumbly through the burned out window frame. "Hey, Mackenzie? You hear me?" Parnell pulled out of his reverie and looked about. "If you will rope in those little ones before they disappear, I'll just fire this place up again and we'll brand 'um right here."

Parnell reached out and grabbed the neck of the violin from Sully's store of kindling. "Don't burn that, Sully," he said harshly. "And don't start another fire in here."

"OK General Sherman. We'll spare this one for the Rebels." He watched Parnell studying the fiddle neck a moment, then stepped outside to set the fire makings. "I hope you have a match, Parnell. I don't feel like chippin' flint."

"I got one." Parnell tossed a Zippo lighter to Sully and headed out to gather up his mare.

"I think you need a drink, Parnell. You are getting' damn sullen." Parnell turned back with an artificial grin.

"A drink would go well about now," he said. Let's get these dogies branded and go down and have one. A little ice in it wouldn't hurt a bit either." He looked up into the steel blue at the unrelenting sun. "Just scuffing this dead grass might bring on a fire, Sully." Parnell swung into the saddle and trotted off after the straying cattle.

Parnell's mind was elsewhere. There were too many questions in the air. He felt he must somehow hook up with the actress, Catherine, the mad woman who had danced him into the sawdust on the floor of Lake Nine. He vaguely remembered the dance. He needed to be sober when they met this time. Last night was an alcoholic blur and his mind was still not completely straight. He couldn't say the dark dreamscape that filled his morning on this mesa, as disturbingly important as it was, made any sense either. And Sully's story of "the human torch" only mixed confusion into the soup. How did it all tie together with the actress? And where in God's name did he know that one from? Without disrupting his thoughts, Parnell heeled the first of the three calves and dragged her to the fire Sully had kindled. He dismounted and pigged her heels together and went after the second of the three. It would be a few minutes before the irons would be hot enough to burn in the Sullivan double XX brand. Parnell remounted the third time and went after the young bull who had escaped last year's branding.

*I got to see the play the cat woman is doing tonight,* he thought. It would be the final show in Rainbow. He knew better than to ask Sully to go with him. Kate? No. He wanted to see it alone. *Why?* He looked back to where Sully was testing the heat of the irons. He hazed the yearling closer to the fire so he wouldn't have to drag him. *"The Lady Lives Forever"? What was that all about?* He watched as Sully plunged the hot iron into the second young heifer's flank. Smoke went up in a cloud as the calf bleated in pain. Parnell, in a sudden blush of fear, looked about for the falcon. When no bird appeared, he heeled the young bull. He was well along in age to be branded, and a good weight for the mare to drag. Parnell dismounted while Dianna kept the rope tight. He sat on the bull's head while Sully lashed the feet together. No words passed between them as, deftly, the rancher cut the scrotum with his pocketknife releasing the young male's gonads. Sully pulled them out of the sack a few inches. He reached for the hand carved wooden clamp in his vest pocket. He slid it over the bloody twin cords and clamped it securely with a heavy rubber band. Parnell looked into the young animal's eyes. They rolled back white in the sun. The animal bellowed, struggling to escape. Heavy strings of colorless saliva blasted from his nostrils and mouth. His tongue lolled, pink and black. Sully worked with a surgeon's precision. Parnell twisted the bull's ear to split his attention from one pain to another. The pigging rope held. Parnell reached and handed Sully a red-hot iron. Sully grabbed it and cauterized the twin cords below the clamp. He handed the hot iron back to Parnell who tossed it once again into the flame. The bull was no more.

Sully rose. He took up a second iron and burned his double XX deep into the steer's flank. Satisfied, he reached through the smoke and released the wooden clamp. The cauterized cords retracted into the shriveled scrotum and disappeared. Sully undid the pigging rope. Parnell took his weight from the animal's neck and head. It was a full minute before the dazed young steer struggled to his feet. His was a changed world.

"Let's pack up here and head down for that drink, Parnell. I think I could swallow one now."

"Not for me, Sully. I got to get to town." Parnell was drifting in the smoke. He was in a changed world, too. Where was fate leading him?

Sully watched as Parnell trotted on ahead. The rhinestone cowboy wasn't looking back. Soon the mare had him moving at a gallop. Sully watched until Parnell dropped over the west edge of the mesa. *What will be the next adventure?* Sully wondered.

The new made steer sniffed up to his mother. The mother cow butted him off. Sully shook his head. *You're on your own now buddy. No more hind tit for you.* The cow left with her new calf. The new branded steer wandered off in another direction. Sully headed for the ranch. When he got there Parnell was long gone.

# CHAPTER SIX

# THE LADY LIVES FOREVER

Toad was always the first at the theatre. It was his job to be first and he took his job seriously, albeit with a coarse complaint lodged in his mind and heart. He had been working for Catherine for the past seven years and suffered mental scars to prove it. It had grown into a love-hate relationship between them. Toad admired her ability to hold the company together. He wondered at it, too. She had been called on the carpet by EQUITY, the actor's union, more than a dozen times for breaches in her contract. Each time she had waltzed away with nothing more scathing than a firm reprimand. Her actors had gone weeks on half salary and never reported it to the union. Toad had done as much himself. She would, however, sometimes make it up to them with a bonus (not reported to the IRS). Her company had been audited once, but thanks to Wolf's creative book keeping, came away clean.

Toad didn't know how she would pull it off this time. The damn bus was falling apart, the trailer they packed the set in had four bald tires, and the set was in dire need of repair. He held the platforms together—longer screws in the hinges, and more cross bracing. The stage flats were patched and re-patched. There had been no IATSE union stagehands to help with the setup at this stop. The actors helped him set the stage, another breach of EQUITY contract that would go unreported. They were used to it. He doubted if the union even knew they were playing this slot. *Rainbow, New Mexico* Toad scoffed in his mind. It had been an open date before the big one in Santa Fe. *Thank God they had the Santa Fe dates.* Toad crossed himself. He might even go to

Mass in New Mexico's state capital. He hoped his silent prayer would be answered. The stage manager needed time to repair the set he had designed and built three seasons earlier. It had stood up well. Toad knew his business.

But, Toad was tired of this show. The actors were bored with their lines and action. It showed. They truly needed a new vehicle for the stage as well as a new bus and trailer to haul it around. For some reason, The Cat was attached to this old warhorse. She had an obsession about living forever. Toad didn't like to think of the number of times "The Lady" had played. *It's not the "Fantasticks" for Christ sake, and Rainbow is a distant cry from the Sullivan Street Theatre in Greenwich Village.*

The stage manager fumbled his way through the dimly lit Rainbow auditorium to the orchestra pit. Toad had stage managed The Fantasticks during the early years of its run. He got tired of that show too. The Fantasticks was still playing to full houses, albeit small houses, but he was glad he was out of it. Long runs bored him. This show definitely bored him. *It can't go on much longer.* He climbed the steps beside the orchestra pit and set down the jerry can he carried. He ducked off right stage. In the dark he found the switch for the work lights and flipped it. A scattering of bare bulbs flashed on. Large scoop lights left and right stage lit the playing area with horizontal shafts of stark white light.

The Rainbow Opera House was built in 1914—a classic design. The proscenium arch was a gold leaf painted plaster relief. The boxes to stage right and stage left were equally ornate. Raised plaster pink-cheeked cherubs hovered in the cloud-dusted ceiling. They circled a massive chandelier heavy with hung crystals. Toad had to admit it was a jewel of a theatre. In the time of railroad touring companies it must have been popular. It was a faded jewel now. Like his set, it needed extensive repair.

Toad's stylistic western set was made up of various cutout false front buildings. Boardwalks, at different levels, graced the old, raked stage. Up stage center was a hanging gallows, complete with the called for thirteen steps rising to the platform where the noose hung with its ominous, thirteen coils of one inch hemp rope. The cutout buildings flanking the gallows gave the set an accentuated illusion of depth. Up close, in the harsh work lights, the stage flats showed the wear of many performances, many set-ups, strikes and miles of being towed in the old trailer behind the bus. From the audience's point of view, and under Toad's lighting design, it appeared quite believable. Toad was rightfully proud of his set. The backdrop faded from dark to brilliant fresh-blood red. The effect in the work lights was eerie in the absolute silence of the empty house. Toad stepped from the wings into the light and picked up the heavy jerry can. He grimly surveyed the gallows. He set the can down at the foot of the thirteen steps and climbed to the top. He pulled the hangman's lever. The trap fell with an echoing crash. Toad grinned. The grim humor agreed with him. He closed the trap, trotted back down the steps and examined the stage floor beneath the gallows. Toad had to admit to himself he enjoyed playing these old theatres. They were built when the shows traveled by train...*No damn buses to worry about. If you missed an engagement it was the fault of the railroad, not a broken U joint or dry transmission.*

This theatre belonged to the time of vaudeville. Besides being a jewel box with excellent acoustics, the raked stage floor had a sliding trap door. The only problem last night was that Toad's igniter misfired. There was no smoke screen to cover Catherine's exit. *By Jesus, it will go off tonight.* Toad slid back the trap and checked the wiring on his apparatus. It looked good, but one strand proved to be loosely connected. He crimped the lines with a lead collar then stirred up the dust of black powder in the forward flash pan. He next measured out two cups of liquid from the jerry can and poured it in the second long, shallow metal container located just behind the flash pan. He considered his work for a moment. "Screw her." He said, his thoughts aloud and poured another cupful into the tank. "That ought to toast her bleeding cookies." He smiled. "Teddy had damned well better move her out in a hurry, tonight." Toad was speaking aloud to himself; something he seldom did. On most occasions, Toad kept his taciturn thoughts in the cover of silence. He checked the flash powder. It was dry and smelled okay. He added half a cup from the leather bag in his pocket. "There will not only be smoke tonight, Catherine, but hellfire as well." He checked the two fire extinguishers below the tank and flash pan. Beneath the stage, Tommy, his assistant stage manager, would be standing by. *The effect will be a bit hairy but it won't fire the theatre.* "Tommy will see to that.

"It may get me fired," he mumbled to himself, as he tidied up the stage and checked the set. Except for the need of fresh paint and a few repairs, it was almost up to his stringent specifications. The two-week run in Santa Fe would give him time to bring it up to snuff. He might even be able to service the old bus during that gig. Toad slipped the crimping pliers into his back pocket, and screwed the measuring cap back on the jerry can. He wondered, with a tight grin, if Cat would want to test the fire effect? *If so, so be it.*

Toad carried the can back through the auditorium and up into the light booth above the balcony. He would have time to check the lighting and sound system before the company arrived for the run-through Catherine had called for. *A run-through won't hurt. Teddy, for one, needs to trim his timing.* Toad was very critical of every actor. He had to watch each performance from the light booth. He knew the blocking and every word of each play he worked by heart, before they ever went on the road. For the most part, he kept his critical thoughts to himself.

Back in the booth, he cranked up the sound and brought the red fire lights to half full on the backdrop when the fire exit door swung open. A shaft of white afternoon sunlight broke the illusion. Catherine was silhouetted in the doorframe. When he had come into the theatre, Toad had wedged the fire door open for the cast. He wished now he had left it locked. The Cat's elongated shadow cut across the blood red stage.

"Toad! Toad," Catherine cried out. "Are you here?" She shut the door and her shadow disappeared into dark silence. "Toad? Toad?—Damnit! answer me!" she demanded. "Where are you?"

Toad cranked the audio to full and whispered into the mike. "I'm right here, Catherine."

She jumped in the darkness. "Jesus Christ, Toad." Toad heard her stumble over something. He smiled.

"Sorry, Madam … Would you like some light?"

"Turn on the Goddamned house lights. I can't see a thing." Toad heard her stumble again. "Fucking amphibian," she mumbled. He heard that, too.

"I was about to test the special effect, as you ordered, Catherine. Would you like to step into it?" He watched as she groped her way onto the stage. "I added a bit of a flash, which I think you might appreciate."

"Lights, Toad! Give me some light!"

Toad held the mike fuzzy-close to his lips. He was in control and loved it. He whispered loudly: "It's all set to go, Catherine. Step under the gallows."

"Turn on the fucking lights!"

The fire exit swung open again with a crash. The company had arrived. The shaft of sunlight struck Catherine full in the face. "Shut off the fucking lights!" Toad grinned broadly. The Cat was out of control.

Teddy, standing in the doorway, remarked casually: "It's the sun, Catherine. Shut it off yourself."

Wolf pushed past Teddy and looked up to the glass-faced light booth. He was angry at being turned out early for this rehearsal. The stage manager stood, dimly lit, behind the glass plate. "Turn on the lights, Toad," Wolf made it an order. The rest of the cast, gathered behind him, grumbled in agreement. It was early afternoon, early for them to be in the theater.

Toad brought up the house lights and stage work lights. Satisfied, Wolf moved to center stage and took command. Catherine, well out of sorts, unlike herself in front of her troop, slouched on the steps of the gallows. Wolf turned to the scattered cast. "Let's run the cues on this damn scene and get it over with," he said crisply.

Toad's voice came over the sound system. "We are all set to go here, Wolf." Toad spoke normally, now, all business. "Places, everyone." The actors started to move into their opening positions.

"Forget it, Toad." Catherine rose to her feet, contradicting her own order. "I see no need for a run-through. Go home and rest. Every one is on edge—even me." She stepped down stage out of the light. I apologize for the early call." The Cat seldom apologized. The cast eagerly started drifting back toward the fire exit. "Wolf," Catherine said rather sharply. "You, stay. The rest of you may leave. Just run your lines and be prepared for the show tonight," she added tartly. "And," becoming the Cat they all knew, she turned abruptly to the light booth. "Toad, the fire and smoke effect had better damn well work tonight."

\* \* \*

Parnell pushed his old Chevy pickup at top speed to the Pendleton gas station at the south end of Rainbow. It was sometime after noon when he rolled up to the pumps on fumes. Parnell pumped in ten dollars worth of regular and bought two candy bars. He was not going to drink any more today. The sugar would have to suffice. He had no definite plan, except to confront Catherine—The Cat. *Why?* Another unanswered question triggered by fate. Did he want revenge for her putdown last night? She had played cat and mouse with his ego. Parnell was damaged, but not destroyed. Did he think, sober he might score a payback? He signed the ticket for the gas and wolfed the first candy bar as he pulled out of the station. He crumpled the wrapper into a plastic trash bag hooked to the window roll down handle and tore the second one open with his teeth. It wasn't the taste of the sweet he needed; it was the sugar rush to overcome his body's demand for alcohol.

*Alright Cat Lady, for what ever reason, where are you?* Beard the lion in her lair? The logical place to start was Rainbow's Opera House.

\* \* \*

At the theatre Teddy and Catherine's company of actors started easing out the door before she changed her mind and called them back for the run-through. Catherine stood angrily center stage, glaring up toward the light booth.

"Will it work tonight, Toad," she called again. "I want to go out of the second act in smoke and flames tonight, Toad. No excuses."

"It will work, Catherine," Toad said quietly over the intercom. "Fire and brimstone, my lady. It will work."

The last of the troop were moving into the sunlight when Parnell slipped past them into the old theatre. He ducked into a dark aisle seat and sat unnoticed. Teddy and Wolf had missed him. The rest, if they noticed him, paid no attention. As his eyes grew accustomed to the dim lighting, Parnell, studied the classic rococo architecture surrounding him. This was, by no means, the first legitimate theater he had been in, but it was, amazingly enough for Rainbow, the most impressive Parnell had seen.

Catherine and Wolf were on stage. Parnell was in luck and smugly pleased. He took his mind off the cherubs painted among the floating clouds on the ceiling and watched the two of them closely. Toad, in his booth, was hidden by the lip of the balcony above him. Parnell Mackenzie had not been spotted.

Wolf spoke in a troubled, but guarded voice in case Toad or one of the actors was still within hearing. "Tonight is their last night, Cat. Why didn't you tell them?" He put a hand on her shoulder and leaned down toward her seated on the gallows steps.

"I couldn't. I didn't want to spoil it for them." She laughed bitterly. Rising suddenly, she wheeled away from him in frustration. "I'm scared, Wolf. Damn it, leave me alone."

"You are the one asked me to stay. Why?"

"I have a lot on my mind." She studied him earnestly. "I don't understand a lot of it—any of it. I need to sort it out. Somehow we belong here, but I don't know why."

"We belong here?" Angrily he grabbed her by the shoulder and turned her toward him. "We, Cat? Speak for yourself. This grave is your making. It is not mine."

"Just back off," she cried, pulling free of his grip. She turned away, looking for an escape. Wolf made no move to pursue her.

He offered no response. He stood silently troubled in the sharply raked work lights.

Parnell watched them both in silence. Something was coming down here. He made no move to interfere.

"You're losing it, Cat," Wolf cried, "and I want no part of it."

"You are a part of it," she said, firmly but quietly. Her stage voice carried throughout the theatre. Wolf made as if to answer, but held his words. Angry, he spun about and disappeared into the wings. Backstage he threw open one of the heavy stage doors used to load the scenery in and out. He waited a moment in silence. She wasn't coming after him. The Cat didn't even fling an obscenity in his direction. Worried, but curious, Wolf shut the door firmly: loudly enough for the Cat and Toad to hear it and think him gone. He stood in the shadows—waiting—listening—expecting something. *Christ, she has lost it,* he thought. *So? Am I loosing it too? What the hell is going on?*

\* \* \*

Wolf's mind flashed back to the night he had turned down the aging Hollywood star's bed. She was ill, she said. Young Catherine, her understudy, would have to go on to cover for her. The Cat that night had been great, better than the famous star, a falling star at that. The star had fallen in the bottle and almost drowned. Only her name kept her afloat. Wolf slipped up to her room after the evening's performance. She was expecting him—spread, belly down sagging and naked across the feather bed in her posh hotel room. Her buttocks lay loose as two loves of bread dough punched down and left to rise. The corset she used to strap herself together hung from the doorknob to the loo. The star was snoring. The room smelled of vomit. Wolf started to clean the mess as he often had.

He stopped. He'd had enough. His gloves were in his opera cape. He put them on and wiped his prints from the doorknob. *What else had he touched?* He checked the hall, the outside knob. No one had seen him enter. The key she'd given him he cleaned and placed beneath the pillow. He eyed the blackened poker among the brass ensemble at the fireplace. That would do. She loved anal intercourse. No. He'd be suspected. Quietly he went through her belongings. In a pillowcase he bagged diamonds, dollars, a ruby necklace—everything of value—a tidy sum. Then he awoke her. That took some doing. Wolf, however, was determined. She had smelling salts. They worked. She came around. He delighted in telling her of Catherine's triumph in her place on the stage. That was more satisfying than the poker treatment. When she started screaming he lashed the steel enforced bra of her corset over her mouth. It stifled the course sounds. Grabbing the poker, he smashed her again and again until the fading actress completely faded. Breathing heavily, Wolf waited until there was no sign of a pulse.

The stage was set for burglary. The rooms were ransacked with appropriate decorum. Wolf Zimmerman has been her secret slave for much too long. It was his turn now. He would make a slave of Catherine. She owed him. As time passed, making a slave of The Cat never quite worked out as Wolf planned.

* * *

In the light booth Toad had been futtzing about, setting his domain straight. He heard the stage door shut. Wolf had left, or so he thought. He watched Catherine for her reaction. She and Wolf had had some angry words. They made no sense to Toad and he didn't try to put meaning to them. Theatrical relationships were always on the edge. They didn't spur his curiosity. He knew Wolf was pissed. So was The Cat. Toad smiled at the thought. He speculated; something was going down. He shrugged. *What ever it is, so be it.* That was his policy. He wouldn't push it. Not now.

He switched on the intercom. "Have fun, Boss lady," he said softly over the audio system. I'm gone." Catherine didn't look up. Toad took the remaining house lights down and flipped the intercom off. The only lights left in the house were the stark work lights left and right stage. The stage manager made his exit through the balcony fire escape. He pulled the door shut behind him until he felt it click, locked. Catherine watched him leave.

The door closed the daylight off in the balcony. Finally she was alone, or so she thought.

\* \* \*

Parnell, silent in his darkness, was now content the building was empty except for him and the unsuspecting lady on the stage. He watched her turn and climb, slowly, the thirteen steps of the gallows. Her back to him, Parnell slid from his seat and moved closer.

He was here to see but not be seen. It was a start. *Am I here to have the Cat Lady beat me again?* Parnell vaguely remembered the dance. He was sober now. He determined it was not going to happen again. His mind snapped back to the morning; the fire on the mesa. His life was twisting on the thread of his dream—or—was it his dream? Where would this flight land him? *So here I am.* So what. *I will live through it.* He hadn't taken his eyes off the woman on the stage. *I am here for the ride wherever it takes me,* he thought. He leaned back, front row center, and let it happen.

The Cat's shadow projected in multiple distortions left and right stage. She climbed, counting the steps softly. It was an eerie sight. At the thirteenth step she turned majestically and faced the empty auditorium. For a long moment she held the pose, then with a lost sigh, she sank beneath the weight of her problems. Sitting on the top step, her head between her knees she uttered the single word, "shit." It was a sigh of despair she would never allow herself in front of her troop or in front of anyone, unless the character she was playing on stage called for it. She couldn't stand human weakness. Catherine didn't like playing that kind of character. She despised weakness in anyone and most aggressively in herself. She slumped lower. "Shit." She pulled herself together loosely and gazed out into the empty house. "It's all coming apart" she said. Then she saw him.

Sitting front row center, a grin graced his dark tanned face. Catherine, caught in this act, hid her shock and spoke with bored resignation.

"You want a replay of last night, Cowboy?"

"I came for the whole show, this time, Catherine of Enid, OK?"

"You may not be totally entertained." She stood and started down the steps. Her footing was more secure. "There is something about you, Parnell—. That is the name, right?"

"Right." Parnell was intrigued. At the same time he was beginning to question his motives, his sanity. He was definitely not secure. "Jack Parnell Mackenzie" he answered, "but Parnell will work."

"Well Jack Parnell Mackenzie, there is something about you I don't understand." She stepped out of the light and into shadows. "I don't like being in the dark," she said.

"Who does, especially in your line of work."

"Sometimes it helps." Catherine moved to the unlit steps leading down over the orchestra pit to the seat level. "Do you like the theatre, Parnell?"

"All the world's a stage."

"My, my. That _is_ clever." Parnell chose to overlook her sarcasm.

"At the university I played Jacques in Shakespeare's As You Like It."

"Did you? And did you remember your lines? Did you graduate?"

"I dropped out to tread the stage of life." Parnell said, awkwardly thrusting back with a worn cliché. "That was my only stint—at sham."

"Sometimes the sham becomes quite real." She leaned over and, surprisingly, kissed Parnell gently on the cheek. Cocking an eyebrow, he gave her a sidelong glance.

Catherine continued with her thought. "Sham can be delicious even." She sat beside him. "And even terrifying." Parnell felt the chill. It cut through his brain first and then snapped to his heart. That organ stopped operation for a beat. Not long enough to stop the world but long enough to make him think of stopping it. The Cat was winning again. He wished now, he had spent the night with Kate, and was with her still. Kate was safe.

But coming here had been his move—his step into the pit. He hadn't meant for his heart to stop.

He had felt that pause before. An emptiness—a blank moment—a nothing. Would there ever be a stroke of nothing he could understand—hang onto? A thread of the present—or even the past? Who was he? At points in his life Parnell had been sure of his being, his own person. Right now he wasn't certain if he were here—or in his dream? He knew he was in a limbo. Did this limbo count against him? Had he reached that point, or was he only sliding toward it? He shook the feeling off.

"Who are you, lady?" He slid his arm along the seat behind Catherine. She didn't object. At least she didn't throw it off, or get up and leave. Or was she just tired. He leaned forward to study her face. Her eyes met his. For the second time in a few minutes she seemed strangely familiar, vulnerable, even. *We have been here before*, he thought, with a chill—*this close— dressed in danger. Except,* he thought again, feeling another wave of the chill, *I was the one in control, the one with the power of death—dominance.* "Where the hell are we coming from, lady?"

"In time, Parnell," she said softly. There was a tear in her left eye. Parnell watched it build and roll down her cheek beside her perfect nose. He leaned in and caught it on his tongue, tasting the salt. Catherine held him off but didn't push him away. She needed, if nothing else, the illusion of control. She would make him believe it. Her tongue gently caressed his. Another tear salted the taste. The kiss grew in sad intensity.

Wolf, shrouded in the black drapes, watched soundlessly. This wasn't the first time he had witnessed the Lady Cat make her moves, but in his role of voyeur this encounter was growing to a new height, a new meaning. This was not the Catherine he was accustomed to. Wolf entertained a dark secret passion of his own. If he couldn't have Catherine to himself, he would only share her on his terms. Her fantasies were his to enjoy, if only in a deep, masochistic well of his making. *Be patient and eat the leftovers while both of us relive the moment. Mental masturbation, perhaps, but better that than the alternative.*

The lover's scene played out before him. It unwound in the semi-darkness like a lantern show in Boston candlelight. Even in her tears, Catherine teased, caressed and held Parnell at bay. Wolf struggled with his thoughts and held his silence.

Parnell, like a schoolboy on his first date, strove, fruitlessly to overcome his passion. It was no good. The Cat opened her shirt. (she wore no bra) and allowed him to lip her erect nipples—for seconds only, then she pushed him off.

Wolf had seen the tears. *Why? Why tears? What was happening?* With Wolf, her nipples never came erect, and the tears had been of laughter. In the act of their love making, if he could call it lovemaking, The Cat spoke or thought of other things—other times, with other men. He was nothing but a stand in, a substitute. Wolf was tempted to cry out and expose the damn charade for what it was—for what he thought it was. Somewhere, in his subconscious past, he felt the truth. His tears were of frustration. Angrily he rubbed them from his cheek and kept still. There was no clarity. In the maddening darkness of his indecision, he clutched his manliness for what it was; a piece of meat to flog.

Cursing silently, Wolf could not—would not cry out. There had been occasions where Catherine had accepted his watching secretly, even enjoyed him doing so. It was a game with her. But this was different. This was private. A shadow of the dead—dark shades of the past. Wolf vowed in silent anger he would not be treated in this manner without revenge. Who was this man? *Where do I know him from, Parnel MacKenzie? When and where have I seen the two of you together before?* He dug his fingernails into his twisted flesh, wiping the past picture from his mind. Wolf had been another man then, a different person. *There is no such past!* he cried in blistering thought. *We'll all be dead tomorrow.*

Wolf wondered at that black deliberation, then cast it off, forcing himself into the present. *Hell, after tonight it will all be over. Even Toad will be out of work tomorrow.* His mind was wandering. *So will I be out of work tomorrow. So will we all. So will The Cat. So be it, as Toad would say. We'll all be dead tomorrow—.* There it was again.

He grabbed the moment for what it owed him, for the last breath of lust he could drain from it. He let his eyes search out the torture in his heart.

* * *

With a dancer's grace Catherine twisted from Parnell's grip. He gasped in agony, reaching for the shadow that eluded him. In Jack Parnell's mind, he was the schoolboy in the back seat of a battered Chevrolet. He leaned back in defeat and spread his empty arms along the chair backs and looked up at the conquering female above him. He held still as she knelt. To his helpless wonder, Catherine took his glistening totem, his helpless sign of manhood between her lips, and --- In a circle of cruel seconds, left him empty, left him drained. He was not rejoicing. Parnell had not seen God.

"I do better on the gallows," she said. She walked off, keeping her back to him. The Cat felt tears building up behind a dam of sorrow. "See you 'round, Jack," she said. She pushed through the fire door into the afternoon's slanting light. The door fell shut behind her leaving Wolf and his proxy stunned.

Parnell didn't move for many seconds. Then blindly, things spinning in his mind and heart, he raced from the building. The Cat was nowhere. Parnell walked to his truck trying to rake things together. He left the Chevy where it was and climbed the rusty fire escape steps to his room above the long closed Corner Bar. He slid the bolt, locking the door behind him, and flopped down on the bed Kate must have made before leaving the other morning. *That seemed weeks ago.* He stared at the cracked ceiling.—*Or was it, in truth, years ago?*

*It was many years ago. Why had he come back?* Kate knocked on the door, but he didn't answer. Parnell had never locked his door. After five minutes Kate still didn't turn the knob. She gave up.

* * *

99

Parnell lay for hours, not thinking—not daring to sleep. At 8:15 he kicked off the bed and changed his shirt. Down the hall, at the communal washstand outside the toilet stall and tub, he splashed water in his face and headed back to the opera house.

Curtain time was 8:30. The first row center seat was empty. Parnell took it.

# CHAPTER SEVEN

# THE LADY LIVES FOREVER

Except for a few scattered seats in the balcony, the house was full. The curtain had gone up at eight-forty-one. "Eleven minutes late," Toad noted on the yellow pad lying beside him on the light-board. *This town is dead. Where did the god damn people come from?* "We drew them in like flies to bad meat," he mumbled to himself.

\* \* \*

The final production of THE LADY LIVES FOREVER was well into the second act with good audience support. Toad wondered at the actor's perfect timing. *This is the best show they've done in ages—even without the run-through. Something sparked this performance. The cast is hotter than* I've *seen them in weeks.* He wondered about it. He also wondered about the special effect he had arranged for the highlight of the second act. *That will bring the house down—or blow it up.* He grinned ironically. "Catherine of Enid will go out with a bang." He mouthed the words soundlessly. His eyes never left the stage. Toad knew every actor's line and every light and sound cue impeccably. He could quote the actors words in or out of context. Much to the actors consternation he noted each mistake made in any one performance. Sound cues he didn't even think about. This show had no "canned" sound to speak of. Wolf did that from the pit.

Toad noted Wolf was strung pretty tight tonight. Wolf produced the overtures and mood music. He hadn't missed a beat, but he was damn nervous. Something was wrong. *He and The*

101

*Cat had fought that afternoon.* "He's always licking her boots," Toad mumbled. He had the mike to back stage and the dressing rooms keyed off at his end. He could hear everything they said at the other end, however. Toad liked to know what was going on. It was his business. Right now, he had his eyes and ears on Wolf.

Wolf directed the orchestra and vocals, as well as taking care of his other tasks. Catherine demanded lyrics in all her productions. Toad didn't approve of The Cat's vocal qualities, but he had to admit she could sell a song. The five piece orchestra (Wolf insisted on calling it an "orchestra") consisted of his fiddle, a second fiddle, a cello, drums and Freddy McTavich, who providing he hadn't dipped too deeply into the sauce, played a number of various wind instruments with surprising bravado. The band (Toad insisted on calling it a "band") doubled as the chorus, and three of them joined the singing ensemble when called to do so. Acting was a craft Wolf would not lower himself to. He was a "musician". Toad let it go at that.

The play they had been touring for the past two years was originally set in New England during the times of the witch trials. In Toad's mind, it was a fair piece of dramatic literature. Catherine rewrote it, however, giving it a western flair and background. Instead of drowning the witch, in Salem, Massachusetts, as Toad would have preferred, The Cat's production hung her in rural Colorado. Catherine added music, dance numbers and brought the date up from the seventeen hundreds to the early nineteen-hundreds.

Cat loved the West and the Rocky Mountains. She was crazy about ranches, riding horses and rock climbing. A number of times she had made him stop the bus so she could scale a mountain. Although pissed that they had to stop, Toad had been impressed by her rock climbing skills. She could go up a steep rock face like a fly on a wall. She could come down like a bird on a string of nylon rope no bigger than a spider's web. It was something she learned in Europe, she said. She found it exhilarating. Wolf had gone with her on occasion. But Toad could see that climbing frightened him. He did it to save face. Toad had been afraid she would stop the bus yesterday to climb up the rim rock they passed on the ranch road. *The woman is crazy.*

These thoughts ran through Toad's mind as he fingered the switch that set off "The Red Devil Special," cue one-eighty-six. *She might find this exhilarating, too,* he grinned at the thought. Toad knew the flash would singe the wardrobe and possibly a bit of hair, but it would startle the shit out of the audience. Catherine would love that, even at her own expense. He raised his eyes, looking once again through the plate glass window down onto the stage. He also watched Wolf in the orchestra pit. Wolf fed the pace to the drummer who beat the cadence followed by the chanting actors on stage. He nodded to second fiddle and to Freddy McTavich, checking that they were ready to come in with him when the music underscored Catherine's big speech. McTavich screwed the mute into his trumpet. The Cat's big moment would come up in a minute. Toad drummed his fingers on the console in time with the music. He was a bit exhilarated, himself. All was in order. He looked from the red devil switch to the stage. His lips twisted into a smile.

Catherine, in a tight red slit riding skirt, boots and fringed leather jacket stood handcuffed on the hanging scaffold. Calmly, she studied the oversized rope tied into the ominous noose. The towering hangman stood in black behind her. A sheriff's silver star of authority glistened on his chest. Ceremoniously he removed his wide brimmed Stetson and drew a black hood, with eyeholes cut into it, over his polished, baldhead. The actors, arranged at the foot of the scaffolding, following Wolf and the beat of the drum, picked up the pace of the chant,

"Hang the witch—Hang the witch—" The volume grew as they built toward the fiery climax.

In the audience, in the front row, in exactly the same seat he had occupied that afternoon, Jack Parnell Mackenzie sat mesmerized, his attention riveted on Catherine. The audience beside and behind him was totally absorbed, as well.

On stage, the hangman/sheriff stepped forward. He offered Catherine a simple hood to cover her eyes. Her hands cuffed behind her, she spurned it with a dramatic flick of her head. The long loose strands of auburn hair flashed in the light like flames. Toad watched it all, his fingers stroking the toggle switch to the Red Devil. The hangman dropped the rejected hood over the handle of the wooden lever that would release the trap.

Below the platform the chant continued to build in intensity. The hangman casually positioned Catherine in the center of the deathtrap door. With diabolical pleasure he settled the noose over her trim neck. Slowly he arranged her flowing hair outside the rope and positioned the base of the knot snuggly behind her left ear. Satisfied with his work, he stepped back to the lever and gripped it firmly. He looked down to the blood-crazed inhabitants of the small Colorado town for approval. The chanting came to an abrupt halt. Silence reigned. Parnell, in a state of confused agitation, half rose from his seat… as:

"Hold in the name of God!" His hand still on the lever, the hangman turned angrily to locate the source of the interruption. From right stage a priest, calling out urgently, forced his way through the crowd. At the foot of the thirteen steps the priest in scarlet Catholic robes threw up his hands in supplication. "She must be given one final chance to confess and redeem her tortured soul." The hangman stepped away from death's lever. The execution proceedings were temporarily stayed. There was an audible sigh from Rainbow's unsophisticated audience, even a few scattered cries of relief and a smattering of applause. Parnell settled back into his seat. Nervous coughs and a general rustling of settling bodies accentuated the silence as the audience relaxed into a nervous sense of false security.

On stage, the actors reacted angrily. They didn't want their blood lust interrupted. The priest solemnly climbed the gallows steps to face his challenge. At the top he crossed himself and kissed the crucifix, which hung in beads about his neck.

"Aberdeen Sadillo McQueary, forgo the occult!" he cried in deep resonant tones holding the cross before him as he spoke Catherine's stage name. "I plead, in the name of our Savior and his holy Mother, for your soul. Forgo witchcraft, Aberdeen. One last time I beg of you and offer you this final opportunity for redemption. Confess your dark crimes. Cleanse your Spirit in the eyes of your Merciful Lord, Jesus Christ and the Virgin Mary who bore him with God's blessing. Let me open the doors of Heaven for your tortured soul. Let you be redeemed, my daughter. In the name of all that is Holy—<u>Repent thy sins!</u>"

Catherine glared at the man of God in silence.

In the orchestra pit, Wolf, one eye on the scene, played softly as he led the second violin and cello. Freddy McTavich, under Wolf's critical eye, took a quick slug from his silver flask. The cymbals brushed quietly. Aberdeen Sadillo McQueary, played by Catherine Rexwroth, spoke out directly to the Priest. The carefully articulated words reached every ear in the hushed house:

"I shall live again as I lived before. The year is nineteen-O-one. You, man of God, if such you are, must open your eyes and mind to this world entering a new millennium. You and your church are no longer in the dark times of the frustrated, tortured genius, Galileo, who proved the world to be round; who proved our insignificant spot of dirt and rocks, our planet, orbited the sun. Your Pope, and you who follow him, must not do now as your church did then. I will not be forced to recant, as Galileo did. Threatened with a tortuous death he signed a false state-ment swearing all his proven findings were incorrect. He died anyway, man of God! And on his deathbed he recanted your church-forced statement, saying with his last breath: 'No one can deny the seasons. Although you may walk in a darkness of your choosing, your church can not deny the daylight and the night. The earth moves, as I have proved it does,' the great Gali-leo said. At that, he died." Catherine looked down at the angry silent crowd at the foot of the gallows, and raised her voice. "I shall not cease my experiments. I shall not deny the truths I have discovered. Do with me what you will. I shall return! This lady lives forever!"

"Defensively the priest held the crucifix between them. "Woman, you make the court's decision irrevocable—-"

"It is a court of fools."

"You will retract those words," the hanging sheriff cried. He stepped between the lady and the man of God, pushing the priest back. "I shall be the judge here, and I have passed my judgment and the true judgment of this fair city! Lady, you will hang by the neck for your crimes." The actors surrounding the gallows cheered. They were not to be denied their blood.

Speaking quietly into the cue mike, Toad reached for the Red Devil effects switch. "Cue one-eighty-six coming up, Tommy."

\* \* \*

In the wardrobe room beneath the stage, Tommy, the assistant stage manager, was kibitzing with Geraldine, the wardrobe mistress. Recognizing Toad's voice, he adjusted his headset. Reacting to the order from above, he moved quickly to the effects apparatus Toad had loaded that afternoon. "Got'cha. I'm on it, boss". He keyed off the mike, climbed a stepladder under the trap door and took a quick look to be assured all connections were secure. His eyes bugged in a double take.

"Jesus, Geraldine," he looked back to the woman ironing Catherine's upcoming third act costume, "this fucker's full."

"Full of what?" Geraldine answered laconically.

"I mean for the fire effect. Someone could get hurt."

"So what?"

"I mean this is serious, Gee."

"Toad throws the switch. What you got to worry about. Last night, Catherine asked for it. She'll get it."

"She'll get it alright," Tommy said with heavy concern. The Cat could get hurt, Geraldine. If it weren't for Catherine, we wouldn't be working. Work is hard to find in the theatre."

The wardrobe mistress reluctantly agreed with that, but she didn't like to admit it.

"I mean, I like my job" Tommy continued. I mean, I like having one. Catherine's OK, just a bit mad—in her fashion. I hope she can keep us going. This is a tough business, Gee, I mean, tough!"

"It ain't easy," Geraldine agreed. She came to action, crossing quickly she climbed to the effects box. She took a look and reacted quickly. "Screw Toad. You're right. We got to drain some of that shit before it's too late." But it was too late. A shot sounded from the stage above them. The trap slid open. "Duck!" Geraldine cried. Both of them sprang for cover.

On stage, the death trap dropped.

Our savior, Teddy, dressed as a hero of the range, complete with devilish van Dyke beard, and mustache worthy of Beelzebub, fired a second stage shot and rushed toward the gallows. This shot was cued to cut the rigged rope. It did. The stage lights blazed blood red as Catherine dropped through the trap into Teddy's arms. It had all taken no more than a second.

The Cat's drop was Toad's final cue. He threw the Red Devil switch. An explosive flash from the stage brightened his maniacal expression.

The startled audience rose with a scream. The brilliant red/orange fire effect washed over them. The "Whommm" of the explosion set them all back in their seats as quickly as they had sprung from them. Heavy smoke filled the stage and washed into the auditorium with the rush of a crowned forest fire.

Catherine and her hero were obliterated in the cloud. In the confusion, all the actors ducked for cover. Toad's effect was beyond success. It was overkill.

Screaming in the front row, Parnell recovered first. "No, no, no, no Cat!" he cried. In a state of horror his mind snapped to the fire in his recurring dream, crazy fear reflected in his eyes. He leaped from his seat, vaulted into the orchestra pit and tried to clutch his way up onto the stage. Wolf grabbed his legs and pulled him back into the pit.

"It's only an effect, asshole." Wolf cried as he struggled with Parnell. "It's meant to be an illusion. Keep down. Stay down here in the pit." Wolf fought a losing battle.

The scene on stage and off was barely contained hysteria. A stagehand, watching from the grid above the stage, was engulfed in smoke. Choking, he made a dash for the old pin rail. Looking down he saw Teddy and Catherine surrounded by other actors making a getaway. "At least they look alive," he said with relief. "That Toad is crazy." Thinking the theatre might well go up in flames, he started down the ladder to safety.

Teddy was in a state of shock. Along with his ten-gallon hat, his false beard was missing. The male lead was frozen in fear. It was Catherine who dragged him to comparative safety.

In an equal state of disarray the priest, his collar askew, rushed up to them. "Are you two alright?" Catherine looked at him blankly. "Shall we go on?" he sputtered. Cat still hadn't gained her voice. "I mean it's a mess out there. Shall the <u>play</u> go on is what I mean."

His last line snapped The Cat to attention. "We're alive aren't we, Andrew?" she said, recovering. "You can see we are alive, Andrew. Jesus Christ, yes, the play goes on. I'll kill Toad later."

"But there is some cowboy from the audience wrestling with Wolf in the pit."

"Shit… it's Parnell." She muttered it under her breath.

"Your new boyfriend?" Teddy said with a tight grin. Teddy was beginning to recover from the blast. Tommy and Geraldine, carrying fire extinguishers, raced up the stairs from below. Geraldine brushed Teddy out of the way and studied Catherine for a moment.

"Thank God there is not much harm to your red dress. I'll have it ready again by tomorrow night."

"Is my third act change ready? That's what I want to know, Gee."

"I'll have you stripped and changed in no time, Catherine."

Tommy waved his arms for attention. "Toad is waiting for the word, Catherine. Do we go on with the show? There seems to be no live fire on stage, or in the auditorium. Is it a go?" He paused, his eyes wide. "Toad's waiting for the word."

"That amphibian is going to get more than a word when this night is over. Yes, Tommy, we go on. And tell him it may well be his last act. Come on, Gee." She pushed the wardrobe mistress toward the stairs. "I got to change."

Tommy spoke into the remote mike softly. "The word is go, Toad. I believe all here are alive if not well. That was some special effect"

Shielded in his booth Toad surveyed the wrath he wrought below. It had all worked out surpassingly well. The great old theatre was still intact. There were no fatalities. The provincial audience had been goosed appropriately. They got their money's worth and will have something to talk about for years. So would the cast and crew. Toad smiled. He would go down in a small corner of theatrical history.

"Then go it is, Tommy," he said. "Cue one-eighty-seven coming up." He glanced into the pit where mayhem was still in progress. "Music, Maestro, please," Toad cried into his mike— "That is, Wolf, if you can shake that cowboy off your back?" The scuffle was still in progress between the orchestra leader and Parnell. Toad watched, further amused. He noted that those of the audience who had fled into the street were now returning. This show was too good to miss. The fire doors were open to clear the smoke. The air was almost breathable. People found seats as best they could.

The main attraction now, however, was not the play to watch. It was Wolf and the cowboy. Toad, with devilish delight, brought up the Wolf special which illuminated the pit during the pre-show music. The audience didn't know what to expect, but with the smoke clearing, they were game for anything.

Toad watched Wolf rip open Parnell's shirt in a valiant attempt to hold him down. No go. The cowboy took a wild swing at the Maestro. Wolf ducked the blow but tripped from the dais into the drums. Parnell took advantage of the free moment and grabbed the lip of the stage to pull himself up. Freddy McTavich and the second fiddle gave him a boost. They had enough of the cowboy in the pit. Let him take the limelight somewhere else.

On stage, Parnell grabbed an actor and yelled: "Where is she? Is she alright? Where did she go?" Toad instinctively brought up the follow spot to track Parnell's actions. This would, indeed, go down in the books as an historical performance. Toad would relish the telling of it—to another company. He figured he had closed his door on The Lady Lives Forever. He would catch a train out of Rainbow tomorrow and be glad to be gone.

Helping Wolf to his feet, the second fiddle said: "I don't care where he went. I just wanted him to hell out of the string section." Freddy McTavich picked up his trumpet, removed the mute and prepared for a fanfare. Wolf drew himself together and gave the downbeat. The music started. It was a bit ragged, but with a high trumpet over ride it was meant to center attention once more on the show. But what show? Toad actually guffawed.

With the fanfare and lights, the audience now had a new and even more interesting distraction. Parnell, center stage, was in the spotlight, his back to the audience and totally confused. He grabbed the preacher by his flowing, singed, scarlet robes and yelled into his face: "Where is she? Where did she go? Where did you put her?" The priest stared at him, speechless, in blank disbelief. "God damn it, where is Catherine?" Parnell shook the actor violently.

"In her dressing room, asshole," the preacher hissed through his rattling teeth. "Now get off the God damned stage! This show must go on." He shook himself free of the cowboy. Two stagehands grabbed Parnell to drag him into the wings. Parnell struck out at them, fiercely serious. His attackers retreated toward the pit where Wolf was trying to subdue McTavich who was now doing a mariachi turn. Seeing Parnell face to face, the audience broke into spontaneous applause. Toad at the follow spot had proudly outdone himself. Parnell was suddenly and painfully aware of where he was. Followed by wild applause, he fled into the wings and out of sight.

Grinning widely, the stage manager brought down the spotlight. The actors regrouped and took their places. However much in disarray the performance was, the show would go on. Toad joyfully keyed the back stage mike. "Cue one-eighty-seven coming up, Tommy, and so be it." It was a resounding finale to act two of The Lady Lives Forever. The actors and the theatergoers of Rainbow, New Mexico would remember it forever. Toad knew he would. It was the highlight of a long and varied career.

# CHAPTER EIGHT

# ACT THREE

From the back stage area, still in minor turmoil, a harried Parnell clumped down the stairs leading to the bleak subterranean dressing rooms. He stumbled into a hallway. Four numbered doors lined the narrow passage that led to the wardrobe room, toilets and showers. Catherine's dressing room had a chipped gold star painted on it.

Inside, the star's quarters was a row of light bulbs bordering three sides of a cracked mirror above the eighteen-inch-deep makeup counter that ran the length of one wall. There were two straight-backed chairs, one at the counter and one leaning against the back wall beside a narrow full-length mirror. The room measured approximately eight feet by five feet. Opposite the makeup bench, a row of metal acorn hooks for wardrobe changes and street clothes, were screwed to the wall. In the corner was a small sink. The cold-water tap worked. The dull, smudged, once white walls of the room were graced with theatrical graffiti.

Catherine, in red silk bikini panties, stood in front of the full-length mirror checking her near perfect body for possible bruises, or burns. Fortunately, there were no marks other than a slight fringe of singed hair. The Cat was in magnificent shape, a fact she was well aware of. Even under these trying circumstances, she took time to admire herself.

In the hall outside her room, Parnell opened the first door he came to. No one. He headed for the next. Geraldine, carrying Catherine's costume change, rounded the other end of the hallway.

"What you doing here?" she hissed in a stage whisper. It is the unspoken law to remain noticeably quiet below and back stage.

"I got to find her." Parnell was not quiet. His stage whisper barked back at her like a pit bull. "I got to find her," he repeated intensively.

"The one thing you got to find, mister, is your way out of here." Parnell ignored her. A big mistake. He started to open the door with the gold star.

"Nobody fucks with Geraldine." The dresser might not out-weigh Parnell but she had the determination of a nose tackle going for the throat of the opposing quarterback. As the frustrated Parnell reached for the door Geraldine's shoulder hit him at waist level. Teddy stepped from his dressing room just as Geraldine made contact. He shuddered in disbelief as the two of them crashed headlong through Catherine's door. Feet and shins thrashed wildly in the hallway.

Inside, from beneath Geraldine, Parnell looked up at Catherine, his nearly naked nemesis. "Darling," he croaked, "The fire. Are you alright?"

Teddy stepped into the doorway and posed in full camp. "More to the point, oh silver spur of the range, are you all right?"

Catherine had been through enough in the past twenty-four hours. She shook her head in disbelief. She didn't need this. "You do get around, don't you Mr. Mackenzie?"

"You know this person, madam?" Geraldine asked, holding Parnell pinned to the floor.

"From somewhere, Gee, I know him—and for longer than I care to remember." Parnell twisted from under the wardrobe mistress and tried to straighten his torn shirt.

"Godamn it, Catherine of Enid, or whoever the hell you are or wherever you come from, I just met you. I never saw you before in my life." He managed awkwardly to gain his feet. The reflection facing him from the full-length wardrobe glass was a harried mess. *What is driving me to this madness,* he wondered. His nerves were stretched like fiddle strings. His brain, the heavily rosined bow bearing down on them. Would they hold together? In his troubled subconscious he knew The Cat was right. They <u>had</u> known each other.

*From where?*

*Another world—?*

*another life?*

"Christ… what is the matter with me." But he knew he had no control. He looked helplessly into the distorting glass of the old beveled mirror.

*Who the hell am I?*

"Geraldine," Catherine said, observing the disheveled Parnell. "It is quite alright. You may leave. This man and I have known each other for a long time." She paused. "Right, Doctor Mackenzie?" Parnell made no reply. "Or perhaps in our previous encounters the name was different, also known as, AKA, etcetera, anonymous—John Doe. I believe, however, the experience must have been more than a one-night stand."

*Doctor? Where had that come from?* Completely shattered, Parnell found no comeback, nor would he find one. Catherine flashed him a saccharin smile before turning to her dresser. "Oh, be a good girl, Gee Gee, and take Teddy with you." Teddy, leaning back on the opposite wall of the passageway, had no intention of leaving. He wanted to witness the whole act. Geraldine gave the star a dark look, rebuking Cat suitably, and gathered herself together. She checked Catherine's costume for any damage that might have developed from her rumble on the floor with the intruding cowboy. Finding none, she hung it ready. She paused in the doorway and spoke with her back to Catherine.

"If you need me Madam…"

"I'll scream, Geraldine." The dresser kicked the door shut behind her and grabbed Teddy by his wrist. "Come on Poopsy." He had no choice.

"My, my, Gee Gee," Teddy swished. "What was <u>that</u> all about?" Geraldine glared at him. Turning back she knocked on Catherine's door and spoke sweetly.

"You have twelve minutes, Ma'am, before you're on to open act three."

"A dozen minutes is more than enough time, Geraldine. Just don't bother us until the call." Beyond the door Geraldine's eyes rolled up to the ceiling. Poopsy grinned. The wardrobe mistress gave him a sharp kick in the shins and headed back to her duties.

Inside the star's dressing room, still reaching for his equilibrium, Parnell steadied himself. He was on his feet, but not securely balanced. The rip in his open shirt exposed the long jagged liver colored birthmark on his right shoulder. Leaning back against the makeup counter across from him, Catherine wet a finger on her tongue and ran it along the unusual blemish. The marked man caught the reflection of the birth-brand over her shoulder in the mirror. He shifted his shirt to cover it.

"We only have twelve minutes, cowboy. Now that you've arrived and haven't been expelled into the dark of the night, what did you come for?"

Determined to win this round, Parnell placed his finger across her lips to silence her. The Cat opened her mouth and bit down almost hard enough to break the skin. Parnell pulled away, instinctively. He looked at the blue teeth marks expecting to see blood, and strangely sorry there was none. He was once again losing. Frustration and anger boiled within him building a false masculinity.

"Eleven and a half minutes. It's your move," she taunted.

The game, if it was a game, was on. Despite her arrogance Catherine knew she was vulnerable. She made no move of denial as Parnell reached out and gripped her narrow waist in his callused hands. Tearing his eyes from hers, he dropped to one knee and passionately pressed his head between her breasts. Catherine's left hand reached out to explore the once again exposed birth-brand. She rolled the discolored flesh between her fingers. Parnell, unaware of her touch, or much of anything except his anger diminishing in the salt taste of her flesh, brushed his lips harshly down and around her bare midriff. Unconscious of what her left hand was doing, Catherine looked down at him.

"What now, Jack Parnell? It was dance all night, play all afternoon and you are back for more. Are you insatiable, Parnell?" She smiled. "Can nothing keep you down?" The smile built into a soundless laugh. There was no reply from Parnell. The laugh faded as Parnell pushed forth urgently, drawing down the V of raw silk that molded the down of pubic hair encompassing the pink. He felt a shudder ripple through her. Her thigh muscles clenched, willing her legs to open further. Parnell circled the truth, tasting her need, his tongue and sun-blistered lips feeding on it. Glancing up between her breasts, her eyes met his again. Her staged smile had been replaced by an expression of fiercely charged desire.

It wasn't Parnell she was looking at. Her thoughts were lost in another time, another man—as his were lost in the heat of space, and a flaming emptiness he must fill. Parnell closed his eyes to concentrate on the flesh before him. He missed the flash of fear, the passionate sorrow that filled the windows of Catherine's memory as she fought to gain control. The Cat's eyes blurred in a growing pressure of tears. She shut them down. But behind the closed lids built a mystic vision of another truth— another dream—a blinding image outside reality—beyond the present, behind the life she now lived.

In her mind view, Catherine was suspended above a still green sea of contained energy. Her fantasy swayed above a body of mirror still water. The blurred image in her sightless eyes was slime-green foliage and wildfire flowers. Mist rose from the defused surface of the green. She was cradled in the rough-barked natural curve of a gnarled yet graceful limb of ageless cedar. It reached out inches over the green, warm water pool. The limb swayed gently, brushing the surface, dimpling the mirror with gentle ripples that spread to the rich moss-slippery, rock-lined banks. Laid back, cupped in the crook of the large cedar, she and her lover moved within the rhythm—

"It's my fantasy, Parnell," she breathed. "Theatre is my reality. I don't know you, Parnell. Do I? Do you?" Her strong fingers gripped his shoulder fiercely. "Your brand, your scar— your mark. Does it hurt, Parnell?" If she were saying the words aloud he wasn't hearing. "Did it hurt when you were cut? Did it burn? How long ago Parnell? This scar you bear, this mark, was it born with you?" Her fingernails sank into the flesh, drawing sharp lines of bright red, new threads of fresh blood. Parnell thrilled in the inflicted pain. He pressed his open mouth hard against her flesh. Their acute suffering reveled in a rush of sexual exhilaration. Parnell's tongue held the fierce pressure until Catherine came a second time. Tasting the joy of success, Parnell backed off.

The tears came now. Catherine wept with soft intensity. Parnell rose up into the rippled, antique mirror's reflection. The Cat leaned back against the cool glass. She slid her hands down, knowingly, linking them behind his waist. Parnell, his eyes tight closed to avoid his image in the glass, leaned back into her grip until feeling him, she pulled him forward into the rain forest of her aching soul. Through a half-lidded blur she watched him burst inside her. She felt his rush and joined it. They were lost: balanced in their personal consummation, apart, but reaching for the souls in their desperate wish to be together.

\* \* \*

The dressing room door quietly swung in upon them. Geraldine observed the couple. Other than a raised eyebrow she showed no reaction as she broke in on their total concentration.

"You have less than a minute, madam, before you come on."

Brought back to the present, Catherine released Parnell. With tissue Gee offered her, she cleaned herself then wiped the tears away. Briskly, she held her arms out to be dressed.

Parnell, cut free, suddenly embarrassed, tried to cover himself. He turned to the wall and clumsily tugged his jeans up about his waist.

"I've never missed an entrance yet," Catherine said quietly. Gee zipped up the back of her fresh costume.

"You might this time, madam," she said matter-of-factly. "But as for my part, your wardrobe is on and ready." She combed the singed hair away with Cat's camelhair brush.

"Thank you Gee-gee." The Cat nudged Parnell aside and checked herself in the full- length mirror. She liked what she saw. "You can't be rid of me, Parnell," she said absently. "I'll be back you know." She paused. "You know—I've come back before." Stepping out, Catherine turned in the doorway. She was puzzled by what possessed her to make that last remark. Parnell was out of hearing: out of mind. He hadn't heard a thing.

Toad's unmistakable voice came quietly over the two-way intercom speaker on the wall of her dressing room. "You are on, Miss. Catherine."

"So I am." The Cat dashed out and up the stairs. Jack Parnell Mackenzie was left behind in wonder.

"Who is she?" he whispered. Geraldine shrugged. "Where did she come from? Why? And who the hell am I?" He cried.

Geraldine looked at him and shook her head. "Damned if I know," she said. From above came a roar of applause. Catherine had made her entrance. "I've got work to do, Cowboy." The wardrobe mistress left Parnell brooding in the mirror. "When you leave, don't slam the door."

There was another roar of applause. "Yes, do close the door quietly." It was Toad's voice over the intercom. Parnell realized the two-way connection had been left on throughout his visit. The rhinestone cowboy fled. Above he found the stage door ajar and slipped into the cool darkness of the alleyway.

Jack Parnell Mackenzie had had enough of theatre for one night.

# CHAPTER NINE

# A BALL OF FIRE

Above the mesa on the Sullivan ranch, the red sun came up with a roar. Balanced on Tinaja's thrusting volcanic plug, it framed itself, a ball of fire, in the long ago charred window of the adobe ruins. The peregrine, perched on the blackened windowsill, barely gave it notice. She tore at the warm, bloody flesh of a young rabbit, her first kill of the day. Pausing, she cocked her head and listened. In a cloud of dust, Parnell's old truck rocked toward her silent refuge. Reluctantly the falcon left the balance of her meal and rose effortlessly to the chimney above the ruins. The top of the smoke hole was covered by a large flat slab of stone balanced on four corner rocks to keep rain and snow from washing down into the fire. The flagstone had protected the mud and stone all these years, helping to make that corner of the ruins the most permanent. The sheltered chimney formed the peregrine's home. The big falcon ducked under the slab and watched.

Parnell pulled the truck to a grinding halt. Old Tom Sullivan was with him. Under the bird's dark eyes the two men sat quietly. The old man stared absently into his lap. In the hush of red dawn, Parnell was half absorbed by the spectacular view. *Red sky at morning, sailors take warning.* The seacoast proverb flashed in his mind. But his mind was not primarily on the wonders of nature. He stepped out of the pickup and circled the ruins thoughtfully. He stopped under the chimney corner. Silently, he studied Tinaja's red sun-splashed peak, but in the serious periphery of his focus was Tom Sullivan. Tom was slumped in the seat of the truck, his head bowed. The old man's attention, what there seemed to be of it, was concentrating on his thumbs circling each other in the crotch of his lap.

\* \* \*

Early that morning, while doing the barn chores, Tom's brother, Sully, had found Parnell asleep in his truck by the corrals. Parnell had driven to the ranch following the evening's theatrics. In Sully's estimation Parnell hadn't been drinking, but he was, in the eyes of Sully, exhausted—washed out. Sully woke him and told him as much. He invited him in for breakfast.

Old Tom had the pre-dawn meal, sourdough hotcakes, bacon and eggs on the table. There was plenty to go around. Parnell hardly touched his plate. After a third cup of coffee, and not a word from his troubled friend, Sully Sullivan excused himself. "I got the flatbed trailer hooked to my pickup. Got to head for the Abbot ranch on the Poniel creek for a load of winter hay. It's the first cutting," Sully said, "and a good price." Parnell made no comment. His mind was somewhere else. Sully studied him. Something beside a quart of bourbon had taken place in Parnell's life last night. He wouldn't push the quiet man to bare his soul right now. It might come out later. What ever had transpired, Sully felt certain the mad woman from Enid Oklahoma had been at the core of it.

Sully shook his heavy bearded head and wondered why his poor friend just didn't cuddle up to Kate—if Kate would take him back? Sully thought she would. Kate was a forgiving woman. She had helped Parnell the other night when she should have kicked him in the ass. Parnell needed a gentle hand and a rich forgiveness. "Forget the mad woman, Parnell," Sully reasoned quietly. "The Mad woman is just passing through." Sully hoped she was just passing through. She was a very unsettling personality. Sully also hoped Parnell, although a fool at times, was not fool enough to join her circus. *It would be a three ring mad house: Parnell, the faggot and the crazy fiddler—and the Mad Woman.* "Four rings," he sighed quietly. In Sully's mind, that show would cross the border into the land of the absurd. He shook his head again. Parnell had not looked up. "Told Abbot I'd be by. You want to ride along?" He slapped Parnell on the shoulder. Parnell winced. The raw birthmark beneath his shirt was sore. The blood drawn last night in The Cat's dressing room had dried to the torn cotton denim.

"You hurt?"

Parnell shrugged. "No. Just a scratch. I need to patch it up is all". He had heard Sully talk of how there wasn't enough water on the Sullivan ranch to raise alfalfa. The Sullivan brothers had to depend on neighbors for the winter hay. "You want help loading?" he offered lamely.

"Don't need it. Abbot got a lift. Come with me if you want, or kick back and relax." Sully eyed Parnell under a raised eyebrow. "You look like you could use a little R and R, friend." Parnell didn't argue. "I'll be back by noon or a little after. You still here, I'll put you to work ... unloadin'." He grinned with his lips. Sully was worried. He nodded to his brother. "Old Tom here is a hell of a seamstress ... or seamster, if you will. He'll patch your shirt up for you in no time. And if you're scarred, there's Bag balm in the medicine cabinet – and in the stables." Mention of the time honored country cure in the well-known green can brought on a half smile from Parnell. Sully was encouraged. He pushed a little. "But Parnell, may be best you get Kate to see to it. She might could patch your head, too, cowboy. You look a bit torn up at the corners."

Parnell looked up. "You're right about that, Sully".

"Hell, invite her out. It would be good to have a good woman here for a spell. Maybe she could raise a corner of that dark quilt the Enid witch laid on you."

"Bueno, Sully. That's enough. I'll be okay." Parnell protested quietly. "I need to stay out of that town for a while. Get my head back together."

"Good thinkin'. Kate might help." Sully nodded to his brother, Tom, pouring off the bacon grease. "Take care of Parnell, Tom. Sew up his shirt. Don't let him do nothin' rash." He laughed, trying to brush off his dark feelings.

"I'll keep a hawk's eye on him." Tom giggled. "And I'll get the needle and thread right off."

"You do that, Brother. See you both about noon, or one."

\* \* \*

Parnell walked out with Sully. The rancher turned to him seriously. "Tom lost his medication somewhere."

"His medication?"

"Ya, his pills to keep his mind at rest. You know. I gave him some the day we was branding. Remember? Right now he seems to be OK. Just keep an eye on him. He don't know what he done with them pills."

"What can I do, Sully? Will he be alright?"

"Nothing serious. He's lost them before. Probably just misplaced. I'll pick up some more while I'm gone. Just keep an eye on him, would ya? No more birds in the smoke?"

"Sure, Sully. He'll be OK, just like you said." Parnell watched as Sully got in his battered Jimmy ¾ ton with the rusting flatbed trailer hooked to it and rattled out over the cattle guard. Thoughtfully Parnell went back in and helped Tom with the washing up. Old Tom's actions seemed perfectly normal, that is, normal for old Tom. Parnell dismissed Sully's words about the missing medication. Tom would hang in there. Parnell covered his conspicuously marked shoulder with the drying cloth and gave the old man his shirt to mend. Whistling through his teeth, Tom stitched it up while Parnell dried and put away the dishes. When they had finished Parnell sat and had another cup of Tom's coffee. He ran the events of the past few days through his brain. A plan was half forming in his troubled mind.

"How about I take you with me for a drive, Tom? You can show me something more about this country," he said.

The prospect of getting out of the house and away from the headquarters pleased the old man. "As long as you don't drive me to town," Tom insisted. "Sully don't like me goin' to Rainbow. He's afraid I might get in trouble."

"Don't worry, Tom," Parnell assured him. "I won't lead you astray."

"You sure led Sully astray the other night." Tom shook his head remembering the morning he discovered the two of them off the road in Parnell's truck. "You wouldn't do that to me, would you?"

"Don't worry, Tom," Parnell repeated himself. "You'll be safe with me." Parnell didn't know what his plan was for sure, but his mind was too churned up to do nothing. Something was driving him, and it wasn't something he had complete control over. *Let fate take the lead,* he thought. *I'll follow.*

Old Tom giggled with excitement. He finished the shirt and handed it to Parnell. "Can't go out-and-about half naked." He giggled again and flustered about the kitchen in hairless rabbit eared slippers setting things to right. All was ready in less than five minutes. Parnell had to remind him to put his boots on before they took off.

"Where we a-goin'?" Tom cried as, boots in hand he climbed in the pickup barefoot. Parnell noted the old man pulled his boots on over no socks.

"We'll just drift around," Parnell said evasively. He didn't want to lose Tom's excitement. "You can teach me something about this country." He knew taking Tom to the ruins would go against Sully's grain, but he couldn't see that it would do any real harm. Parnell was driven to find out the root of the story that had him so confused. Old Tom had seen the bird when Sully didn't. Old Tom might have answers locked up somewhere in that muted mind of his. Bringing the story into the open might even help Tom Sullivan to straighten out his troubled think-ing. *Who knows?* Parnell knew he was making excuses for his actions. He wanted to take his mind off last night. Yet, somehow the events of last night were directing him this morning. How and why?

Tom chortled and bounced on the seat as they drove off. Parnell took a roundabout route to the rutted cut-off leading to the top of the mesa. He wanted their arrival to look accidental.

As the truck turned into the mud-dried ranch trail toward the ruins, Old Tom's mood took a turn, as well. A vertical dive, you might say. He was no longer alert and interested in the surroundings. His head slumped over, and no amount of talk from Parnell could snap him out of it. Parnell, determined once he was committed, drove on.

Something definitely got a grip on Old Tom. *What the hell could be the problem at this place?* Something definitely flipped a snag into the old man's brainpan. As he drove, Parnell was aware his own brainpan was not in the best working condition.

* * *

Now, at the ruins, Old Tom hadn't stirred or uttered a word since the turnoff. Parnell stepped up to the passenger door and opened it. Tom still didn't move, that is—anything except his thumbs, busily twiddling in his lap. Parnell took a deep breath. He hoped to learn a few truths, and at the same time bring the old man out of his shell. Parnell Mackenzie spoke with quiet authority. He was in this far—might as well go for the gold.

* * *

"What happened here, Tom? What happened here years ago when you were a boy?"

Old Tom, still in a trance, straightened up in the seat. He looked about absently then shrugged and giggled with no trace of humor. Parnell reached for his elbow and coaxed him out of the seat and onto the ground. Tom lowered his head again, but raised his eyes under his battered sweat marked hat brim. Avoiding Parnell and the ruins he turned toward the canyon rim and walked slowly in that direction. Parnell followed with frustrated hope.

"What do you know here, Tom?" Parnell knew he was pushing it. "What is it locked up in your heart that shut down your head?"

The Falcon, unseen beneath the flagstone lid of the chimney, watched, cold and unblinking. Old Tom picked up a rock and tossed it over the edge of the rim rock into the depths of the canyon. He listened to the sound of silence and seconds later the clack of stone on stone. It echoed from the further wall of the deep canyon. The peregrine in the chimney corner rousted her feathers. Tom stopped cold. He knew the warning. Parnell mistook the sound for a rattlesnake's advice for caution. He looked about. The rattle or rustle, perhaps wind in the tumbleweeds, had come from behind them, close to the old burnout. Parnell felt a chill pass through him but could see no danger. In the old man's presence he hid his uneasiness.

Tom turned and started back toward the ruins. From the look of him Parnell knew Tom's mind was more unsettled then usual. He looked frightened but alive—more alive than Parnell had ever seen him. Tom's mind was working. *Things were coming together*, Parnell thought, or—*perhaps they are coming apart, —shattering*. Parnell decided he better not push the old man further right now. He would let him find his own way, if he could find one, and hopefully come up with something. If nothing came of all this in a short time, Parnell determined to drive Tom home. He didn't want to upset the cart and spill all the brains out. Had he made a mistake bringing Tom up here?

This place scared the hell out of Old Tom. That was obvious. Sully had warned him to steer the old man clear of it. There was something about this place, this location: the ruins that gave Parnell the shudders, too. Ghost stories. He recalled how he had acted the other day. He couldn't remember all of what he had done, the fire and all. He knew it was crazy. Sully had been a witness to it. Sully might rightly have blamed it on the after effects of too much to drink. Parnell hoped that was all it was.

Jack Parnell leaned back against the sun-warming adobes and rested his hand on the windowsill. In a moment of terror, he jerked the hand away. A mess or fur and sticky lengths of fresh guts stuck to him. In horror he tried to shake it free. Rebounding like a yo-yo, the rabbit's warm entrails wrapped about his wrist like a hot snake. Grabbing a stick he found at his feet he desperately started scraping at the bloody offal. To his sick dismay he discovered the wood scrap he was using was the broken neck of the fiddle he had discovered in the ruins two days before. He remembered he had left it on the hearth. *How did it get out here?*

Parnell heard Tom's rambling voice inside the ruins of the burned adobe. Was he talking to himself? Off by himself in the midst of some farfetched tale, or perhaps one of his childish verses? Parnell desperately scraped at the bloody mess on his hand and arm. He dragged his wrist across the edge of the windowsill where it had become entangled in the first place. As he detached the sticky, twisted entrails, he became vaguely aware of what Tom was saying.

"Up here on the mesa, the winter wind will blow the hair off a buffalo." Tom went on with his disconnected thoughts. He wasn't talking to Parnell. His worded thoughts were just going into space. "There's a spring at the bottom of the canyon," he went on, "where I threw the rock. When I was a kid I hurled enough rocks down in that wet hole to fill it up." He looked toward the canyon. "Sully hates that spring. It spills warm water year round. I couldn't throw the rock today out far enough to hit the water. I used to could do that. That water is warm year 'round. It won't freeze—doesn't dare. You crawl down there you'd think that water too hot to drink. I've drunk it. Tastes like sulfur. Stinks too. You can smell the stink up here where the sun lifts it when the wind's right. On a hot day like this you sometimes can smell it. The doctor used to say it was real healthy. It's good to soak in it he said. He soaked in it. "

*Doctor?* Parnell was listening carefully now. His hand was still a bloody mess but he had cleared the worst of it free. Wiping the balance on his jeans leg, he looked in through the window to Old Tom. "What doctor?" he said. "What you talking about, Tom?" But Tom Sullivan was back into some odd corner of his mind. He wandered out the fallen door and toward the drop-off again. He was no longer speaking. Realizing he was making a mess of his britches Parnell held his bloodied hand away from his side. He followed Tom, carefully closing the distance between the two of them. "What doctor, Tom?"

Tom reached out and clung to a limb of the dead cedar his brother had held onto two days before. He leaned well out over the edge and spoke as if to himself. "He had big plans for that spring. He used to soak in it." In silence, Old Tom leaned out further. Parnell stood ready to grab him if he slipped. It was unlikely the tough old limb would snap. Parnell didn't want Tom to fall, but he also didn't want to startle him, or break him out of his reverie. He wanted to keep him talking—to keep him think-ing—putting his thoughts into words.

Tom was in his own mind with memories. There was nothing else within miles. In that mind, in the past, Old Tom watched someone in the depths of the canyon. Parnell leaned out but could see no one down there. *Did I expect to?*

Tom was silent, but he clearly saw someone soaking in the green, moss lined sulfur spring below. Parnell shook his head. It was all in Tom's twisted thinking. Parnell watched and hoped for him to go on. A long silence and he did:

"I used to watch. I would hide up here. I would creep up on my belly to behind my hiding rock and watch 'em—". Another silence. Tom digested his last statement as it echoed. He looked about, searching for his hiding rock—. He listened to the echoes from the green spring hole. He heard them and jerked guiltily. He wheeled and stumbled, blind and tripping back toward the ruins. Parnell followed closely. Tom crawled inside the ruins. Drawing his body into a tight fetal position, he huddled, trem-bling on the hearth of the fireplace. *Is he in a trance?* Parnell wondered. *Is Tom perhaps a diabetic? They went into trances, or fits—same thing.* Parnell tried to remember from his long ago interrupted medical training. He wondered what was in the pills Old Tom was supposed to be taking. If he took them every day, it could take thirty six hours or more for the effects to ware off.

* * *

Parnell thought about his interrupted medical career. It had been a short one. He got his BA and BS at the same time. The BA was his. The BS belonged to his father. BS *Bullshit.*

His father and uncle were both doctors of medicine. Parnell's father liked the medicine so much he became addicted to the drugs he prescribed, at which point he switched to the practice of psychiatry. That was when the boy's mother moved in with his uncle. Parnell was left with his father. Parnell's father and uncle came from a wealthy Philadelphia family; a family with a medical history. The male side of the Mackenzie family had been doctors back to the time of the Revolution. One of his great, great etcetera grandfathers had been Benjamin Franklin's personal physician—had sat in front of Franklin's stove—had accompanied the great man to France. Parnell had been bored by the story so many times he hated it.

Parnell Mackenzie had been an unexpected child. At the advent of his birth his mother nearly died. He was born early, but not early enough for her. When she was presented with the child, she ordered him taken away. Parnell grew up with tutors and in private schools. His only friends were his literary fantasies. Kipling, Edgar Allen Poe and Rabelais, had been his favorite authors. Shakespeare and Samuel Johnson were close seconds. But his father and uncle had laid out his future for him. To receive fanatical aid from them he had to continue his schooling and medical school was the only viable offer they would consider.

Parnell cursed himself for cowardly bowing down to their demands. But school was easy. Parnell was blessed, or cursed, with a photographic mind. He refused to volunteer in class, but would study the night before a test and pass as one of the best of his class. For him school was a free ride. It was much easier than hard work, as in manual labor. He would drink and live his fantasy life on the side. He took plenty of time for that. Life was easy and he wanted to continue on that track for the rest of his life. In a bizarre way, his secret prayers were answered his second year of medical school. His uncle, the eldest of the brothers, and childless, died and left his wayward nephew a sizable legacy: everything he had. Jack Parnell's inheritance was well over a million dollars.

His uncle's lover, Parnell's mother, was forced to move back with her husband, Parnell's father. She was furious, but had no choice. Her son had not only messed up her life by forcing his way into this world through her womb—he had now screwed her again. With the money sitting there in her worthless son's account, she was penniless. Parnell hated her. He would see that she wouldn't get a cent of it.

For Parnell, there was one drawback to this great windfall. And it was a great drawback. The principle of his cash inheritance was to go to his legitimate children when they reached the age of eighteen. Young Parnell would only receive a portion of the interest, not to exceed five hundred dollars a month.

Parnell's father accepted his wife back as if she had never left. He was living in his wonder world of barely controlled dope ridden fantasies. His habits were financed by a string of mind-boggled patients crawling to his door and paying through the nose for dope and his dubious psychological help.

Parnell's wayward mother, thinking of the future, now demanded her son sprout progeny. She dragged wealthy and willing partners to the flat where her son was now immersed in the works of Zane Grey and William McLeod Raine. Visions of horses and wide-open spaces rode his brain waves. The thought of raising fat babies for his mother to vilify did not appeal to his free spirit any more than finishing medical school and falling into a practice in Philadelphia's upper class of "cesspool" society, as he called it. He fled. Riding the range was better than studding the gaping emptiness presented to him by a mother who, if she thought it would not land her in prison, would put out a contract on him. She wished she had done just that, months before he burst into her world, a festering boil for which there was no cure.

On his way out of civilization, as he despised it, he stopped by his uncles law firm and made arrangements for the remittance to follow him on his wayward path. He would survive and keep them supplied with general delivery addresses. So far he had.

He wondered now, in his troubled search for fulfillment, what in Christ's name had brought him to the brink of this canyon? *What was this address?* He was standing in the flame-ruined dream of a lost cabin and a lost life listening to the babbling of a crazy old man. He was, however, deeply haunted by this location. He was forced to stay and find the answers. He had to. He twisted his thinking back to Old Tom.

\* \* \*

Parnell realized he might have opened a can of worms. Old Tom was the can and the worms were crawling out. *I should have followed Sully's advice and never brought his brother up on the mesa.* It was too late for that now, and despite the feeling of guilt shadowing him, Parnell wanted to know the whole story. In some way he was implicated in it. *How? Why?* He wanted to know. It was ridiculous. *To know what?* Some vague strange stuff was squirreling around inside the old man's head. Parnell was certain, or at least feared, he might find some connection between the two of them. Perhaps he was crazy, too. He listened closely as the old man whimpered in his sudden sleep—trance—or whatever. Tom's words, at first, had been garbled. Now they were sharp, anguished and clear:

"It wasn't like I sneaked up to watch," the old man cried, tears running down his withered cheeks onto the dirty hearth. His arms wrapped tightly beneath his thighs, he made no move to stop them. "The first time I didn't mean to watch," he wailed pathetically. "It just happened. I couldn't help myself. All I wanted was to be friends with her. She was friendly when I started visiting her daytimes at the house. Even the doctor was friendly, but he was mostly gone." Old Tom's head rose, the watering eyes looked blankly around the nonexistent room. Parnell wondered if Tom were seeing the room like he remembered it as a boy. Had the old adobe resurrected itself in his mind as it had burned in Parnell's dreams? Parnell forced himself to be patient. He waited with trembling excitement. The old man squinched his eyes shut. His small tight body shuddered visibly. After a long moment of silence Old Tom picked up his painful narrative.

"But then I watched. It all changed when I watched them together. I didn't mean to. I just happened to look down and then I couldn't help myself. Blackie, my horse, was tied at the corral by the barn. He was way back, safe out of sight. I checked the barn and the house first to see if she was there. He had been gone the day before, the doctor. She had been here alone. I liked it best when she was alone. Sometimes, when she was alone, she would go down to the spring by herself. Maybe she had gone down today, I thought, so I walked over to the rim. If I saw her I was going to call to her. But, if she was there, I wanted to just watch her for a while first without her knowing it. I don't know why. She said she sometimes lay in the sun on the big rock, or went swimming. She had told me we should do it together some day. I guess I thought maybe she would wave me down. I don't know. I didn't think about it then. I just got on my belly and crawled up to the rim behind my hiding rock. —She was there—but so was he, the doctor. They had no clothes on. They were there on the flat rock in the sun. They were together. I watched them. She was sitting on him—moving. I watched. I was bad ... wicked." Tom Sullivan was quiet for a long time. "It was my fault."

What Tom was saying was barely audible but terribly intense. His eyes were now tight closed. Only tears squeaked through. Parnell looked in wonder at Tom's trembling old body. He was sitting, drawn up into himself on the fireplace hearth. The old man's head dropped between his knees. His thin hands clutched at his crotch, massaging it in a guilty daydream of his youth.

"Jesus Christ," Parnell mumbled, in pain and sympathy. "And I thought my dreams were bad."

"Naked!" the old man screamed suddenly. He stretched out to his full length, and rolled from the raised hearth to the dirt and flagstone floor. "Down there she danced in the sun," he cried. "On that big flat rock for him! —She danced for him!" He screamed again, pounding the hard packed earth. "With no clothes on she danced for him! The steam from the spring rose up around her like a curse. Bare naked she was—She would—-"

Tom's eyes fluttered open and, despite his years, he scrambled nimble as a young boy, to his feet. He spotted Parnell staring at him from the blackened doorway. "What are you doing here?" he cried. "You don't belong. This is my place, mine and hers," he yelled in Parnell's face. "You are gone. It is just us now!" He spun about trying to shake the crazy visions from his brain. Then he spotted the rabbit blood on Parnell's arm. He looked up at Parnell accusingly. "Whose blood is on your hands? Where did the blood come from?"

Parnell held out his bloody hand. "It's alright Tom. There was something bloody on the windowsill. I touched it without meaning to. That's all." Tom moved forward and studied Parnell's hand. Then he looked at the windowsill. Remains of the rabbit were still there. Tom moved in and studied it closely.

"It's hers. It belongs to her." He started giggling; reverting to the Old Tom Parnell first met. Parnell felt himself relax, almost. He wondered how many days Tom could go without his medication. The old man picked up what was left of the rabbit and looked expectantly into the sky. "Funny thing she would leave it."

"She? Who are you talking about, Tom?"

"The falcon. It was the falcon. It wasn't her mate. This is too big a kill for him. Her mate is smaller—if she has a new one. I don't think so." Tom studied the sky with silent intensity for a full three minutes. "I killed him," he said quietly. Parnell considered this last statement a moment.

*Why and when had Old Tom, or Young Tom as it might have been, killed the bird's mate?* It was too bizarre to comprehend.

The female is the biggest?" Parnell asked. It was a mundane question, and, Parnell thought one that shouldn't cause any mental hysteria.

"She is the biggest, the fastest—and the boss." Tom giggled again, switching back and forth from semi-sanity to his enfeebled mind. The giggling stopped suddenly. Tom became serious. "That Falcon whipped her mate into shape," Tom said with a reverence. "Always did, ever since I first met her. I was a boy. You don't see him now. He disappeared—her mate." Tom's lips twisted into a cruel grin. "Good thing too."

Parnell wanted to ask what had happened to the mate. How had Tom killed him and why? An inner voice told him to drop it.

Tom picked up the rabbit parts, sniffed them and then dropped them back on the windowsill. "Fresh." He smiled. It was not quite a giggle.

"She'll come back for this," he said. You better get out of the way. She can be mean. She will be mean, too."

Parnell picked up a handful of dust and rubbed it into his hands, trying to eradicate the last of the blood. "You've known this bird a long time, right, Tom?" He asked surreptitiously.

Tom followed Parnell out through the doorframe and watched him trying to clean the bloody hand. Parnell gave up with the dust and started scraping off the blood against the rough wall around the chimney corner. Either Tom didn't hear the question, or didn't care to answer it. Tom studied the rabbit blood dripping under the windowsill. Dropping to his knees he sniffed it again. Something about the blood jogged his mind. He tasted it. His face changed. Old Tom became completely sane and rational.

"Just like that night—the fire—." Tom's voice cut the air with a sharp edge of steel, cold steel. Parnell felt the chill.

"What fire, Tom?" He was afraid to move in closer, but he had to know. Would the old man go on?

"Papa brought me here. There was blood on this window. Some one had crashed the glass to get out. Papa wondered why they didn't use the door. The door was open." Tom looked away toward the canyon. "The blood was burned black on the sill," he said. "But bright red underneath, and still wet when I touched it. It was on the ground, too."

"This blood is fresh, Tom," Parnell said in the silence that followed. Parnell was worried. Old Tom was a different person. Whoever he was now was frightening. "It's rabbit blood, Tom. That's all it is. It's nothing to—"

Tom got to his feet and stepped quickly away, then turned back on Parnell. For the first time he looked Parnell Mackenzie in the eye. The look was not friendly. It was not the look Parnell was used to. Parnell guessed that Old Tom was now in reality, his mind running over. Words jumbled out rapidly, unintelligible. To Parnell's relief the old man turned away. Once again Tom Sullivan was totally alone with his ghosts of the past.

"It's like the dancing—and the fiddle," At the mention of the fiddle, a frightening change came over Tom. His voice was younger and much stronger. It changed to the high cracked register of a boy in the cruel throes of puberty. Parnell was not comfortable at all. Goosebumps shivered up his legs and back as he watched Tom turn, as in the grip of witchcraft, and walk with a youthful bounce back toward the canyon rim. Parnell, subconsciously still wiping blood from his hand, followed cautiously. Old Tom was not talking to him now; may not at this point even know Parnell was there. *If he is speaking to the wind, so be it,* Parnell reasoned. He tried to catch the words the old man was passing off like so much gas.

\* \* \*

From her vantage point, in the dark at the top of the chimney, the peregrine's sharp yellow eyes followed Parnell. Flying, the peregrine falcon can spot her prey crouched, hidden in the grass and rocks hundreds of feet below. From this distance it was not a friendly eye she laid on Parnell. But Parnell, wrapped up in Tom's narrative, was only vaguely aware of some unknown presence raising chills through his nervous system. Every few minutes he searched the area. *For what?* Embarrassed by his superstitious weakness, he shook off the feeling, only to have it strike again; a sharper blow each time.

Twenty feet in front of him Old Tom balanced at the edge of the drop-off. He was gazing down at the sulfur pool. The spring was only partially visible from where they stood. Tom was thinking, but had stopped talking. Gently Parnell egged him on: "What fiddle, Tom? Who was dancing?" The old man ignored him. He mumbled incoherently, then:

"Papa found out—he must have—he beat me. He did, and rightly so." Tom cringed in this attack of guilt. He felt again the laying on of the sharp horsewhip his father seldom used on the team. It cut through the boy's clothes and into his skin bringing on an ooze of blood that, when it dried, stuck his denim shirt to his young back. Old Tom shrank back, vividly remembering.

He swung out from the dead cedar with surprising energy and strength for a man his age—for a boy, Parnell realized. From the dead limb the boy hung out from the tree, a hundred feet of open space gaping hungrily beneath him. Young Tom swung in circles around and around the gray cedar to avoid the lash. Parnell, afraid Tom would lose his grip and go over, dared not interfere. If he moved closer he was afraid Tom might mistake him for his enraged assailant—father, whoever—and would prefer death to further confrontation.

"I am guilty of a wicked truth," the boy/man cried. Then, thankfully, the beating stopped. Apparently having slipped into another dream, Old Tom swung back and crumpled to the ground. Hanging half over the precipice, he broke into shaking sobs. His fists pounded on the sharp volcanic basalt, bruising the knuckles, tearing the skin until it bled.

"Truth is good, Tom," Parnell interjected, truly concerned and trying to reason with the old man. "You wouldn't be beaten for telling the truth." Tom didn't hear him—couldn't hear him. He was the boy, the young Tom, and living the boy's guilty dream of forbidden manhood. He looked back down at the dark quiet pool surrounded by alder brush and the tall sprawling cedar that rooted through the great boulders, splitting them like slow, silent thunder over the centuries. Tom dried his tears on the rough sleeve of his shirt. He crawled back behind a dark rock, his hiding rock, where he would not be seen from below. He raised his head stealthily and peeked around it:

"They are in the water, right down there; the green water. It's sulfur. It comes from the bottom of the earth: from Hell, the last gasp of the eruption: a furnace of the underworld. 'It's the water of sin,' Papa said. I didn't believe him. I wouldn't! I saw them. I knew what they were doing was wonderful and beautiful. I wanted to be a part of it."

Awed and naïve, the young boy watched from his hiding rock. "I saw the man take his clothes off first. He plunged in the water and called to her to follow. She took her time and pleasure. She let her hair down, like flames, tumbling to her waist. Then with Amazing Grace, like the song she used to sing, her blouse and riding skirt slid to the rocks. She stood in her high-buttoned boots and flowing silks. Tall and trim she stood, her small breasts in a lace harness. I had seen my mother like that, but these clothes were different. So was she. The man lay back in the warm sulfur water, like he was hungry for the candy of each move Katrina made."

*Katrina?* It was the first time Tom had named the lady of his dream. *Katrina?* Parnell listened in disbelief and wonder. The picture was too vivid to be untrue, and *Tom relived* it by the heartbeat. Parnell was definitely listening to and watching, a young Thomas Sullivan now. He was fully alive and no longer the mindless old man, Sully's halfwit brother. Young Tom, in his secret world of fantasy, lived in a world of beauty, horror and truth. The boy went on:

"The water was green and clear and they were naked, swimming sometimes and sometimes lying on the rocks, thick blankets spread beneath them. After the first time, when I saw them by mistake, I would sneak back here and watch again." Tom rolled back and stared up at the sky in silent torment. Then he threw his hands over his face. "That was my truth, my sin. My sin now is that I can remember. Father said 'forget it. Forget it, Tommy! It never happened. —But it did happen. I can remember. I do remember. I want to remember! That is my sin, and I will pay for it. That is the way it is, the way it has to be. The way it always will be.

"I am a boy. I am thirteen. I wonder why the hair begins to grow between my legs. I wonder why my—'thing'—gets hard. I wonder why it feels so good it hurts when I watch the lady and the man together." Young Tom rolled back on his belly behind his hiding stone and watched again as Katrina danced upon the large flat rock that made a stage for her performance; the gray-green flat rock that reached out from under the limbs of the greatest cedar tree—the giant tree—the tree of love.

Parnell could almost see it. He tried to shake the vision from his mind. It was too strong. It was Catherine. The words of The Cat's fantasy came back to him. *Or am I insane?* Tom was going on:

135

"She would get up and dance on that rock; in a long red silk scarf, or cape she called it. Oh, she would dance." Tom sighed. "She moved like a mountain cat, or bird in the wind. Sometimes at night when the moon was at the full: those nights I would know and I would sneak out under the frosted light to watch—and each time I would sneak closer …

Sometimes when the doctor wasn't here, when he was riding in his buggy making rounds, she called them rounds." Tom pounded his balled fists on the rock behind which he hid. "She would dance alone. I pretended she would dance alone for me. I'd watch and watch. And each time I would sneak closer. Down the secret trail that she knew well, that he knew, too, and that I knew even better. Until in time my secret was down there with them, beside them, feeling their bodies in my mind. Close and warm and holding myself, I watched.

"It was different down there then from up here. I could see everything full size. At first it frightened me, being so close. From above, from here, they weren't as real and I was free to move. From here I couldn't see it all. I couldn't see the truth. But when they lay on the great cedar limb that reached across the water like a snake, I saw the truth then. I knew. I saw them moving in the sun and moon of truth. It frightened me. I was frozen, stiff and still as death, I was safe, I thought, safe in the dark shadow of a halfway cave just big enough, I thought, to hide me.

"The doctor balanced and walked out on the great rough cedar limb and spread a blanket to protect them from the bark. The edges of it dipped into the warm water. He sat down, naked, balanced, safe, in a crook in the limb. The limb raised and lowered with his weight, barely touching the steaming green water. He called to her to join him. But she was dancing on the rock. She wasn't ready yet. I wanted her to keep dancing. I didn't want her to go to him. But I knew she would.

"She loved to dance. I watched from my hiding place close enough to smell her smell, the smell of her perfume, the smell of her, the beautiful smell, the smell I loved to taste."

Old Tom … young Tom lay on the brink of the hundred-foot drop-off inhaling the rich memory of her aroma, the fragrance of her sex. The old man's chest heaved as he gulped the air.

Parnell leaned out and looked down—.

Jack Parnell could see them too. He shuddered at the thought that had come to life before him. He saw, at first shadows swirling about, light upon the moonlit rock: a shower of crimson silk, reaching for the wind that washed over her. With Tom, Parnell now felt the fire. Unknowing—knowing he was there.

And then she dropped the cape and with her dancer's balance, walked naked out upon the limb and let herself down astride the waiting man. Parnell and Tom watched in awe.

"I'm crazy," Parnell whispered hoarsely. He wrenched himself away from the haunting image. He looked back toward the ruins of the adobe cabin, and tried to clear his mind. Tom's hypnotic words and pictures had left him blind to reason. Behind him, on the brink of death, Young Tom cried out, as the bodies met—as she touched him, as slowly he sank into her. She moved more slowly, in control of her passion—and her life—slowly, until he closed his eyes. Steam floated up around their bodies in the act of love. Parnell fought the vision: closed it from his mind. Young Tom went on, his mind in flame.

"From where I was—I watched her face," Tom said, his voice hushed in reverie, barely heard.

Was Tom, indeed talking? Had he said anything at all, Parnell wondered, or *is this a mad, masochistic vision of my mind in Hell?*

Old Tom's boy's voice was charged with youthful wonder, filled with fear and questions. The boy's first close view of the human sexual act was explicit in its animalistic strength and beauty. And yet, in the darkness of his father's words, he now truly believed the act of sex, or love—or knowing sex with others to be his sin. *What happened after that, Tommy?*

Suddenly, as if reading Parnell's thoughts, Old Tom, behind his black hiding rock on the mesa's edge, clawed his way to a sitting position. "Sex? Sex!" he cried out plaintively. "I'd never even heard the word, yet father, when he found out I knew that I was naked, beat me for it: for knowing what the Bible meant. He whipped me when he found out I knew the truth. Hanging to this tree, I screamed at him: I screamed, 'what they were doing—what—we—were doing wasn't dirty—wasn't wrong. It was good! I screamed. And then silently, I screamed, because there was no way to reach him, because he couldn't see the truth. Papa had no eye for beauty. Papa's eyes and heart were dead while he was alive."

Tom's face fell into the canyon of his old age. He wilted out of the beauty of his youthful innocence. "It was later—" he whispered. "It was later." Tom was once again terribly aware, alive and thinking clearly, shaken with the sudden cold panic of his ruptured youth. Parnell watched the revulsion spread across the old man's countenance. Old Tom had given up. His voice was barely audible. Parnell leaned forward to catch the words.

"It was much later." Tom stumbled on his words. "Or maybe not. Time has a way of telling lies. —It was with the other man.—the fiddler—that the dirty and the ugly came."

Old Tom closed his wild eyes and threw himself back behind his rock. The moment passed. His voice found its youthful cadence once again. He looked back down and saw Katrina on the rock. He saw her before her trouble crossed his path with blood. He was in awe and innocent again.

"And there they were," he said, "On that great cedar limb. It rocked gently until it brushed the surface of the water making little waves that washed across to where I lay in hiding. They were mountain lions mating in slow motion on that limb. It was beautiful. I wished I could be with them. I sneaked closer and then—And then, one time too close. She knew that I was there. She looked right at me. She saw me. But she didn't say a thing. She didn't cry out as I was afraid she might. Instead, she—she smiled. Her face was beautiful—Her eyes were—Her eyes were open. I saw he kept his eyes closed, tight closed. She didn't say anything to him about my being there. She didn't tell the doctor I was there watching them. Then she got that look on her face, a look I grew to know, and love – and she cried out.

138

"I thought he was hurting her. I started to get up to help—to protect her. I didn't know then what was happening. I was a boy. I was thirteen. But she shook her head "no!" It would be our secret together. I stayed still—scared—happy—until he fell asleep. And then – And then—Katrina came to me. She came to me."

# CHAPTER TEN

# LOSS OF INNOCENCE

Old Tom gave vent to a great heart throbbing sigh and threw himself full belly on the rock-hard ground behind his hiding rock. Through the old man's tears Parnell made out words spoken by a heartsick boy.

"She is wonderful. I love her. I am thirteen. I am a boy and I love her like nothing else that ever happened to me." Tears rained down his withered cheeks. "When the doctor left, gone 'on his rounds' as she said, as she called them—I would pretend I was the man. I was the only man. Not at first. At first I was ashamed when she pleased me. I cried quiet tears by the green spring, that first time with the man asleep on the limb. Then she told me to slip away quietly and come back later when the doctor was gone. She wanted us to be close, she said. A little way from the sulfur spring, where I thought I wouldn't be heard, I ran like a coyote, a frightened one. I stayed away for a week until Mrs. Doctor, as my mother called Katrina, came to the ranch house and told my mother the doctor was away and she needed help to fix the corral. 'One of our steers had knocked it down to get at the water,' she said.

"When I saw her coming I ran to the barn and hid, pretending to clean the stables. Mother found me and told me about the broken corral. 'It might be one of our steers knocked it down,' Ma told me. 'I want you to stay there until the job is done right,' she said. 'Get your horse. Your father would go if he was here, but he ain't here. Now you have to be the man.' She turned and started toward the house. 'I'd rather you went than your father anyway,' I heard her say. 'Your father could get in trouble up there.' She didn't mean for me to hear that, but I heard and I wondered about it.

"Katrina was waiting for Ma at the house. When Katrina saw me bring in my horse Blackie and start to saddle him, she said 'goodbye' to Ma' and 'thank you'. Then Katrina started riding slowly up the steep trail that lead to the mesa. I would have ridden bareback but I thought I better take the saddle with the bags, so I could carry tools. I thought the corral was really broken. I was nervous anyway. She might be angry. She couldn't of forgot about the spring and me hiding there. I stopped at the house for a drink of water.

" 'She don't ride so good,' Ma said. 'She uses that fancy, fool sidesaddle. 'Fraid she'll get bowlegged,' she sneered. Ma didn't much like Mrs. Doctor, I don't think. 'You ride along, Tom,' she said. 'You'll catch her before she reaches the flat. You be careful, mind you? Don't get into no trouble. Just do as you're told.'

"Blackie is a good horse. I'll be OK, I said.

"I started off at a trot. I didn't look back, but I felt Ma watching me and Blackie until we were out of sight."

\* \* \*

"Once on the flat of the mesa, Katrina had moved her horse, with the strange looking saddle she rode, at a fast lope. I couldn't see her when I crested the rim. I pushed Blackie into a lope, too, until I saw their adobe house and wood slab barn. Katrina was in the corral pulling the saddle from the back of her mare. Scared, I slowed Blackie to a walk. I watched Katrina go into the barn to hang the saddle. She came back and started brushing down the mare. Water from the windmill was trickling into the stock tank when I got there. She had the mare tied to a corral rail to hold her back from the water, letting her cool from the fast gallop that had brought her there well ahead of me. I studied the corral rails. There seemed to be no break that I could spot right off. I got down slowly and walked around the rough log railing, pretending to study it closely. But my mind wasn't on the logs, or looking for a break.

"Katrina kept brushing her mare. The animal was breathing hard from the fast mile and a quarter run. Katrina was flushed red and breathing hard too. I could tell. We hadn't looked at each other yet—not matching our eyes. She was nervous, too. At least, I thought she was. I don't think she really was. I don't know."

Parnell watched the boy/man walk back to the ruins of the barn. Tom put his hands up, as if leaning on the poles of the long gone corral. The past became the present in his mind. Parnell Mackenzie listened, astounded by the shift back to the reality of Tom's dream. Parnell could see it happening before him again—-. The barn was now standing, the corral back in place. He could see it building together as in his dream before the fire. He could hear Young Tommy speaking in his youth.

* * *

"I don't see any break in the rails," Young Tommy said, his voice high and strained. "I brought tools."

"I hope so." Parnell heard a woman's voice answer. He looked about, startled. She hadn't come into focus yet. Would she? He could see the barn and the rails of the correl.

"Where's the break?" asked Tommy. "Ma said that one of our steers might have broken through." Parnell saw small dust clouds rising from the earth of the corral as the ghost of the woman and her mount moved to the water trough.

Tommy's eyes followed Katrina, her back to him as she followed her mare to the water and watched it drink thirstily. As the animal drank, Katrina dipped her hands in the cool water and splashed it on her face. Parnell heard and saw the water splash.

"The doctor is gone, Tommy boy," she said. "I told you he would be gone."

"I'm sorry about the other day," Tommy said, kicking a booted toe into the dust.

"Why?" Tommy watched her unlace her high boots. Parnell watched the surface ripple as the water made way when she stepped into the hand hewn wooden tank. It was chipped out of a huge fir log. The old bandit, who had sold the place to the doctor, carved it out years ago.

Tommy's fantasy shaped itself in Parnell's mind as, with her riding skirt still on, she lowered herself into the cool water. Tommy looked away as long as he could, listening to her splashing more water over her face. It soaked down into her white, buttoned blouse. Parnell saw the newly wet cotton close over her firm breasts, the dark nipples standing out, eagerly. He couldn't pull his eyes from this apparition growing from the past. Stealthily he stepped closer.

"You'll get wet," He heard the boy say.

"I am wet," the woman said. "Do you remember, Tommy?" She started to unbutton her blouse. "I asked you to come up, Tommy. But I had to go get you, Tommy." Her horse was still nosing the water, but had had its fill of drink. Parnell watched as she kissed the mare's soft white nose. "Now go away," she said, pushing the animal gently from her.

Tommy started to leave. He didn't want to go. "I don't want to go home," he said softly. "I don't want to go away." The boy was still hanging onto Blackie's reins for security. He had barely moved a step or so. Parnell watched him closely kicking into the dust.

"I didn't mean for you to leave, Tommy," the woman said. "I'm nervous too."

"But you said—"

"—Go away to the mare." She laughed, but it wasn't a making fun laugh. It was just fun. There is room enough in here now for you." The mare had crossed over to scraps of hay in a manger where the eves of the barn sheltered it from the weather, unless the wind and storm came from the east. An east storm would wet the hay and grain. "Come here, Tommy," she said. 'We are all alone. I am very alone, —and you are a beautiful young man.' She had let her blouse fall into the water. Her firm breasts were bare and shining in the wet and morning sun.

Parnell stared. He couldn't move any more than young Tom could move.

"Tie Blackie's reins up to the rail," the woman said. "We are all alone. I want to touch you like I did the other day. I want you to touch me. Don't be afraid."

The boy dropped the reins. Blackie was trained to ground hitch, but Tom wasn't remembering that. Parnell watched him slide between the rails and move slowly to the water tank. She was beautiful. Parnell couldn't take his eyes off of her.

All Tommy could see in this world now was Katrina. He stood by the tank and fiercely made his eyes shut until tears crept out and down his face. Katrina, her hands shaking, reached out and undid his belt. The tank edge was a little under buckle high. She splashed cold water on his boy's belly and laughed when he jumped back. She hung onto the belt and pulled him to her.

"Your shirt will get wet," she said. Tommy's britches fell down around his white thighs and ankles. He kicked them off.

"I don't ware long underwear in summer," he stuttered, his eyes still closed to everything but tears.

"I wear nothing underneath my skirt, either," the woman said softly. "It feels better that way, don't you think?" Gently, she opened up the boy's shirt and kissed his belly. Her mouth was so soft Parnell could feel it—gentle, warm, and cool, too, from the water she had splashed on her face.

Tommy opened his eyes, and turning away, rubbed at the tears. Was this getting into trouble, he wondered? Was this what Ma was thinking when Blackie and me started up the hill? "I better get dressed, Katrina," he said.

"You better get in," she said. "You have come a long way to go back without me. And I have waited for a week without you."

Young Tommy was having trouble getting out of his cowboy boots without falling in the water, or the dirt. She held the boy close and let him sit on the edge of the wooden tank. Finally, Tommy just fell back into the water. His boots were still on. "I'll have to hide those wet boots from Ma," he said. "What will Ma think about me getting my boots wet, Katrina?"

\* \* \*

The vision faded – dissolved like a scene from a movie, too sad, or tender to be built upon. Parnell felt jaded. He hadn't taken a breath in minutes, perhaps longer. Tommy stood, dry and no longer young. His body sagged with age and loss of faith. He wandered, broken, toward the ruins of the old adobe. Parnell, broken, too, but breathing now, followed at a distance. Old Tom went on, breathing dreams of his exhausted, overflowing youth:

"After that time, I visited Katrina whenever I could. Every chance I got. When I was supposed to be looking for stray cattle," Tom laughed, "I'd stray right up here." Old Tom grinned, dryly, remembering.

*He's happy,* Parnell thought. *Christ, who wouldn't be—. In the past Old Tom was safe.* The man/boy spoke with warmth and love. His mind, if in that past, was altogether. *This woman had a problem, albeit mental, and the boy had fallen through the crack. And in that void, unknowingly, Katrina had taken the boy's life from him,* Parnell thought. *But who am I to be the judge—the voyeur. Who am I in all this? Who was—who is this woman? Where had she come from? This enchanting, hungry woman who had taken young Tommy too far into her pleasure?*

"She treated me like the man," Tom said aloud and clearly. "She made me the man. She taught me. At first I knew nothing about pleasing her. She taught me what to do as she was teaching me to speak good English. No more 'aints,' she said. 'There is no such word as aint.' I learned a lot from her. Our time together made me a man, she told me. It made me a strong and gentle man. She wanted a gentle man, she said. And she said, although 13, I was old enough to be one—and strong enough. 'The doctor wasn't always gentle.' She said. 'He could be mean,' she said. 'But you are gentle, Tommy, and strong, too. There is nothing wrong,' she said. 'What we did at the sulfur spring— what we do now is right and good.' I touched her gently. I would do anything for her. —I did.

"And then, one day." The boy pulled himself up and peeked around the edge of his hiding rock. Below, beside the pool, he saw Katrina sunning on the great flat rock. "She was spread upon the blankets that were kept dry in the cave, the shallow cave I first had hidden in."

Parnell watched Tom's face turn cold in memory. *What happened?* There was no humor in his eyes now, no love. *Something was changed.* Parnell watched carefully, standing back, watching the pool and the boy/man. It was as if Tom were a ghost, a ghost, seeing something for a second time.

Parnell felt the chill that passed through young Tommy Sullivan; the same cold wind the boy felt. Parnell crept to the edge and studied the sulfur pool closely. In his sight there was no one there. Parnell was relieved at that. The pool was still and green: translucent.

Parnell concentrated. Something started swirling in the depths, something that didn't break the surface—something thick and deadly. The sun dimmed on the great flat rock beneath the cedar tree. Parnell looked up. There was no cloud in the sky, no shade in the stratosphere. Between here and the white fire of the sun there was nothing. And yet, below, the pool; the rocks bordering its shore, were in a cold and bitter shade. Tom's words cut through the icy circle:

"That day the doctor was away. I knew he was away—but she had told me not to come. She would be busy, she said. I remembered her saying it. But I had to come. I was hers now. My life was drowned in her love, in the water of her love. I was a part of her. I had no choice. I disobeyed her wish. I had no choice. I was a fool boy. It was my sin. I was a boy again and not a man."

Parnell only saw the boy on the periphery. His tunnel vision sought the pool and its icy shadows. In the heavy distance of many years, Tom went on.

"Why did I disobey?" he cried. "Why did I have to see? But now, it was too late. I was only looking down instead of being down there with her. Papa had asked me to look for strays in the lower canyon but I had ridden up on the mesa. I had to see her. I thought of going down anyway. I watched Katrina stand and step under the cedar, out of sight. Her reflection spun in the still green water like the Falcon's. A breeze rippled it, cut her to pieces, scattered fragments of her naked body. I lay terrified—. I watched, knowing I should not go down, knowing I should run—wondering why she had told me not to come—. But I lay still, staring, in the hands of fear." Parnell watched Tommy stare, horrified, down into the green spring. The old man's body tightened, shivering in cold memory. In seconds, old Tom's voice changed to bitter hatred.

"And then—I knew. Then I saw the man. The man stepped in front of her reflection, shattered it like broken ice, on the green surface. He blocked it, turning what was left of my dream into a nightmare." Tom shuddered and turned away. "This man was not the doctor." Tom forced himself to stare back into the canyon.

Parnell followed his gaze into the depths again where there was still no sun. This time, he saw, Katrina, or her shadow, naked in her truth, step into the cold gray of his imagination. She took off the new man's open jacket and his shirt.

"She is down there with another man!" Tom cried accusingly, pointing. You see?"

Parnell, to his horror, did see. The woman had her back to him. The man was in shadows. Old Tom wasn't talking to Parnell. He hadn't talked to him since they arrived at the ruins, and yet Parnell saw the vision. And then—the picture faded. Parnell cut his eyes away and looked to Tom. The old man had his britches down to his knees. Unknowingly, he clutched his lank penis, crying out.

"There are two of them now, you see, and one of me. I was the boy again." His voice faded away, almost lost. Katrina wasn't dancing just for him. Old Tom lay hidden in the shadow of his hiding rock. He rolled, face down to the cold earth and cried aloud, his words like bullets fired in hate into the earth. "Katrina isn't dancing just for me. She isn't dancing just for anyone —but her. —Just for Katrina she is dancing." Old Tom rolled about and looked up at the empty sky. It was icy gray and cold, the color of burnished steel. There was no warmth from the sun anywhere now. Tom lay, exhausted.

"What can I do?" he cried. "I love her. And I watched them. I couldn't stop myself. I couldn't stop my sin. I held myself as they lay upon each other—and I prayed to kill the other man, to make him dead so he would go away. <u>To make him dead!</u>" the man/boy cried—"<u>to make him stone pressed dead!</u>

Parnell watched helplessly as Old Tom hitched himself around and spoke clearly in the cold light—his new words flat and bitter. "I would <u>make</u> him go away! I <u>could</u> make him go away. It would be that simple. It would be just her and me again. I could do it. I had to do it." Tom rose up behind his hiding rock, his face clenched in determination. He stared down through the cedar limbs into the pool—into the green death of his youth.

Parnell hunkered down, his heart and mind in a state of shock. He didn't move in half an hour. Old Tom's story was absurd, insane. But was it? Had Parnell seen the vision conjured up by a ghost of the boy's memory, seventy years past. Had the boy's description been that powerful, or in truth, had Parnell seen his own ghosts in the corral and upon the rocks below. *God's wonder the old man locked himself in silence all these years.*

Parnell looked away. Concentrating on the present, on today he set himself aside. He brought up his father's idol Sigmund Freud, who's twisted mind turned the world of psychiatry into a phallic nightmare. Parnell tried to analyze the terrors of Old Tom's past. Somehow, Parnell reasoned, Tom's father had found out about the relationship his son had been drawn into. Had Tom's father been watching too? *Like me?* Parnell didn't dare to speculate too far. *Am I seeking truth, or a way out?* He thought.—*And what is my part in all this madness?* Jack Parnell Mackenzie could not deny he saw what Tom had pointed out upon the rocks below. "Fate—shit," he muttered. Parnell forced himself to look back to Tom Sullivan, old or young, down on the ground behind his hiding rock.

The old man, for he was Old Tom again, was silent. His work jeans were still down about his knees. Ashamed, he pulled them up and buckled them. Parnell held still, but turned his eyes away. *Should I sit like a vulture and wait for the end?* Parnell wondered. *Old Tom doesn't see me. His mind is gone—way gone now. He only sees the past, an open sore that ran dry years ago and is now building to a boil again.* He thought of Sully's warning. 'Never bring my brother up onto this mesa.'

"I opened up the past and put the boy through it once again," he bitterly chastised himself. "And I do nothing." He looked at old Tom curled tightly in the sparse grass. "I squat on the sand pile of my morbid curiosity, and listen to this old man, this boy, whoever, suffer? Christ almighty, must I know the painful, the entire truth?" He cursed himself for his desire.

Parnell's legs were numb from squatting down so long. It made no difference. His mind was numb as well. He didn't make a move to change the situation. He would listen to the ghosts. Old Tom spoke again, his mind deep in the present of the past.

"I went and got my rifle," the boy said with dead determination. "I had to do what must be done—what I must do—. I carried the gun every day after that. I told papa I had seen coyotes on the mesa. That was why, I told him, I carried the old 30-30 in the boot beneath the saddle skirt. I never used a saddle much before. I liked to ride bareback on Blackie. But I needed the rifle—. I needed to do what I needed to do. I had promised to do.

"I thought about the doctor. The doctor was there first, I reasoned, before me. It was only right to let him be, if I must—to let him stay—to let him live. But in my truth I knew the other man would have to go. I thought, perhaps, the doctor would agree. The other man would spoil everything if he was near her. He would hurt her. He would destroy us. I couldn't let that happen. I said it was for both of us, me and Katrina. But in truth it was in my heart the hurt was festering. I couldn't see that then. I was blind. I only saw that she was mine! Katrina was mine to hold, to keep from harm. I was ready. I must do it in secret—where Katrina wouldn't know. I was ready. I kept the rifle with me.

"For weeks I never saw the other man. I never asked her who he was, or told her I had seen him. I didn't want to warn him. I didn't want her to know I knew about him. All by myself, this was my secret. I waited. If that fiddle man came back, he would be dead and never come again." Parnell watched as Old Tom stood and looked about. He smiled, proud of himself and did a little jig step to imaginary music. "If he never came back that would be good," Tom said. "If he did come back I would be ready. It would be even better. I was the man. Katrina still said. I was the man. I would make it right."

* * *

The falcon sharpened her vigil. Tom had turned away from the canyon pool. He focused his attention on the ancient, burned adobe now. Puzzled, Parnell watched the old man become a boy again. What he didn't see in the boy's mind was the crumbled building restoring itself. The barn and corrals rose to attention. Tom walked slowly toward them. Blackie, the small gelding grazed where years ago Young Tom had ground hitched him by the corral. The reins drooped to the dry earth. The gelding wore no saddle. Young Tom stroked the horse and spread hay before him.

In the present day, the falcon dropped noiselessly from her chimney perch. She stooped in silence, flashing within inches of Parnell. Startled by her sudden presence, Parnell leaped to his feet. His legs below the knees were numb from hunkering in the squatting position. He knew he couldn't run or even walk without falling. But the peregrine ignored him after the first rush. She rose hundreds of feet in the thin atmosphere and hung there, playing the twisting air currents. *That bitch is watching every move I make,* Parnell thought nervously, *but from where? I must be on my guard.* Damned if he knew why the bird was out to get him. Right now, if he had a grip on the 30-30 Old Tom had been babbling about, he would blow the blue-feathered bastard out of the steel blue sky.

Young Tom turned away from the black gelding he had ridden in that summer evening in 1905. In the adobe, or somewhere close, were vibrations of fiddle strings. Maybe Katrina had the windup Edison playing. He wasn't certain where the music came from. It made him uneasy. Tommy slipped up to the window just south of the fireplace; the remaining burned out window. Parnell watched him move about the ruins, listening. He tried to interpret what was happening in Tom's head. Parnell moved closer, listening. Tommy paid him no mind. *Is he speaking,* Parnell wondered? *Am I imagining the words?*

"That night the doctor was away. I knew he would be gone. She had told me he would be gone. I sneaked out of bed and rode bareback. I was excited and in a hurry. I didn't take the saddle or the 30-30." Old Tom retraced the boy's moves from where he left his horse at the corral. "I heard music and crept up to the window by the fireplace."

Inside, the room was as the boy remembered, everything neat and clean. Prints and paintings of actors and dancers decorated the mud-plastered walls of the one large room. Katrina was dancing. She faced one of Young Tom's favorite paintings hanging above the window he was looking through, a portrait of her dancing in the costume she was wearing now. Tom saw tears in her eyes as she moved in with slow passion. She had told him the painting was done in the east where she was a dancer on the stage—until she met the doctor. The doctor had talked her into coming west. She had given up her career to join him.

* * *

"I loved him. I loved the doctor," she told Tom. "He is a very jealous and a very possessive man. He frightens me, as well. Fear brought me closer to him than I had ever been to anyone before. Maybe I'm foolish—masochistic." She laughed ruefully. Tom didn't know what the word meant. There were many words she and the doctor used he didn't understand. Sometimes she would explain. She was teaching him. Katrina liked to teach him. This time he didn't ask. "I like the excitement of taking chances," Katrina said. "Here I don't have many chances to take chances—except with you."

Katrina was very slowly taking Tommy's clothes off at the time. It was raining and they were in the house. "There are some chances in life that must be taken slowly," she said. Before I left Boston the doctor told me I could have no friends except on his terms." She sighed and stroked Tom's cheek where he knelt between her legs. She was sitting on the ledge of the fireplace in a loose linen dress. The storm outside hissed big drops against the window. Young Tom, now naked, looked up at her in adoration. His brow twisted in troubled thought.

"Does the doctor know about me seeing you?" the boy asked. "About us. That I love you Katrina and that you——"

"And I love both of you, Tommy," Katrina said. "And he knows about you. He knows you take care of me when he is away. He knows you keep me happy when I am alone. Doctor Mackenzie knows I need you when he is gone. He has watched us together."

Tom jumped to his feet and turned away. Shaking visibly, he held his back to her. Katrina didn't move from where she sat.

"I don't like him watching us," the boy cried. "I don't want him to." He turned back to her, tears of anguish in his eyes. His fists were balled up at his naked thighs, his eyes blazing. "I won't have it!" he cried.

"Tommy," she said sternly, a teacher talking to her adolescent pupil. It was the first time he had heard that tone in her voice. It startled him. His fists unclenched He dropped his eyes. Which way to go? He didn't know. "Tommy," she repeated, quietly this time. "You watched me and the doctor many times. You watched us making love." The boy's face and neck turned crimson. "You watched us from the rim of the mesa and then you started coming closer and closer each time. Don't deny it. It is not a good thing to lie." When he looked up, Katrina's eyes were with his. There was no love there.

"How did you know?" Tom stammered. "How?"

"The doctor spotted you on the rim." Her words were cold. "We thought perhaps you'd go away. You didn't. We accepted it. We accepted you."

"I'll go now," he cried. "I hate you. Why? I hate you both," he cried.

"Why do you hate us? Or why did we accept you?" She smiled.

Young Tom raced for the door and out through it, racing naked through the night rain. He heard her words behind him. "Your clothes, Tommy." The boy stopped. His jeans were on the floor in front of the fireplace. His shirt and boots were there too. His feet were in the mud. He looked back. Katrina was there. She was standing, naked in the doorway. "Come back, Tommy," she called into the storm. "Nothing has changed. I still need you." There was a long quiet moment. "The doctor needs you too." Young Tom started back. He stood a long time dripping outside the door. Katrina was beautiful. He held out his hand. She took it. She kissed his wet fingers. "Come in, my man," she said. Tommy went in. Katrina didn't wait for him to dry off.

From that day on, Tom Sullivan understood his weakness. He accepted it. He belonged to Katrina—and the doctor. He belonged to them. Katrina led him in and laid him down on the floor, on the thick rug in front of the fire. He watched the flames make hot love on the hearth above. He watched himself dissolve in the heat surrounding him. That night, his boy's manhood burst within her again and again.

"We are in love," he cried.

"We are one, Tommy," she answered, "and we will always be as one. I love you, but not you alone."

Young Tommy came again in his desperate burst of youth. He released himself completely, mind and body. He was hers to do with as she would. He knew now, she was no longer completely his. He was hers. He mustn't—he wouldn't care.

\* \* \*

Standing that night at the window, Tom watched her tenderly. She had asked him to come. But something was wrong. The music was not coming from the windup Edison. Someone was in the high-backed chair. They had their back to him. That was where the music came from. Whoever it was played the violin. Tom saw the bow rise and fall with the music. Katrina whirled about with a flourish and leaned over the back of the chair to stroke the musician's hair.

It was the other man. Young Tom knew it. He knew the man played the fiddle. He didn't know how he knew, but he knew. The man touched the violin the way he touched Katrina. Tom remembered: he remembered them upon the rocks by the pool. The man played on. Some times so gentle you could barely hear a breath of music. At other times he bore down on her until she screamed.

Parnell saw Tom turn away from the burned out window. The boy covered his face and screamed in agony. There was silence for a long time before Tom spoke.

"She kissed the man and they opened up some wine that he had brought. She must have sensed that I was here. She asked me to come—to be here with her—she didn't like to be alone, she said. I didn't know that he would be here. She hadn't told me that he would be here. I told myself she didn't know he would be here." Tom stopped a moment and stepped back out of the light. "She looked toward the window, but I was in the shadows. She said something to the man. He grinned. She set down her glass and came outside. The man watched her as she stepped out the door. It was as if they had it planned. I should have known. The man laughed and picked up his fiddle and started playing once again.

"There was a 44-caliber rifle hanging high on the back wall of the room. Tommy knew that it was loaded and wished he had it in his hands. He would blast a hole right through that fiddle. That would stop the music. Then he felt Katrina close behind him:

"Katrina left the door open. She moved into the dark and took my hand. It was a warm night with a full moon. She said nothing. She led me around the chimney corner—out of the moon light, into the shadows of the night."

Parnell watched as Tom moved with the action as he spoke. Embarrassed to be the voyeur, Parnell was forced by some fateful hand to follow. He knew—he thought—he was invisible to Young Tom, and to the ghosts surrounding him. Tom was completely in the grip of his tortured mind. That mind brought up the past and ruled it with a cold and vicious fury. All Parnell could do was listen to the happenings that had filled a lifetime with a macabre love—and joyless emptiness.

Tom looked around. "There was a blanket lying beside the adobe wall. She must have put it here. She had planned the evening. They had. She pulled me down beside her, and whispered she was sorry. I was nervous. The other man? I said."

"Don't worry,' she said. She told me not to worry. "The doctor hates him," she said, "take off your clothes. I love him, but I left him, Tommy. This is our chance to take a chance with him."

"I couldn't move. 'I'll help you.' She said. And she did. I didn't want her to take off my clothes, not with the other man so close. I hated him—I was glad the doctor hated him. But I loved her and would do anything she said. I belonged to her. We lay down close and dark, our skins touching close.

"I didn't hear the fiddle stop. It must have stopped. It wasn't playing when I looked up and saw him standing there. He was naked, now, too. He had been watching all the time. Then he lay down with me between them—in the dark—out of the candle's light. We were in the shadow of the moon. She said 'it's all right, Tommy. Be still.' And she let him put his hands on me—and she did too. He put his mouth on me—She wanted it that way. Now it was her turn to watch."

Parnell cringed. He was forced to watch, as well. Old Tom lay stretched out stiff and tight in the shadow of the ruins. His jaw was clenched, his arms rifle straight, hard at his side, his little fists balled and quivering as he held still in fear. "Don't wake a man in a nightmare," Parnell remembered hearing from his father. The quack psychiatrist was still practicing in Philadelphia. He wondered bitterly about what his drugged out father would say about this one. This one wasn't a nightmare, or lying on the couch wrapped in a Napoleon outfit; this one was alive and happening in the real world. Parnell saw it happening. He wondered if it was the first time Old Tom had relived the frightful memory this close to reality. If, he reasoned, it <u>was</u> the first time, there was a vague chance it would clean the poison from the old man's system. There was a chance Tom would be well and whole again, or on the road at least. On the other hand, he might end up totally insane: completely lost. *What the hell do I know? Should I stop him? But I want to know. Why? God help me but I want to watch.* The old man/boy continued in his agony:

"She said she wanted it that way, so I lay still and let him. I belonged to her. With her hands she helped him—. I loved her. Without her I couldn't love. I love her. I love Katrina—Why did she make me do it?"

Parnell, the voyeur, studied Tom in his midnight dream. The old man lay in the night sunlight by the ruins of the wall. He rolled over and pushed weakly up onto his hands and knees. His old, bald, head hung limp and fragile. He swayed it back and forth like a sick old bear drooling with a toothache.

Parnell took the moment to check the sky above them. The peregrine still hung there, wings extended in the steel-gray of the sky. She was balanced on the updrafts rising from the depths of the canyon. The ultimate voyeur, it was always her turn to watch. *I hope she is entertained,* Parnell thought bitterly. *God damned duck hawk.* The term snapped in his mind. *That's what they call them in the east. They live in coastal regions close by the water. They prey on shore birds. What the hell is she doing here where beneath her there is nothing but sulfur springs and now and then a flash flood?* Parnell looked back to Old Tom, then back to the bird. She was hanging in the wind three hundred feet above them. *She sure ain't just passing through,* he thought. *That bird is a killer. She knows what she is up to.*

"Christ Jesus!" Old Tom cried, startling Parnell. The old man struggled to his feet. Katrina and the man had vanished. Old Tom pounded weakly on the chimney wall. "My life has been in the grave with her for sixty-four years. Why is it born again? It should have stayed in the black and empty space it kept." His pale blue eyes, the pupils in a pool of reddish/yellow jelly, watered once again. He leaned into the wall. His old head banged helplessly against the rain-washed mud. There was a long silence. Was it finished?

Parnell hoped the story was finally out—out and over with. Finished. It was time to get back to the ranch—back to a normal life. He reached to comfort the old man. It was a big mistake.

* * *

Tom jerked away from the touch. Becoming aware of Parnell for the first time in over two hours, he faced him in a fury, crying out in fear and anger: "Don't you touch me! Don't you ever lay a hand on me again"!

Parnell stepped quickly back. "For Christ sake, Tom," he cried instinctively, "it's me, Parnell.—We got to get back to the ranch," he added lamely.

"Doctor Mackenzie, right!" Tom fired back with a look of hate. He was in two worlds. He didn't understand his feelings in either one. He acted on the moment and all his moments now were blessed with madness. Tom skidded wildly, on his schizoid track, from the young boy's personality to the old man's.

"The doctor, right!" the boy cried. "And you," he pointed accusingly at Parnell, "you came back and found all three of us. You went crazy like Katrina said you got some times."

"Who, Tom? Who are you talking about? What God damned doctor?" Parnell tried to assert himself. Maybe he could snap the old man out of it. But, m*aybe I'm locked into it,* he thought, dumbfounded at his own acute imagination.

"Everybody knows Doctor Mackenzie," Tom croaked, his young voice hoarse. Parnell was stunned by the desperate, pleading cry. Was Old Tom giving him the name of this phantom doctor? Parnell's past, a previous personality? Or was old Tom just as crazy as he talked? *Or, did the phantom doctor bear my name in actuality? My name?* "No! Impossible!"

"But nobody knows your crime," Tom hissed in a screeching whisper. "Nobody knows your sin—our sin—your truth and my truth, <u>Doctor</u> Mackenzie. We are naked here, the three of us! All of us but you."

Parnell stood stock-still.

Tom turned around, looking down where he had recently been lying. He pointed. "We were right here, the three of us, where you tried to wipe the blood off your hands. The blood you and the falcon spilled." Tom dropped back down on the ground. He was the boy again. Parnell backed away. "I saw you coming first," the boy cried to Parnell. In the darkness we hadn't heard you drive up in your buggy. I saw you strip the harness off and take your mare into the barn. You gave her hay and grain. I tried to get away. I couldn't move. You—You didn't know we were lying here. You didn't know—yet! I tried to tell Katrina that the chance she wanted to take, was taking, had taken—this exciting wonderful chance with me and this fiddle player was running out. I couldn't."

Parnell was desperate and confused. He <u>was</u> loosing it, now. "You're crazy, Tom" He yelled, backing further toward the faint ruins of the barn. "It's not me, Tom. God damn it, what are you talking about? <u>It was not me!</u> It <u>is</u> not me! I am no fucking doctor. I wasn't even born till years after all this all happened, Tom—-." But Young Tom was in the soup of truth again. He was looking to where the barn had stood. He didn't hear Parnell. Parnell knew he couldn't hear him. Parnell knew when to give up. He made a quick check to see that the falcon was still in place. She was. Circling and watching. *Fucking bird.* "This is all crazy," he mumbled. But deep in his heart he felt something horrible was tugging with a wicked turn. He was back at the rock foundation of the barn where he felt safe: where he could safely watch Tom and still keep an eye on—*the fucking bird.*

This thing is getting out of hand. It is frightening. And Parnell is drawn into the thick of it. He had desperately wanted to know—but know what? *And do I want to know, now? Christ, no.* If Tom is reliving the truth, it is a truth Parnell definitely did not want to be a part of. *But I am*—"I am a part of it," he cried up to the sky. "I know it now."

Old Tom's demons had possessed him. The old man yammered on, but Parnell Mackenzie knew in his heart it wasn't the yammering of a mad man. The man/boy wasn't speaking in tongues. He was terrified, as in a nightmare that wouldn't end. Would young Tommy wake up from this one? Would Parnell? Parnell knew about nightmares. He looked from the ruins to where the barn had stood beside him. There was an eerie familiarity that flashed, bright and dark like grainy, scratched frames of poor quality black and white film. He couldn't shake it off. He caught Young Tom's strangled words:

"I couldn't move. I tried to cry out to warn Katrina, but no sound came. My mouth was dumb. My heart dried out. The two of them were through with me now. They were doing it with each other, the licking thing I didn't like. I hated that man. Right now I hated the doctor, too. I knew what he was going to do. Katrina had taken her chance and lost. I was scared." Young Tom's voice dropped to a plaintive whisper. "Why was I here? I loved Katrina. I would do anything for her." Parnell watched the old man bang his head against the adobe wall, perhaps in an effort to clear his thinking.

Parnell was about to take a chance himself. He stepped forward as if to speak to Tom again when the boy snapped his eyes back to the barn. He drew back frightened and cried out in a hoarse whisper that cut the still air.

"The doctor spotted my horse. He said my name in a whisper. 'Little Tommy', he said and laughed a mean hard laugh. He took his doctor bag and rifle from the buggy and sneaked toward the house. I guessed he wanted to watch me, with Katrina. He couldn't know yet about the fiddle man.

"Katrina and the fiddle man were in a lover's knot and paying no attention to anything but themselves." I left them. I crept to the corner of the house and around it where I watched, terrified.

"They didn't see the doctor coming. They weren't seeing anything but mirrors now. The doctor crept up to the window, thinking, I guess, that we, the two of us, were there, inside. He would watch and then scare me. He had done that before. He liked to scare me. He liked to watch the two of us. He didn't know about the man.

"Then Katrina cried out, the way she did—in love, or—pain. She always said to me that love was pain—. Life was the child of pain, she said. Katrina said a lot of things I tried to understand. The doctor heard her cry and ducked back to the chimney corner. That was when he saw them naked in the dark. Maybe, at first, he thought the man was me. But then he recognized him. And that's when he went crazy. The doctor definitely knew that man. He hated that man. He called his name and kicked him in the head. He called him lots of names. He screamed that the man had followed Katrina. 'This will be the last time you follow her,' he cried. 'Dead men don't follow anyone.' He yelled like he was crazy and raised his gun and shot two bullets into the ground on both sides of Katrina and the fiddle man. I was afraid he would hit her. The doctor didn't care. He was crazy like I never seen him. He might kill her. I had to stop him.

"I raced around the house to get behind him. I leaped on his back and started pounding him. I <u>had</u> to make him stop. But I couldn't. He threw me down on top of the two of them. He fired again and then again as close as he could get. He nicked the man. I saw blood spurt out of his leg, close to his crotch. It was not enough to kill him. We three were naked, like worms trapped in a can. Like worms, he made us crawl into the house."

* * *

Parnell watched, dumbstruck, as Young Tom, in reenactment of that night, crawled along the chimney wall and through the door. Helpless, Parnell followed.

It was a huge step back into time for Parnell Mackenzie: a big step back into a bigger truth. Inside, the room Parnell saw it as it was in 1905, when Tommy was thirteen. Parnell, to his horror, recognized the walls and roof. It was the dark of a moon lit night. Was he watching shades of what was really happening or was he in his dream-state. Was he the doctor of his dream?

Parnell Mackenzie stood in helpless awe as the ghostly shade of the bleeding fiddle man hunched into the fireplace corner and cowered there, naked, looking very much like the man who played the fiddle for The Cat. *Good Christ!* Wolf, *is that what she called him?*

The voice of Old Tom picked up fragments of his story: "The doctor told the fiddle man not to move or he would die that much sooner. He slammed the door and bolted it." Parnell saw the door shut and the bolt slide into place. Old Tom's voice went on: "He told me to sit down and shut up or die." Young Tommy crawled to a corner and huddled there, terrified, waiting—waiting for what would happen next. The old man's voice went on as the frightened boy: I wished the doctor would kill the fiddle man. I would be happy to help drag him to the canyon wall and throw him over. But the doctor only grabbed the fiddle. He smashed it on the flagstone floor, poured coal oil on the scraps and lit the lot." Parnell saw the flames leap up. Through those flames the fiddle man squeezed shut his eyes on a flood of tears.

"Why don't you just kill the fiddle man?" Young Tommy was back in voice again. The black and white shades disappeared. Parnell was glad the ghosts were gone. But the walls were still surrounding him. And Tommy was still talking. He was talking to Parnell: "Or give me the old forty-four on the wall. I'll shoot him for you." Parnell saw the rifle hanging above the fireplace. Tommy was looking at it, then once again back at Parnell. The fire flared up on the flagstone floor. The ghosts returned:

"You touch that gun you're a dead little boy," the doctor said. Katrina knew it, too. She made a dash and tried to unlock the door. The doctor clubbed her with the rifle in his hands and knocked her down. Tommy started to get up to help her. From where she lay she shook her head, 'no'. The doctor looked down at the naked boy. 'She's right, you know, little Tommy. You've had your fun. It's over now,' he said. 'If you get in the way I'll have to kill you too. No one will ever kiss your little piggy-dick again," he said. Tommy cringed, certain now the doctor had been watching them. The ghosts grew dim.

Parnell, horrified, watched Young Tommy, clutch himself defensively. True grit of determination speared across his face. The boy glared in defiance at whoever, in his trance, he was looking at. Then his eyes opened wide and he flashed a telling glance to the right.

\* \* \*

"Don't do it, Kat."

Where had those words come from? Parnell heard them, but he was watching Tom and Tom hadn't moved his lips. Who the hell said it? It wasn't Sully's voice. Sully wasn't due back with the hay for another two hours. But Sully was a dream. Parnell barely remembered Sully—if there was a Sully. Perhaps the falcon spoke the words. That son-of-a-bitch was full of more surprises than Mackenzie cared to understand. But the falcon was no ventriloquist and she was three hundred feet above them. Or was she? At least she wasn't in the house. The house was whole again. Had he spoken the words himself? —A terrifying thought.

"Kat, the doctor called her." Old Tom's voice spelled it out. "K, A, T. Kat for Katrina. "While the doctor talked to me Katrina tried to get to the rifle hanging on the wall. The fiddle man did nothing. He just lay on the floor and moaned. He wasn't bleeding bad any more. The fiddle man was a coward. Katrina was a queen. She would have saved us all if I hadn't given her away by looking. The doctor saw my eyes follow her and he spun around.

"Don't do that, Kat." This time Parnell heard the words plainly. He saw a blurred shape of the man who spoke them coming into focus. The picture was in black and white. In sharp relief now, the man was Parnell's build. He had a dark Van Dike goatee waxed to a point and pencil thin mustache. Dressed in pinstripe tight britches, a silk vest and tailored jacket, Tommy's doctor was a dandy from the early nineteen hundreds. Aside from that, the man was disturbingly familiar. Parnell knew him from the past—from somewhere before. The doctor, in dark silhouette, turned as he spoke. Parnell followed his glance. Once again he saw Katrina. In that flash of recognition, Parnell's vision went Technicolor.

It was no wonder young Tommy worshiped her—bewitched by her would be a more appropriate term. Katrina had the exquisite body of a dancer. Her face and naked body were all to familiar, but in this setting and under the bizarre circumstances, it only flashed in Parnell's swirling mind for an instant. Incredibly beautiful, Katrina stopped just short of the hanging rifle. The picture blurred back into black and white. The shades moved as under water. Parnell backed against the wall in terror. The man, who spoke out of his shell, went on:

"You are going to dance for this sniveling thing who came to find you, to take you back to Boston, Kat, to make you the biggest twinkling star on Scully Square." The doctor's shade crossed to the man lying on the floor. He poked the fiddle man in the crotch with his rifle barrel. The light from the burning violin on the flagstones enhanced the darkness of the night within the mud walls of the rough adobe. The glass chimney of the oil lamp was smoked to black. Parnell fought off the vision. He knew it was daylight and no walls were there, but here he was crouched in a corner, in fear, pressed back against a wall that was not there.

Young Tom's eyes followed the shadows of his imagination. Tommy saw everyone but Parnell. Parnell saw only shadows, heard only voices stretching through the years.

"If I was going to go with the fiddle man, Parnell," Katrina said to the man with the rifle, "we would have been gone long past this hour."

"Parnell?" Parnell recognized the voice she spoke with, but who's from where? *Was madness catching? Old Tom's mad dream rubbed off on me? Or is this my dream, my dream of flying?* This was worse than one of the Irish fairy tales his father used to spout off to scare him when he was a child. *All that's needed are the trolls and leprechauns.*

Helpless as he was, Parnell wanted to grab Old Tom and drag him out of there, slam him into the truck and take him home. Parnell was powerless. He couldn't move. He was slave to the action, taking place before him, unseen, but very much a part of it. He saw Young Tom, in Old Tom's body, naked, crouched against the wall, watching. He could not shake off the images. Tom's macabre world swam before him. *Christ in His grave.* The door was bolted shut behind him. He was a shadow among shades locked and helpless to change the course of action.

"You shall dance for us, Katrina." The doctor spoke with a disarming smile. "You shall audition for your promoter here." He indicated the fiddle man with the point of his weapon. "Open your trunk, Kat. Let us see your wardrobe on the floor."

"No." she cried. "Don't destroy my things—my dreams. I had no plan to leave you, Doc.—I love you. —In a strange peculiar way, perhaps, but indeed I do. I gave up my dreams.—I gave up everything to be with you. You are my dream. I see no friends here, Doc, no one. I have no friends but you. You take me nowhere. I see no one, but you." Her voice was desperate in its pleadings. "Tommy is my only friend when you are away. But I love you. I have stayed for you. I will stay." The lady beseeched the man —beseeched Parnell. Young Tommy got up beside her. The doctor slammed him back against the wall where he slumped unconscious. Tommy had no chance to speak.

Parnell watched this bad, "B" rated, late night movie. Except, he couldn't change the channel. He couldn't turn it off. The boy's head hit the wall hard enough to take his senses from him. He slid to the floor an old man again, blood running from a cut above his ear. Katrina tried to get to him, but the doctor forced her back.

"Had you come back tomorrow as you planned," she cried, "or as you said you would, our life would not have changed. Where could I go, Parnell?" She looked to Tommy, unconscious on the floor. She looked to the fiddle player cowering naked against the wall. "For God's sake, don't hurt Tommy, Doc. And this poor man," she looked to the fiddle player, he is no threat to you. Tomorrow he would be gone, and gone alone. He will be gone." She stood helpless in her nakedness. Smoke from the fire burning on the flagstone floor was slowly drifting to the only sucking ventilation in the one room house. It slid up the chimney like a venomous snake. The fire was no more real, to Parnell, than the people he was watching. But what he watched was real. And he could smell the smoke.

"Do as I say," the doctor ordered Katrina. Stoke the fire. His voice was ice, his mind, beyond reason. "Do it, Kat, or little Tommy will be the first to go." The doctor swung the muzzle of the rifle to the boy's temple. —The actors, fading in and out on Parnell's twisted mind screen, now held firm.

Young Tommy began to stir. The doctor casually nudged him behind the ear with the muzzle of the rifle. Katrina, taking the threat as a truth did as she was told. She added kindling to the shattered violin smoldering in the center of the room.

Tommy stared around, trying to orient himself in the smoke shrouded mad situation he awoke to. Reliving his horror story, he burst out. "No, Katrina! No," he cried. The doctor mashed the barrel of the rifle against the boy's nose, flattening it against his face. He grinned down at him, cutting a sidelong glance to Katrina.

"No Tommy," the woman said, shaking her head, tears in her eyes. Her long hair almost brushed the live coals she gathered from the hearth. Parnell snapped back, as if rewinding a videotape reviewing a horror scene his mind had played before. "I'm sorry, Tommy," Katrina whispered. "Doc won't hurt you. You'll be alright. It's just another game, Tommy." She laid wood kindling, split pinion, on the polished flagstones and ox-blood mud floor of the adobe. In seconds the pitch splinters caught. She stirred them into life with the ebony neck of the violin. Flames danced light and gay. The draft from the bee hive fireplace sucked most of the smoke up the chimney hole.

"It might be better he didn't live to remember this routine, Katrina," Parnell heard Doctor Parnell say. The words echoed in his heart.

"Open her trunk, little Tommy and get Katrina's costumes out." The boy looked franticly at the woman he adored.

"Do as he says, Tommy." Katrina rose from the floor. She stood naked and heroic in the firelight. "Do as the doctor says," she repeated. "Remember, it is just a game." She smiled at him and nodded to the steamer trunk that held her prize possessions. Tommy opened it as he'd often done, to choose a costume for her to dance in. He loved the costumes, the silk, the feel and smell of them—the scent of Katrina that inhabited the polished steamer trunk—the rich scent of Katrina.

"Throw them on the fire, little Tommy," the doctor ordered quietly. "They will dance in the flames."

"No!" the boy screamed. "I won't!"

The doctor slammed the young boy back against the wall again. Tommy stood in his naked rage and stared back at him. "You can't make me do it. I don't care what you do! You're bad."

"Then watch me do it, Tommy boy. You watch and be amused." The doctor held the rifle up and ready.

"Don't move, Tommy," Katrina said. "Doc won't hurt you. Those costumes are old anyway. I need some new ones." Helpless, Katrina glanced from Tommy to the bleeding fiddle player in the chimney corner.

"That man won't ever get you anywhere, Kat," the doctor said. He stepped up to the body on the floor and kicked it savagely. He snatched up the rosined bow that lay beside him and used it to snag Katrina's wardrobe from the open trunk.

And while the fire caroused in its destroying pleasure on the floor, the costumes Katrina loved, the doctor cast onto the flames. For a moment they smothered there. He stirred them with the rosined bow and flames broke through again. Thick smoke sucked into the flue and up the chimney. The doctor salvaged the red silk veil she danced in on the rock beside the green pool and draped Katrina in with it.

"No!" Tom cried. He was old or young again, remembering. "It's my favorite. By the green water she danced for me in that." He started forward.

"Don't move, Tommy," Katrina cried. "He'll kill you." It was not a game any more. Tommy flattened back against the mud wall and watched in horror as the doctor draped her in the yards of bright red silk.

"Now dance for him again," the doctor laughed. Dance about the flames. Dance, Kat lady. Dance Katrina, dance for your Boston friend, as well," the doctor cried. The man was completely mad. "Dance for all of us. Dance the fire dance," he cried, "Ghostdancer, the fire dance of death."

* * *

Young Tommy turned old in Parnell's mind. Tears streamed down his withered face. Alone and old, he cried out, wailing in the almost silence of the room. "Only days ago I watched you making love. I don't understand. Stop!" he cried. "Stop! Don't make her dance like this. Young Tom jumped out to stop the mad man with the gun. The doctor hurled him across the room into the chimney corner with the fiddle man. The boy convulsed and pulled away. The fiddler made no move. He was naked, cold and shivering. Tom couldn't stand to touch him. The doctor laughed.

"Lie still, Tommy," the woman cried. Tommy watched in horror as the doctor pulled a short white silk and lace ballerina's outfit from the open trunk and thrust it at the woman. "He can't go much further, Tommy. He's not crazy. He's just jealous. We'll be out of this soon. Katrina begged." The doctor laughed.

*Does she believe what she is saying?* Parnell wondered. He thought not. But he was an onlooker in a world of the dead, powerless to interfere. In terror, Katrina pulled the costume up under the red silk and over her nakedness. Tom screamed, but the fiddle man held him down. The doctor fastened the hooks at the back of the stark white silk chiffon. From the trunk he tossed her the silken padded toe-dancing slippers. He watched her fit them on, tie them snug around her firm, trained ankle.

The doctor stood back admiring his work for a brief moment. He wasn't through. In his eyes she wasn't fully prepped as yet. With her back turned and bent gracefully to finish tying up the toe shoes, the doctor casually reached for the galvanized can with the spout for filling lanterns. He drenched Katrina in the kerosene. In an instant he soaked her hair and dress. She rose with a start. The coal oil, cold and shimmering down her thighs and calves, reflected brilliant orange in the firelight.

Tommy screamed and rose up to stop him. The doctor fired a round, narrowly missing him. The spot of lead ricocheted about the room.

"Stay down, Tommy," Katrina cried. Don't move or he will kill you, too."

"She's right, little Tommy. Stay quiet like the naked fool beside you. I am promoting this show just for his approval. It would go over well in Boston. Just sit and watch the lovely dance I have prepared for you and Mister Boston. The Lady who lives forever is going to perform one more time, Tommy, for you and her insipid fiddle friend." He turned to the lady. "On your toes!" he ordered, and jabbed Katrina's flat belly with the rifle barrel.

Tears surged from Katrina's eyes, they glistened, diamonds on her oil drenched perfect skin. Obediently she rose to her full height and struck a pose, one Tom had witnessed many times. The doctor grabbed a second fiddle packed, unseen in the steamer trunk. He lobbed it across the room to the Boston Man. "Play a good instrument!" he ordered. The man tucked the ebony chinrest beneath his trembling jaw and drew the rosined bow across the strings. "The Fire Dance, fool," the doctor cried, "and make it hot for the whore masters of the East."

With the downbeat, Katrina began to move. The dance was desperate—impassioned and precise. Her body flowed in the eerie light. The dancer was a bird in flight. Tom was hypnotized. The fiddle man had closed his eyes. Young Tommy followed every move his love was dancing, every step as, almost imperceptibly, the doctor inched Katrina closer and closer to the fire built on the floor; closer to the hungry flames.—until—she burst—like a wild flower, into flame herself.

* * *

Parnell, snapped from his cold reverie, heard Young Tommy scream. He saw the doctor knock him almost senseless with the rifle butt. In this world of ghosts Parnell felt helpless. He watched in horror what he realized, now, was most assuredly his personal nightmare, his dream of dreams—his flying destiny.

"Dance," the doctor cried. "And dance, Kat lady, dance. You are the center of attention now. In the spotlight you are the flaming star, the prima Donna ballerina you always thought you were," he cried maliciously. Parnell could smell the smoke no more, but he saw the fiddle man and Young Tom, choking in it. The doctor threw the bolt and flung the door back into the night. Katrina leaped for her escape.

"Go Kat. Upon your toes my darling," the doctor cried out in his madness. "Dance out upon the rocks. Dance like a bird out on the air."

She burst into the night, screaming voicelessly, limbs stretched in agony. The doctor didn't stop her this time. She leaped and twisted in the midnight sky. Following the dancing star—the doctor, Tom and fiddle man rushed out into the fire-lit night. Parnell followed.

Katrina, engulfed in flame, her steps, by rote, still executed with precision, made her final leap over the canyon's rim. If she was thinking at all it was only to wish for the comfort of a quicker end.

She hung there—like a bird—the falcon, wings extended, resting on the updraft, flaming in the air. And then—Katrina disappeared.

* * *

Ignoring young Tom, the doctor forced the fiddle man to the edge. Young Tommy took advantage of the diversion and raced back into the burning house. Not yet a total inferno Tom fought his way to the fireplace wall where the second rifle hung. Tommy grabbed it and dove back out through the door.

On the canyon rim, Tommy saw the fiddle player looking out over the rock edge in fear. He knew the end was here. He had given up all but begging. "Walk." The doctor ordered.

"No. In God's name," the man cried out.

"In God's name indeed." The doctor slammed him at the base of his skull with the rifle butt. The fiddle man went screaming down in silence. The man of medicine turned in search of little Tommy.

Tommy stood outside the ring of firelight. The gun he had taken from the wall was trained on the doctor. The boy waited. The doctor thought correctly that perhaps Tom had gone in for the other rifle. Looking for him, he dashed into the blazing house. Tom stepped out of the shadows and shut the heavy door behind him. He quickly propped the 44 beneath the latch and checked to see it was secure. Then he backed off to watch.

Inside he heard the doctor, in a panic now, struggling to force the door. It wouldn't budge. As the flames licked up around the house the boy stood back. The man inside kept slamming at the door. The doctor was dancing now, beating out death's rhythm on the heavy planks.

Silently, naked in his tears, young Tommy climbed on his horse and galloped toward the ranch. Parnell collapsed.

# CHAPTER ELEVEN

# THE REALITY

Parnell woke in a cold sweat. He was used to that, but he usually woke up in bed. Right now he lay staring at the steel blue sky trying to orient himself. If he was in bed, he was still dreaming. If he was awake, Kate wasn't with him. *Did I pass out?* Gradually, the wild dream he had just experienced came alive in his mind. If it was a dream, Parnell could remember it this time. It wasn't good. He rolled on his side, dredging up the past few hours in his mind. *I'm on the mesa, or still on the mesa.* He was lying close to the ruins. *The sun was the only thing blazing.* There was no fire or smoke. The ruins looked cold and as old as they had been when he found them two days earlier. His truck was parked beside them. Parnell forced himself to his knees. The joints were stiff as if he had been lying for hours on the rocky ground. *Tommy? Where's Old Tom?*

Still on his knees, Parnell turned clumsily to the east. Old Tom sat on a rock looking with despair into the canyon. Parnell recognized the rock. Young Tommy's *hiding rock.* Parnell's mind swirled in strange worlds, words and pictures in and out of focus. He had brought Sully's brother up on the mesa, to the ruins, to find the answers. *Well, I found a few,* he thought ruefully. *All they have done is spin a maelstrom of madness in a crazy old man's warped mind—and in mine.* "Why did I stir the pot? Why in Christ's name did I bring the poor old bastard up here? Sully warned me. Sully?" He looked at his watch. "Shit. It's not even eleven. I feel like I been here two days, —or years."

Parnell was talking to himself. It was something he seldom did. *Keep your thoughts to yourself, Parnell.* It looked like the old man was talking to himself, too. At this distance Parnell couldn't make out the words. He shifted position easing the pain in his knees. He didn't want to disturb Old Tom. He wasn't even sure Old Tom would see him or recognize him. Right now Parnell was not sure of anything, least of all himself. Had he really been through what he vaguely recalled going through? *An installment of my favorite nightmare.* He got stiffly to his feet and checked the ruins. They <u>were</u> cold. *<u>Definitely cold</u>.* But they held a new meaning for him. *Sweet Jesus, what?* Old Tom got up and started towards him. The old man was babbling again. His vision cut through Parnell into the distance.

"I ran away." Old Tom had tears in his eyes. "I fled. I am a coward." He mumbled the words.

*He is not talking to me? Who?* Parnell was not about to make a guess. Suddenly remembering the bird, he checked the sky. The peregrine was nowhere to be seen. Parnell was relieved. Then the bird's absence troubled him. *Where is the son-of-a-bitch?*

"I ran away," he heard Old Tom say again. "The falcon saw me run away." Parnell tuned in. He tried to convince himself Tom's story was just a myth, the ramblings of an insane old man. *But the bird? The God damned falcon, wherever it was, was real.* Parnell listened.

"At home, I never even took Blackie's bridle off." Old Tom mumbled. "I left him in the yard and crept through my window into bed … until Papa called me. I had left my clothes behind. They were burned up. I told Papa I had lost them. Papa wanted to know what had happened? Why and how would I lose my clothes? 'You been swimming with that "woman"? 'Where were you,' he yelled, standing at my bed holding Blackie's bridle. 'You never even took your horse's bridle off. Where were you riding in the night?' I burst into tears. Papa beat me with the bridle reins.

"He yelled that the doctor had been looking for me. The doctor told him I had been at his house and had run away. I cringed. The doctor must be still alive. Papa beat me with Blackie's bridle reins again and said I would have to come with him. 'The stupid doctor was a mess,' Papa said. 'He was burned, his beard half gone—and bleedin' all over the place,' Papa said. Your ma patched him up. She's a better doctor than that asshole. I lent him a horse to ride back up there. He was in a hurry. From what he told me there was no hurry' Papa said. 'Anyone goin' over that cliff is dead. Dead is dead,' Papa said, 'and there is no hurry in tryin' to change it.'

"Dead? I wished right then I stayed at the fire and, for sure, made that doctor dead."

Old Tom walked past Parnell with no sign or recognition. Parnell watched him wander in and out of the ruins. Mackenzie made no move to stop him.

"Papa dragged me with him—to help look for her—Katrina—the woman I loved. To find her burned dead body; the dead body of Katrina, the only person I loved. I couldn't tell Papa that.

'We're going down, boy,' Papa said, yanking me into the kitchen. He made me put on clean clothes. 'We're going to see if there is any truth to what that nut-brained medicine man told me.'

"I knew the truth. I knew what we would find. I knew it was true. I said nothing. I went with Papa. I had no choice.

"My 30-30 was still in the saddle boot beneath the skirt. If I had saddled Blackie the night before I might have saved Katrina. I hoped Papa wouldn't see it. He didn't. He went on ahead. Mama came out and looked at me in wonder. 'What were you doing in the night?' she said. She gave me a burrito with eggs and bacon in it. I wasn't hungry. She said, 'take it anyway.' I did. She said, 'why are you taking the 30-30 with you, boy?' I said, for snakes. But it wasn't a snake I planned to kill."

Parnell tagged behind as Old Tom stumbled aimlessly about the ruins, talking, cutting in and out of his insane tragic story. The old man led Parnell almost to the canyon rim when, without warning, he swung back and glared at Parnell in cold hatred.

"It is the doctor I will kill with my 30-30," Tom cried. For the second time only since Parnell had leaned back into the bloody windowsill, Old Tom spoke directly to him. It was unnerving. Instinctively Parnell stepped back again.

"But the doctor was gone by the time we got here." Old Tom said angrily. Doctor Mackenzie had run away, a coward, now. I knew he would come back. I would be waiting for him when you did come back. I would wait a century—and I have." Tom said it quietly, with cold intensely. "You never did come back in nineteen-0-five, or nineteen-ten—or nineteen-twenty-nine. I knew it might take years. I would wait. That morning, I only found the fiddle man."

"Katrina—-?" Parnell questioned in a whisper. Old Tom's eyes strayed off, somewhat lost—. He scanned the vast colorless sky. Parnell was relieved to have the fierce pressure of Tom's eyes diverted. He let out a long heavy sigh. He had been holding his breath.

"Katrina?" the old man said, still looking at the sky. "Katrina? —She never landed."

Tom looked puzzled. He turned to look out over the edge of the rim rock. Parnell stepped up beside him. He looked down too. Were they both searching for the dancing ghost? There were a million questions in that canyon. *Were the answers there?"*

* * *

In the chimney hole the falcon rousted her feathers and dropped into the air. She circled the ruins, lifting silently on the hot currents until she hovered two hundred feet above Old Tom and Jack Parnell Mackenzie.

"The falcon was the one," Tom said, quietly. "The falcon led me to the fiddle man. She was the one who kept the buzzards off until I got to him." Old Tom shrugged. He scratched his head. "There is something missing?" The old man mumbled absently. "Something I can't remember." He knocked his head with the palm of his hand, as if to knock the thought lose. He giggled then, as was his custom when his mind was in repose under medication. The giggle stopped and Tom turned slowly to Parnell.

Off guard, Parnell, having heard, the rousting of the falcon's feathers, looked toward the ruins. He wondered now, if perhaps, the peregrine was perched under cover of the flat slab of shale covering the opening on top of the chimney.

In that moment, Tom became truly lucid, insane and dangerous. He recited a foolish sounding childish game. Parnell turned back, listening to the words. They made little sense, but Tom's delivery was softly violent.

"Something missing
Something dark
Something gone
And locked away.
Something dark
Inside my brain
Yet bright as day
If you can guess
You best not say.
You must be gone!
You must not stay."

Dismissing Tom's silly lines for gibberish, Parnell stepped past him to the rim and looked down into the canyon. Tommy watched him cunningly. His mind, his brain, was snapped into focus by the awakening of his buried dream. Tommy, the boy now, angry and determined, having waited over sixty years, made his move. He rushed the doctor. He would seal his pledge, his promise to Katrina. He would send Doctor Parnell Mackenzie over the black brink of basalt she and the fiddle man had crested decades earlier. Tommy hit Mackenzie just above his belt.

Clumsily, off balance, Parnell grabbed the knurled branch of the old cedar: the branch young Tommy swung from evading the ghost of his father's whip.

As if fate needed a helping hand. The peregrine folded her wings and screamed. She stooped into the fray, striking out at her struggling target. Her talons buried in Parnell's shoulder baring the damning birthmark. Parnell Mackenzie lost his footing. Still clinging to the limb, he cried out in pain and anguish.

At the cry, Young Tommy, reacting instinctively, snapped from his trance back to the present time. He grabbed Parnell to save him. It was just enough to change the balance in Parnell's favor. He clung to Old Tom. The old man pulled them both back into a precarious realm of safety. The falcon, in a fury at having her hit diverted, wheeled angrily. Her timing mislead by blinded furry, she dove with uncontrolled abandon on her target.

Parnell, now expecting the flash of feathers and wicked spurs, ducked her savage anger. The falcon missed him by a fraction. It was Old Tom who took the hit. The Falcon sank her razor talons into the old man's chest. Tom stumbled back, tripping on his hiding stone. Beyond it, there was no space to go but down. Parnell, off balance, tried to snatch the old man from the air, but Tom was gone. The peregrine, crying out in desperation at her miss, went with the old man, clinging to his chest, as if to lift him back to safety. It was beyond her powers. Together they plunged into the canyon's depths.

Parnell, stunned and horrified, knew he had been the target. Fate had passed him by. He was still alive. *But why?* His head spun in a dizzying cycle. He was losing consciousness. To keep from staggering off the edge, he dropped on the rough rock-studded ground to reestablish sanity. He was lost now: out of focus. Try as he might, he couldn't gain control. Jack Parnell Mackenzie, once more, drifted into darkness.

# CHAPTER TWELVE

# THE MORNING AFTER

There were a number of early morning imbibers at the bar in Lake Nine: Ranchers and miners who had already done half a day's work. Two men from the night shift at the mines had come in for a day-cap. Balancing their red beers on the polished edge of the pool table, they lingered over a game. A wino was swamping the place out in return for a cool one to ease the shakes, and a quart of thunderbird to go. Kate was bartending. She often did Saturday morning. The bar had been a mess when she arrived. Friday night had been a busy one, especially after the blazing show at the Rainbow Opera house. She hadn't shown up for any of the festivities, but Moe had called at two AM. Before asking her to do the morning shift he filled her in with what he had heard. There was no doubt in her mind, but that she would hear the balance of the tale today. It was already called "the conflagration". She was not looking forward to it.

Kate glanced at the two customers she was mixing Bloody Marys for. She shook her head and splashed in an extra dollop of vodka in each. She put the glasses on the tray and carried them to the corner table.

Catherine "The Great", as Kate had dubbed her in a flash of bitter satire, was dressed in a white, open collared man's shirt, jeans and rubber soled boots; her regular wardrobe. Across from her, Wolf wore jeans and a black turtleneck sweater. The two of them were hunched in serious conversation. They held their words a moment as Kate set the drinks in front of them.

"Well, is the circus over?" Kate asked nonchalantly. She didn't say it with a smile.

"I beg your pardon. —Circus?" Wolf stared up at her.

"I hear it was a pretty hot show last night. Sorry I missed it."

"Circus?" It was Catherine's turn.

"I hear the fire department showed up," Kate cut in. Wolf ignored her and slid a credit card across the table.

"We don't take plastic. See the sign over the bar?" Kate gestured with her tray. " 'NO PLASTIC. WE SERVE IN GLASS. WE GET PAID IN CASH'. Moe likes signs. He says it keeps the ill informed in their place. Like the sign on the door that says TURN THE KNOB BEFORE YOU PUSH. Tourists aren't too bright. Come to think of it, neither are some of the locals."

"You're the Florence Nightingale who rescued the drunk cowboy from Teddy the other night, aren't you?"

"Always on the spot, that's me."

"Well you weren't on the spot last night, honey." Catherine looked coldly at Kate. "You missed the big one. You know, for a cowboy, he wasn't half bad." She slid a five spot across the table. "You take paper, don't you, sweetie?"

"Even from you." Kate whirled away, heading back to the bar.

"Keep the change." Kate didn't lower herself to a reply. Catherine sipped her drink. "You know, Wolf, it is such a pleasure to play the provinces." Wolf eyed her skeptically before considering his drink.

"What are we doing, drinking so early in the morning, Cat?" he said with his own trace of sarcasm.

"What are you always doing, drinking so early in every morning, Wolf? Couldn't you find a young boy to lead astray after last night's flaming display?"

"Can it, Cat. I heard about that episode in the dressing room."

"So? You had him in the orchestra pit."

"The crazy bastard thought the fire effects were real."

"The whole town thought it was real." Catherine barked out a one-syllable laugh. "I was in it. I was sure it was real." She took a reassuring drink. "My crotch is still singed."

"It wasn't the fire that singed that, Catherine."

"You're only jealous, Wolf, because you didn't get your bow rosined last night." She gave him a half smile and held it until he finally broke. After a long pause, he brought up another uncomfortable subject:

"Have you told the company there is to be no show in Santa Fe?" Catherine lowered her head. She picked up her drink and shifted her chair into a position from which she could watch the barroom door. "No?" he questioned, pushing her. She shook her head. He paused a moment giving her time to elaborate. She said nothing. Wolf crunched the wilted stalk of celery Kate had dipped into his drink. "Well they can't say we didn't go out with a bang, Catherine." Cat still made no comment. Her mind was lost elsewhere. Where in elsewhere? Lost here in Rainbow—this town? Wolf was having a hard enough time keeping his own scattered thoughts in line. Secretly he had to admit there was something terribly wrong: wrong with the Cat—and wrong with him. What? There was something in the air, or in the ground. It definitely disturbed Wolf's equilibrium. Rainbow—? *Are were-wolves in control here?* His mind flashed to the Romania of his youth.

Wolf had gone so far as to count people out in the sunlight this morning; a surprising number of them he was pleased to admit. And Parnell? What was this thing with Parnell Mackenzie? Wolf was certain they had never seen the man before in this life. *This life? How many lives are there?* He smiled ruefully, pushing the disquieting thought aside. Yet Parnell was darkly familiar. Wolf found the surrealistic landscape of Rainbow disorienting as well. If the strange shaped mountains, mesas and planes were red he could be convinced they were playing Mars. *Why not? It couldn't be further out than Rainbow.* The ride in the lost bus under the shadow of that strange looking landscape had disturbed him initially. It was familiar in a terrifying way. He knew these images disturbed Catherine as well.

Wolf had to get Catherine out of here. He had a strong feeling he had to get them both out of here. He tried a new tack: "This show, your showpiece, The Lady Lives Forever, has run its course, Catherine." He said suddenly. He gave her a moment as he sipped his bloody Mary. He got no response. "It does not pack the literary punch of Christopher Fry's, The Lady's Not For Burning, or Shaw's, Saint Joan." Catherine gave no sign of reaction. He knew she heard him. She had heard him say this before. He went on. "This show is a God damned melodrama, Cat; a melodrama, nothing more. It played well last night because these people know nothing better than melodrama."

Catherine had not taken her eyes off the door. Wolf hoped she was not expecting her rhinestone cowboy to show up. A thought flashed through his head. It was not a pleasant thought. It was murderous. He realized, in that moment, he wanted Parnell dead. He wanted to kill the man. *What the hell brought that thought on?* He wondered. He knew he didn't like the man, detested him, in fact. *But murder him?* And murder had flashed in his mind. *We got to get the fuck out of this town and get out now! How many times can one get away with murder?*

Wolf dashed down his drink and wished he had another to back it up. He turned his thoughts back to getting Catherine on the move. "We have been running this show into the ground for more than two years. It is nothing more than an old- fashioned melodrama," Wolf repeated himself.

"You are becoming redundant, Wolf."

Wolf realized he was talking to Catherine's back. At least she must be listening. He saw her spine stiffen and was prepared to duck the glass in her hand when, in her rage, it came flying at him. Cat did not take well to criticism. Wolf was out on a limb but he had no choice. The Cat was between him and the tree trunk. There was no place to go but further out and damn the distance to the ground.

"Please listen, Cat. If we come up with a new show for you, I might just be able to come up with the money to keep us afloat." Catherine turned slowly and fixed him with an eye of discouragement. At least it wasn't the drink flying at him. "I see," he said, recognizing the look. "You are going to leave this whole thing to fate, just like you are leaving that cowboy to fate, that Parnell whoever the hell he is." Catherine was definitely bothered by the impact of what he was saying. But more so by the mention of Parnell than the fate of her failed production. Wolf pushed his empty glass aside and leaned in, speaking with quiet passion:

"What is it draws you to this God Damned so called cowboy? What is the connection, Cat? Where in the name of your mad Russian director, Stanislavski, does it fit in?"

"Yes, Wolf," Catherine said with a flat delivery. Her eyes drifted to Kate, behind the bar. The woman couldn't help but catch some of what they were saying. Wolf's voice had risen noticeably. "The cowboy bothers you, Wolfie? And it is not just the fact that Parnell and I had sex—great sex." She let that line be loud and clear enough for Kate to hear it. Kate turned quickly to face the bottles racked behind her. Cat smiled with subtle satisfaction. She had hit that mark. Now it was Wolf's turn. She turned back to him. "There is something else—isn't there, maestro? Something running a fathom or so deeper." Wolf returned her troubled look then turned away. She let him hang there. —"Well, my little Russian Jew from Romania?"

"I never saw the man before in my life," Wolf said without conviction. "In this life I never saw that idiot—Parnell—what was his name?"

"Mackenzie."

Wolf dropped his look back to the table. He saw two fingers dip into his empty drink and lift out what was left of the limp celery stick. He made no move to interfere. The fingers belonged to Teddy. The dancer lifted the celery stalk to his nose and sniffed it. "Infatuation," he said, striking an appropriate pose. "Infatuation, that's what it is. You are both enamored over this, not so young, cowboy." He chomped down on the celery. "Infatuation. I know the feeling." He chewed wisely. "Ah, vitamin C. Excellent.' He took a deep breath, filling his chest to its capacity. After a profound moment he let the breath out and went on. "To stay in shape one must watch one's diet." He burped quietly and turned to Catherine. —"Incidentally, oh great one, a number of us plan to rent a car and drive to Santa Fe. Spending another day in Rainbow is almost too much to ask. We hope the plan meets with your approval. We open there Friday? We will meet you at the theatre. Agreed?" He paused, waiting. There was no response. Teddy started on with his thought: "I, myself--"

"Why don't you all just pack into the bloody bus," Catherine broke in. "Let Toad jolly well drive you to Santa Fe."

"Done." Teddy bowed deeply to Catherine. "Thank you Catherine." He lifted Wolf's glass and chewed an ice cube. "And thank you too, Maestro." He started for the door. He stopped and turned back. "You are coming, too. Aren't you, Wolfie?" He glanced at his watch. "It's almost eleven. Shall we say we leave noonish?"

"I'm staying on with Catherine."

Teddy raised his eyebrows in mock concern. "Good boy. I'll see you in the capital city." He gave them another deep bow. "I'll leave you to your fate." With a flourish, Teddy made his exit. Catherine lifted her drink and sipped slowly. She looked over the rim at Wolf. Wolf was looking at his glass as if afraid to taste it after Teddy had put it to his lips. Outside, sirens screamed. Catherine whipped around to look.

Wolf was still staring at his glass. "Fate it is indeed, Catherine," he mumbled prophetically, almost silently.

Catherine crossed hurriedly to the open door. Kate was ahead of her and out onto the street. The sheriff's patrol car followed by an ambulance raced past them, headed south. Both ladies stared after them. Thirty miles to the southeast, as the bird flys, stood Tinaja's rocky peak with the green sulfur pool in the canyon below.

# CHAPTER THIRTEEN

# INTO THE DEPTHS

"I couldn't spot any sign of him from the rim either." Sully said, deeply concerned. He swatted at a hungry horse fly feasting on the back of his neck. The fly got away. Sully cursed it. He had overcome his fear of heights to climb down the steep narrow trail to the bottom of the canyon. Before his perilous descent he had laid belly down on the rim searching fruitlessly for any sign of his brother's body. He saw nothing other than thick brush and deadly sharp boulders thrusting through the green aspen shoots, choya cactus and tangled alders. When the vertigo got the best of him he rolled back to safer ground and looked up. The view to the sun was safe. Sully had no fear of falling up.

Parnell had called him at the Abbot ranch where he was loading hay. Abbot's wife drove to the hay field to pass the word. They disconnected the trailer and Sully drove back to the phone. He talked to Parnell, then drove to the ranch at a speed faster than safe. His mind was churning all the way. Old Tom's younger brother knew something like this was bound to happen some day. He just didn't want to accept it. He had never prepared to accept it. But the damn bird thing had cropped up again in the corral the other day. Every time that blue feathered hawk showed up it brought trouble. Sully had only seen it once or twice and he denied those sightings. But he had seen it. He couldn't deny that to himself. That was the bird that tormented his brother. The bird was responsible for Tom climbing up on the mesa again. Sully was sure of it.

*A good thing Parnell was with him, or we wouldn't a found Tommy for days.* Although, if his brother was missing, Sully knew the canyon would be the first place he would look. The canyon was the seed sprouting from his brother's troubled mind. *But why the hell was Parnell with him? Sully thought* as he fought to keep the speeding pickup from drifting off the dusty ranch road. Sully kept telling himself he had always done everything he could for his brother: everything he could be expected to do. But the worst had happened anyway. *The worst always happens in the end.* He considered a moment. *That is, if bein' dead is the worst that can happen.*

"There is worse than bein' dead," Sully allowed, speaking with quiet authority. For years his damn fool crazy brother had lived in a nightmare of booze and drugs. *Supposedly, healing drugs.* "Bullshit." Now he had fallen into his worst nightmare. *The way down was probably the longest, most terrifying trip of my brother's tortured life,* Sully thought. *Hitting the bottom would be paradise.* In his mind, Sully looked over the rim. *It was a long way down.* Sully shuddered.

*If by some stretch of the imagination Tommy ain't dead now, he'd be better off if he was.* Sully cursed himself for thinking so. But Goddamn it, life and death is a fact, and some times death is the better of the two. "No one wants to live in a coma the rest of his life." Sully cursed himself again for subconsciously thinking he would have to take care of his brother as an invalid. *Hell, he's always been an invalid—long as I've know him—all my life.* "Shit." Sully cursed his selfishness again. "What can I do?" *Keep cursin',* he reasoned. *It eases life's pressure.*

Sully came around a sharp turn in the ranch road and plunged on, following the narrow dusty trail to the steep banks into the Canadian river crossing. The sun was shining but rain must be falling somewhere. The Canadian, a trickle when Sully splashed through it that morning, was pushing up its banks. To late to stop, muddy water crashed up over the hood and windshield. Sully shut his eyes and hung to the wheel. The pickup washed out sideways on the east bank. Amazingly, the motor was still running. That episode cleared Sully's mind long enough to get him to the canyon.

* * *

Sully stood with Parnell at the bottom of the rim rock. He was looking up for a change and glad to be on solid, level footing, albeit in this hole of a stinking canyon. "What the hell was my brother doing on the rim?" He looked to Parnell accusingly. "I know you said you brought him up here. Did he want to come? Did he talk you into it? Damn it Parnell, what happened?"

"I never should have brought him with me," Parnell answered honestly. "I know. It's my fault, Sully."

"Shit, Parnell. I can't blame you." The big man looked around him at the scattered cedars. He glanced to the north. A thousand yards above the green pool massive Douglass Firs stretched higher than the flat tableland. From the center of the mesa, the flat table top where you couldn't see the drop off, the evergreens seemed to be growing on the level. Sully had always wanted to harvest the Firs and sell them to the sawmill in Cimarron. They would bring a lot of badly needed bucks. He never touched the towering trees. Everything in the canyon scared the shit out of Sully. Then he looked to the thick willow brush that lined the walls of basalt that rose over a hundred vertical feet on both sides of the wide floor of the canyon. The willows were where the truth lay. Tom had to be there. Sully looked up at the sun, now past its zenith. In a few hours the canyon would be in shadows. The west wall, over which Tom had fallen, was already dark. "What the hell did he do?" He turned to Mackenzie. "Fall? What the hell did my brother do, Parnell, fall—or jump off?" Parnell looked away. He couldn't face his friend. At last he spoke, trying not to make it sound like an excuse:

"It was the bird, Sully. The damn thing came out of the sky like a rocket."

"I don't want to hear about that fuckin' bird, Parnell." Sully picked up a piece of shale. He hurled it angrily toward the cliff's face. It fell short. "Tom used to carry on about that Godamed hawk. In his sleep even he babbled about that fuckin' bird." Sully kicked loose another piece of brittle shale. He picked it up and broke it in two. Tommy hasn't mentioned it in over a year—not until you thought you saw it the other day. That bird is a ghost, Parnell," Sully cried in irate frustration. "There is no fucking bird! Got it?"

"I'm sorry."

"Ya, well it's not your fault. Sully tried to control his mixed feelings. He slapped Parnell on the back and turned toward the west face. "Let's just see if we can find Tommy. Once he hit bottom the poor bastard couldn't have gone far. I mean, he had to stop there." Sully dropped the pieces of shale and led off to the base of the rim rock where Parnell had already spent an hour searching in vain. Parnell fell in behind him.

* * *

Following the falcon's vicious strike and Tom's fall Parnell lost consciousness for the second time that morning. He had never been plagued by fainting fits before. *I have never seen ghosts before, either.* He didn't know how long he had been out this time—an hour maybe—probably less. His watch had stopped. The glass face was shattered and the hour and minute hands twisted together. He couldn't remember breaking the watch. *So much for time.* The sun was almost directly overhead. He was perspiring freely; his open shirt soaked in sweat. In his mind he saw the bird and Tom going over once again. The rest in his mind was a fog that would take time to penetrate.

Parnell had crawled to the rim and searched the bottom of the canyon. There was no sign of the old man, or of the bird. They had vanished. He called out for Tom. There was no answer but the empty wind with his words echoing out of the depths. There was no sign of Tom and no marks where he had struck the bottom. At least his body wasn't sprawled across a rock. The old man must have been swallowed by the thick brush and choya. There was no sign of life. *How could their be?*

Parnell rationalized the futility of searching alone for the body. He decided on a plan of action that would bring help. He drove at a reckless pace back to ranch headquarters and phoned the sheriff's office. Without going into details he explained to Liz Romero, the dispatcher, that Old Tom had fallen from the rim-rock into the canyon. Liz was born on the north side of Tinaja. To Parnell's relief, she explained that she knew the area.

"He went off in front of the old ruins. You know where that is?" Parnell asked.

"I know the spot. When we were kids my brothers and I used to play there." She said "I'll get help on the way, pronto.

Parnell then searched the local phone book for the Abbot ranch and called for Sully. Again, without going into the still hazy details, he explained to Abbot's wife that Tom's fall was an accident. "I can't see any sign of him from the top," he told her. And he doesn't answer my call."

"I'll get Sully," she said. Wait five minutes. "He'll call you right back." She hung up. The five minutes took hours.

"Shit." Was Sully's still reply. "I told him never to go up there, Parnell."

Parnell took a deep breath. "He was with me, Sully. I guess I'm to blame."

"No one's to blame, Parnell." Sully was in a state of shock and trying to cope. "I'll get there as soon as I can. We already unhooked the trailer. Towing it would slow me down." Parnell wondered at Sully's calm reaction. "I'll be there within the hour, Parnell. You call the sheriff?"

"Ya. Liz, his sister, I guess. She's putting it together."

"She's a good woman. She knows that place better than I do. Keep lookin' for him, Parnell. My brother is a tough old duck. He may still be alive. Parnell thought differently but made no comment. Sully had to hope.

"Drive carefully," Parnell said. He felt stupid for giving that advice.

"Right," Sully answered. "I'll meet you by the ruins, Parnell, or down below." The connection on the old hand crank, wind-up phone buzzed for a moment, clicking on and off. Some miles of the phone lines were tacked to fence posts. It wasn't the best of connections. Parnell wondered that it worked at all.

"You still there, Sully? Sully?" He listened a moment, then yelled into the static, "They are sending an ambulance. I'm going back on top. If you are still listening and can hear me, Sully, what's the quickest way into the canyon?" The line cleared. An answer came back.

"I suspect he went over where you damn near did the other day."

"That's the spot."

"Just north of there is a narrow trail going down. I mean it is narrow, steep and God damned dangerous, at least for me it is. It ain't been used in years but it is there. And, Parnell, take a dishtowel from the kitchen and hang it from a tree limb to mark where you start down in case the sheriff gets there before me. And listen to me Parnell—go down careful. The trail is deadly. The whole canyon has a death curse on it. It's a tricky som-buck, Parnell, be careful. I'm on the way." And he hung up. This time the phone definitely went dead. Parnell hung the heavy black ear-piece gently back in the forked cradle sticking out the side of the oak box. The hand crank was on the opposite side. The mouthpiece stuck out the front like an elephant's trunk.

Parnell grabbed two of Tom's old red dishrags and headed back to the ruins. After tying one on the dead cedar to mark the site of Tom's fall, it took him ten minutes and three false starts to find the trail down. Sully had been right, it was a som-buck, a New Mexican cowboy's polite term for son-of-a-bitch. He remembered his friend, Sully, saying the other day, while cling-ing fiercely to the dead cedar, he had only been to the bottom once. If this was the way he had made his descent it was no wonder it had only been down once.

The canyon was surrounded on three sides by rim-rock. The only other access was to come in through the mouth where the spring fed into the plains beyond. That end was plugged with a jungle of thick brush. Sully's dad had fenced it off so cattle wouldn't get in there to drop their calves and hide out. Some, like the mother of the yearling bull, got through anyway. It was damned near impossible to get a horse in there to find them, let alone push them back out into the open if the horse didn't want to go.

At the bottom of the trail, Parnell fought his way out through the tangle of brush until he could spot the cedar flagged with the dishtowel. He oriented himself on a determined pinon tree growing in a twisted knot out of the distant east face and a streak of bright green lichen gripping the west face under the flagged cedar. The green looked like bright sewage had been poured over the edge under the dead tree. The two landmarks would keep him in line.

Once under the lip of the rim, however, he found no trace of Old Tom. There were no broken limbs. But then again, he was breaking more brush getting in and out of the area. If he missed a sign he might have destroyed the evidence by his own clumsiness. *It's a jungle down here.*

Parnell was looking for the body, not for the sign. He found no body. *Where the hell did Tommy land?* Parnell backtracked, breaking more brush as he went. He got to a clear spot where he could study the west face beneath the streak of green algae and the red dishrag. There was nothing: no scraps of torn clothes, no body wedged in the rocks, no sign of blood that he could see from that distance. *And, thank God, no bird.*

The heavy bed of willow brush reached a height of ten to twelve feet and was thick as a briar patch. Parnell felt it might have cradled Tom's fall and even saved his life, but if it did, *where the hell had the crazy old man gone to? He isn't hanging in the trees.* Parnell wished he had brought a machete to clear walking space. Hell, he wished he had brought a chain saw. He searched the branches, then wondered if by some chance Tom had caught up on a ledge above. Parnell had fortunately landed on the narrow shelf just a few feet below the edge before it cut in. It had saved his life. If Tom had caught on that ledge, it had been a short stay. From the top Parnell had checked any possible crag that might have slowed his fall or even caught the old man. He had also searched the face from the clearing he had just left.

Looking directly up from the base of the cliff he realized the overhang at the top extended a good six to ten feet out, which explained why he couldn't see directly down to the base. To view the face at a better angle he fought his way to the base of the west face and climbed as high as possible. He spotted the shelf he had clung to the other day and two or three other possible landing sites, or outcroppings, jutting from the cliff's undercut. There was no sign of Tom. In any case, he reasoned, when the bird hit the old man she had taken him out and away from the face. Old Tom would have cleared them all.

Parnell realized he was wasting time. Tom Sullivan had to be somewhere beneath the puke-green algae growth clinging to the basalt. He struck out again for the west wall. He was under the overhang when Sully called down from the rim.

\* \* \*

Now, at the base of the cliff, they studied the situation together.

"If he landed clean on this thick brush there is a chance it might have buoyed his fall, Sully," Parnell said. "He might still be alive—maybe—crawled off or something." Parnell didn't sound hopeful. "I spent over an hour looking and couldn't find a trace of him here, Sully."

"No chance, Parnell," Sully echoed his friends thoughts. "It's over a hundred feet up there—and it's a hundred feet <u>down</u> here. It's a fast drop with a quick stop." Sully shook his large head. "My brother has got to be lyin' here somewhere. Tommy ain't in dreamland anymore. He's dead." Sully was trying to make himself accept the fact.

"Your brother said," Parnell spoke without thinking, "that after the fire they never found the woman's body either."

Sully pulled off his black silk neckerchief and sat on a rock wiping his neck and face. "That was me told you that, Parnell." He looked at his friend. "I told you that the other day when you took to flying. My brother never said a word about her to anyone. And don't never bring it up to Tom. No sense stirrin' up his scrambled brains after all these years. No tellin' what he might do." Sully considered their situation. "Not as you could bring it up to him now."

"Well, what did happen to that woman, Sully?" Parnell asked. "Where the fuck did <u>she</u> go to? And if she disappeared in mid-flight, why not Tom?" Sully looked at his friend and shook his head. "It's a damned strange tale, Sully," Parnell added.

"This ain't a wonderland, Parnell. This is the real world. Things fall, they land."

"Her dancing ghost was never found?"

"The doctor did it, God damn it!" Sully rose to his feet in frustration. "They called her the human torch. —I don't want to even think about it."

"The what?"

"The human torch, Mr. Mackenzie. Shit." Sully collapsed back onto the rock. " I don't know shit about it and I don't believe what I do know." He heaved a sigh. Parnell let the silence hang like the question mark it was. "I don't believe she ever went off the top," Sully said looking up again. "They found some burned rags, that was all. No body—no blood. My old man believed it was all a hoax."

"A hoax?"

That's what my old man told me, and told me to shut up about it. 'Don't never tell a soul', my old man said. The old man might a-been drunk when he said it. I don't know. But until now I never told a living soul what he said." He looked at Parnell then back up to the rim above them. "Some others may of thought the same. The old man said it was the Doc done it, and if you ask me I think he was right. And then he killed the other man, who ever the hell he was, and the Doc and his dancin' lady rode off into the sunset—or sunrise, it bein' morning. God knows where they went. It is so damn long ago now nobody cares. Let the ghosts lie, Parnell. Don't dig up an unmarked grave." Sully got to his feet. He stepped off a few feet and pissed noisily into the dead willow leaves. Parnell listened to the sound and wished there was something else to hear. The canyon was silent as a secret fart. Something was dreadfully wrong. There was no wind, no bird song. Nothing.

"TOM, YOU GODAM SON-OF-A-BITCH!" Parnell leaped to his feet and looked about wildly. Sully whirled and yelled again to the echoing walls. "You are as frustratin' in death, brother, as you are in life. WHERE THE HELL ARE YOU, TOMMY?"

Knowing where the cry had come from, Parnell breathed easier. There was a long pause. Sully angrily buttoned up his fly. "Tom, you old fuck, answer me!" Sully's plea was thrown back at him in ever diminishing echoes. In the end—silence. Parnell settled back on his rock.

\* \* \*

"Sully, where the hell are <u>you</u>? From all that noise I presume you are down there." Sully and Parnell stared at each other. Then it registered.

"It's the sheriff. Up on top." Sully said.

\* \* \*

Sheriff Julio Romero had parked safely back by the ruins. He stood on the edge of the rim studying the bottom of the canyon.

"Down here," Sully called back to him. We're in the brush. He shook a slender cottonwood to show their location.

"Got-cha, Sully," the sheriff called back. "I'll find the trail and be down in a few minutes."

An olive drab army surplus Dodge ambulance lumbered across the mesa and up to the edge of the rim rock. Alonzo Padilla set the break, locked the Dodge in gear and stepped out to greet the officer. "This damn thing rides like a truck, Sheriff," the medic said.

"It is a truck, Padilla," Sarah, his partner answered flatly. She got out of the passenger side and slammed the heavy steel door. "It's an army surplus piece of junk Dodge truck." She headed around to the back of the old, high riding panel 4 by 4, and jerked the double back doors open. Sarah started pulling out rock climbing equipment. "We'll rappel down, Sheriff," she said. "It's faster. We can also check the cliff face. He might have hung up on a crag somewhere on the way down."

"This is the only good thing about war," Alonzo said. "Army Surplus. There's a lot of good stuff left over."

"Ya, well I wish my father had been left over." Sarah jerked out a role of mountaineering nylon rope. "In a way he was, I guess. He was left over in Korea."

"I'm sorry, Sarah. It was a bad choice of words."

"Anyway," Sheriff Romero cut in. He wanted to change the subject. Sarah was short tempered and bitter, but a good medic. She had learned in Vietnam. Her father, a doctor, had disappeared in the earlier government sponsored "Police Action" in Korea. Romero didn't blame her for being bitter about it. He was bitter himself. Two of his younger brothers had been bagged and shipped home out of Hanoi. There would be more of the same. You couldn't change government policy no matter who you voted for. "Sarah, we got a man down at the bottom of the canyon," he said, holding the panel door open for her. "That is where we need to get right now."

"That's where we're getting, Julio " Sarah said. She placed rocks under the wheels of the ambulance. "We'll tie off to this piece of junk and drop over the edge. Be down there in minutes."

Alonzo leaned out on the dead cedar. He spotted Sully who had moved into a relatively open area. "Did you find any sign of your brother, Sully? He alive, you think." The medic and sheriff exchanged glances. "You got to hope, Sheriff," Alonzo said under his breath. I understand stranger things have happened here."

"We can't find any sign of him." Sully's voice drifted up to them. The rancher watched from below as Sarah tossed the hundred and some feet of nylon over the edge and buckled on her harness. "What the hell they doin', Parnell?" he asked. "They goin' to slide down that rope, or something?" The big rancher paled at the thought of anyone hanging in space. The trail down had been trial enough for him.

Alonzo slung the medical bag on his back. He wrapped the rope over his back and between his legs. He didn't use a harness. Being an old-fashioned rock climber he considered it a nuisance to put up with. What did you do with the straps when you got to where you were going? As he dropped out of sight Sarah offered an extra harness to the sheriff.

"Nope," Julio replied quickly. "If I can't drive, ride a horse or walk there, I'm not going. I'll take the trail." He noted where Parnell had marked the top end of the trail with the red dishrag. "I'll take my time. I'm afraid we got plenty of time." Sarah dropped the harness and an extra coil of rope in front of the 4X4. She waited until her partner was safe at the bottom and clipped onto the rope. She leaned out over the edge, testing the tie. It was good, as she knew it would be. In graceful bounds she repelled down the face, pausing at possible catch points. Sarah noted the first ledge where Parnell had landed the day before. Below that there were no obvious outcroppings, no signs of torn clothes. *He didn't just trip and fall straight down,* she reasoned. *He either jumped or was pushed. Some force carried him a distance out from the face.* For now, she would keep her thoughts to herself. Where the cliff undercut she slowed her descent and studied the surface. It was clean. At the bottom Alonzo waited.

"Nothing?" He looked at her. Sarah could read sign better than he could. She shook her head. "Nothing on the way down." She checked the area about them. "There is a lot of broken brush here, but those two," she indicated the noisy approach of Sully and his friend, "have been trampling this area. If there was any sign, it's destroyed."

"Sarah," Alonzo said quietly. "The old man either landed or he didn't. If he fell, he landed. The brush is damned heavy here. It may have saved his life. He could have crawled away, but I doubt if he got very far." He glanced up, following the stream of green algae clinging to the face. "But then, I'm told the last person to go over this ledge was never found either."

Sarah gave him a skeptical look. "That story's old enough to be a wives tale, Alonzo. Although I'm a devout feminist, I think we can safely discredit it."

It was Parnell who reached them first. Sully was still struggling through the undergrowth. "This one isn't an old wives tale," Parnell Mackenzie said, picking up on Sarah's last line. I saw Tom Sullivan go over the edge. He did go over right above us, but there is no sign of his having landed down here."

"How far were you from him when he took the fall?" Sarah asked. "Did you look down immediately?"

"I didn't see him land, if that's what you mean." Parnell couldn't explain even to himself why he had passed out. He had seen nothing following the falcon's attack. The whole truth and nothing but the truth was too farfetched to be reasonable: a mind-boggling can of worms best left in the dark. He shrugged. "Parnell," he said, introducing himself. "I'm Parnell Mackenzie." He held out his hand. "And who might you be?"

"Alonzo," the man said, shaking Parnell's hand firmly. "The lady is Sarah. She's the best of what we got." Studying the area, Sarah made no move to accept Parnell's hand. He drew it back. "What I should say, flat out," Alonzo went on, "is that Sarah Pasquale is the best search and rescue medic in the State of New Mexico."

Parnell studied the lady dropping the sixty-pound equipment pack from her shoulders. She wasn't over five feet, plus maybe three inches tall, but she moved like an athlete. He had seen her bounce down the rough rock face. She was an athlete. "I was back a ways when Tom fell," he said, avoiding the fact that he had collapsed, unconscious. "I looked down as soon as I could. There was no sign. I don't think he could have tucked back under the overhang. I searched this area carefully. On my hands and knees, I have been all over it. There is no sign to follow."

"You were with him when he went over?" Sarah asked, probing. Parnell nodded. With her eyes Sarah followed the line of the rope back up. "With all the thrashing around you have done here there is no sign now." Parnell let the pointed accusation drop.

"Old Tom Sullivan fell just north of that dead cedar where you slid down," Parnell said. "If he dropped straight he should have landed right here."

"You saw no broken limbs? Nothing?"

"I'm sorry, Lady," Parnell said, controlling his mounting anger. "I didn't find a trace of him." He thought about the bird that had gone over with Old Tom. He had thought about the falcon constantly since he got to the bottom and could not find Tom. Was the bird supernatural? Had the falcon magically swooped the old man to her nest somewhere? Parnell thought better than to mention this madness. *Where was the peregrine now? What was she up to? The bird was the only one that knew.* Parnell would keep it to himself until he had the damn bird by the throat. Sarah looked at him coldly for a long moment. It was Alonzo spoke up first:

"Let's get looking, Sarah. That's what we're down here for. Right?"

"Right." Sarah pulled a roll of surveyor's flagging from her pack. "We'll flag the areas as we search, OK? That way we won't be doubling our work load."

"And we won't be missing anything," Alonzo added.

Sully, hat in hand, pushed up to them. He pulled his Stetson back in place. He had lost it twice, snagged by the thick brush. Sully didn't like being in the brush. Even more, he disliked being without his horse. "Howde, Alonzo," he said. "Thanks for commin'"

"Hello Sully" Alonzo said quietly. "If your brother is alive we'll find him and pull him through, Sully," he said. "I'm awful sorry about this." Sully shook his hand.

"I don't hold much hope, Al, but we got to find him. Thanks. We got to find him one way or another."

"We'll find him, Sully," Parnell said dubiously.

"He has to be here, Mister Sullivan," Sarah said. On seeing Sully, her attitude had changed. "With all of us working together it shouldn't take long." She turned to Parnell and handed him the dumb end of a fifty yard tape measure and a roll of bright surveyors tape. "Stand right here and hold this," she said. "I'll work through the undergrowth and tie the surveyors marking tape fifty yards ahead." Parnell nodded. He handed her the loose end of the bright surveyors plastic ribbon. "Thanks," she said, and almost gave him a smile. Parnell was relieved.

# CHAPTER FOURTEEN

# THE SEARCH

The sheriff was at the head of the trail Parnell had marked with the red dishrag. He was about to start down when he spotted a black 4X4 cresting the distant edge of the mesa a mile to the north. It parked for a while. No one got out. Julio stood still and watched, curious. Then the vehicle moved slowly toward the search and rescue site. "More help?" he mumbled. "I doubt if it's a tourist looking for Tijuana." He had got that weird call two years ago. The lost gringos had seen a sign and arrow pointing off the paved road toward Tinaja. They misread it as the direction to the infamous Mexican border town, Tijuana. Somewhere on one of these dusty ranch roads they had run out of gas and been stranded for two days. A cowboy a-horseback reported them. When Sheriff Romero located the van with the lost souls crouching inside, they were terrified. "Banditios," they cried, clinging to each other in fear of mass rape and pillage. One of them, a Ph.D. in Latin-American studies it turned out, tried to communicate with Julio in Castilian Spanish. It took Julio some time to convince them they were still in the United States.

Sheriff Romero studied the black 4X4.moving in his direction. "If it's help," he murmured to himself, "we can use it." The sheriff considered waiting for the vehicle to pull close enough to find out who was driving. He watched for a moment. The 4 by 4 stopped again. "Hell, they can find their own way," he said to nobody. Sheriff Romero moved down the trail out of sight.

The sheriff's had not been the only eyes watching the black Chevrolet 4 by 4. The falcon, crouched in her hidden nest missed nothing. The Chevy pulled to a slow stop just below the chimney corner. Catherine got out of the passenger side and observed the ruins with quiet curiosity. She stepped inside over the low back wall and studied Tinaja's peak through the charred window frame. Traces of dried blood were still evident on the sill. She touched the stain and smelled her fingers. There was no scent. As she stepped out through the leaning doorframe the right hand window of the 4X4 rolled down. Catherine sensed it and spoke without looking. "I told you I want to be alone here. Leave." The driver wheeled the vehicle around and drove off angrily. Catherine paid no attention. She gave the sheriff's pickup a casual glance and headed for the rim's edge where the Dodge ambulance was parked. She noticed the rocks placed as breaks under the wheels and checked out the rope attached to the sturdy bumper. On the ground, a few feet from the truck, she spotted the climbing harness and the extra length of nylon rope Sarah had left. Catherine picked them up.

That was when the falcon chose to leave her hiding place. She circled Catherine a time or two without threatening her, then glided out to the center of the canyon. The rising air currents elevated her a hundred feet or more at an exhilarating pace. Catherine watched her in awe. *You are here, too, my feathered friend. Is your nest close? You are the peregrine falcon I saw the other day. Good. We are here together. I am very glad to have your company and hope that good feeling is returned. I need a friend.*

\* \* \*

Below, in the shadows of the giant cedar, Parnell sat quietly on the limb that stretched across the slick, moss green water. Claiming the call of nature, he had left Sully and the medics to search the base of the cliff. Parnell's mind was lost in the memory of Old Tom's story. The telling was too realistic not to be believed. He had seen "shades" of the people Tommy had spoken of here under this very tree. That, and the premise: a young boy's first love in a sate of fear—the fear of discovery—fear of the sin—of illicit love. Beyond love, the forbidden acts of the flesh—sex. Young Tommy didn't even know what the word meant. The doctor and his woman had drawn the boy into their game—their game of lust and intrigue. Or was it simply Katrina's need of love? Was she an innocent, too? *Not entirely innocent,* Parnell thought. *Her values were desperate. Nymphomania?* Parnell thought desperation was more in line with her actions. *Desperation, loneliness, and fear of loss. Did she care about the price to be paid?* Where was the good doctor all this time? *Or was this whole story a young boy's fantasy?* Parnell knew better than that. He felt a chill grip his spine. It shot up and down his backbone like a twisting length of barbed wire that cut through to his lunges and took his breath.

Parnell got quickly to his feet, nearly loosing his balance; he leaped for the safety of the great flat boulder split by the roots of the gigantic cedar. *How do I know this place? Am I insane? Is the past stalking the wrong man?* Parnell studied his surroundings. He glanced up at Tommy's hiding rock, jutting above the rim. They could have spotted the boy from here. *Young Tommy had spoken the truth.*

He looked out over the green, misting pool toward the west bank—. There was a natural cave beneath an overhanging rock slab. Young Tommy's hiding place. The boy lay there now, had lain there years ago in silent and exciting terror, in his cave. —Watching—watching.

Parnell stepped out again on the cedar limb that stretched across the green, heat misting water. He lay back, beckoning to Katrina. Naked, she came out and kissed him gently.

"He is watching, Kat; the boy." He grinned. "Let him watch."

Parnell shook the vision off. His cheek still pressed against the rough bark, he twisted to look. Tommy was no longer there—no longer in his cave. The surface of the pool was still as death. Nothing moved. Parnell stood unsteady in the crotch of the swaying limb. Death surrounded him. He vowed to keep this fantasy to himself, for be it truth, it still was mad.

*Some would think it a sin to even suggest what I am thinking is possible. Christ, I am a fool, or certainly will be taken for one for believing—let alone promoting reincarnation as the God's truth*. "As for Old Tom, if they are fortunate, or unfortunate enough to find the poor bastard alive," Parnell whispered to the wind, "I won't mention the dark dream we shared this morning—not to anyone—not to Sully. Sully suspects some muddy intrigue in this canyon. He is scared to death of it. The falcon, the dancing ghost in Sully's subconscious, dances in the madness of his brother's past. Parnell looked about. Tommy's ghost had truly vanished.

A light mist, or steam, rose from the surface of the pool. Long fine vines of a green seaweed like growth, clustered in circles on the still surface. Through and around the weeds was a clear view of the bottom. Parnell stepped to the rock crusted shore and picked up a dead limb, twelve to fourteen feet long. He crept out, balanced on the rocking cedar limb, and thrust down into the warm water with the wooden staff. The depth appeared to be seven, maybe eight feet and the bottom, a mix of sand and stone. A couple sharp slabs of rock thrust up through it to within two or three feet of the surface. The staff found what appeared to be the bottom. To Parnell's surprise, it sank easily beyond, sucked down into the muck. Curious, Parnell let it slip between his fingers to its full length. There was no bottom. The dead limb sank into the muck like a steel pike into drawn butter. Pulling the limb out was another matter. *Quick sand? Quick muck.* What ever it was, Parnell had to struggle to pull the limb back. He nearly lost his balance in the process.

A bundle of the sticky, vine-like moss clung to the smooth dead limb, adding many pounds to its weight. The disturbing action clouded the clear water beneath the moss.

"Tommy couldn't have fallen in here," Parnell said to himself, securing his footing. He hopped off the limb onto what had been Katrina's dancing stage. He dropped the green draped staff and studied the pool. *Is the water warm, or hot? And where does the spring surface. There is no water running into the pool—none that I can see.* He could hear water trickling out, among the cat and nine tails at the south end of the pool, maybe fifty yards from where he stood. The dark green stalks with brown tails stood six feet tall at that end. The pool was close to twenty yards across at the widest point. The west bank was thick with willow brush. The east bank was steep with a jumble of long ago fallen boulders. There were numerous openings or shallow caves. *Including the one Young Tom spied from.* Parnell checked it out again. Nothing there. *The hot spring inlet must be at this end.*

Parnell stepped carefully down off the big flat basalt stage to the slippery green edge of a moss-covered slab that reached under the water. *Is the water really hot?* It certainly had a strong sulfur stench to it: stronger now that he had stirred it up. Leaning down he slid his hand gingerly through the thick algae cover along the edge.

It was hot, *too hot for regular living creatures to live in, definitely hot enough to sweat out a hangover.* Parnell was thankful he hadn't lost his balance on the limb. "I guess if you swam on the surface and didn't let yourself get sucked down," he said to himself—. "Or maybe the muck was dragged down here by flash floods over the past centuries. The doctor might have dredged it clean. It could be done." He leaned further out over the pool, sweeping back the green scum with his hands.

The shattered reflection of the falcon wind-streaked into his vision. "Son-of-a-bitch," he cried and jerked back for the safety of the solid shoreline. With the sudden shift of weight, the rock he was on gave way. It tipped and slid on the greasy muck to be lost in a dark swirl beneath the surface. Parnell went with it.

It came as no surprise to him that there was no bottom. The shallow shoreline had been an illusion, too. It was a vertical drop. Parnell's head and shoulders went under first. There was no chance to cry for help. He paddled furiously trying to get back to the air. The tough, stringy green vines of the surface growth he took down with him, twisted about his neck and arms. *Don't panic.* Desperately he tried to untangle the weeds about his neck. Now they were around his legs and he was going down. Muck was swirling all around him. Nothing he touched was solid, but it was getting thicker. That was not a good sign. *Don't panic.* He thrashed about with his sharp-toed riding boots, hoping to encounter one the rocks he had seen rising through the muck. *Nothing. No purchase anywhere.*

Then he felt a change in temperature. *Hot, really hot—the spring source.* His lungs and skin burning, Parnell opened his eyes. In front of him the hot water was clear of mud and weeds; a clear black rush from the bowels of hell. Desperately, he broke free of what confined him and struck for the surface. What he found above was solid rock. In his desperation, he had worked his way under the edge of the pool. *Don't panic, and for Christ sake, don't breathe.* Getting a partial grip on the rough rock surface above him, Parnell pulled himself back in what he hoped was the direction to bring him to open water. He only had one chance and maybe five seconds to make it. He came out into the murk again and above him, light. He didn't push with his feet and legs for fear of getting them entangled in the weeds again. He used his arms to pull him up through the morass. At last he gulped air and, eyes stinging, saw the shoreline two feet before him. It was a rock ledge rising four feet straight up. For a few minutes, he clung to it, regaining strength. Taking in deep breaths, he dragged himself along to a gnarled root and got a grip on it. The root was sound.

Parnell was beginning to feel a bit secure when he heard a shrill cry and a roust of feathers. Not quite soon enough he forced himself beneath the riled surface. The fish hawk's talons only slashed through his shirt as she wheeled up into the trees. Parnell didn't wait this time. Anger and adrenaline gave him power to move. His luck held. Before the falcon could circle and strike again he was on the rock shore and able to defend himself. As the peregrine stooped a third time through the steam and mist he hurled a handful of rough gravel in her path. It shot gunned into the feathered Sphinx, almost bringing her down to water level. Then she was gone. Parnell, soaked and stinking of sulfur, watched her rise vertically into the blue.

"Bitch! Bitch of a fucking bird," he cried. "What did you do with him? What did you do with Tommy?" Parnell's tortured cry of anguish ricocheted wildly against the canyon walls.

* * *

High on the rim Catherine was buckling on the climbing harness. She slung the extra length of nylon over her shoulder as Parnell's angry words washed up and around her. She headed north along the rim, keeping back so as to not be spotted.

"You are down there, Parnell," she murmured. "I knew you would be." The Cat found the narrow trail and headed down.

In the brush below Sully stood with Sheriff Romero and the medics. They looked about wonderingly. "What the hell was that?" Alonzo said in quiet awe. Sarah and the sheriff watched the falcon rise into the blue distance.

"Sounded like Parnell." Sully looked up to where Sarah and his friend Julio were staring. The falcon leveled out and circled gracefully. "But I don't think I want to make a guess what it's all about," he added quietly.

Sarah was concentrating on the bird. "A Peregrine," she said. "She's a rare bird. My God, she is beautiful."

"So are buzzards," Sully said quietly—"at a distance."

Sarah was still studying the falcon. "Do you have any more of them here?—a pair, maybe?"

"She's the only one I've ever seen, if she is a she," Sully mumbled. "She acts like a Banshee."

"Magnificent," Sarah sighed with admiration. Alonzo Padilla nodded in agreement. Sheriff Julio Romero said nothing. He was watching Sully.

"A real work of art," Sully said bitterly. "Just like the rest of us." Sully walked off into the brush to pee again. His prostate was acting up.

"That bird, that falcon is a magnificent creature. If nothing is done to save her and her mate from the horrors of modern bug extermination—DDT. That bird will be extinct in another fifteen years. But there are people trying to save them. I happen to be one of them.

"Come on," the sheriff grunted. "We're down here to find a body." He looked at the two search and rescue staff. "We don't exactly have an army. My fault. I thought we'd find the old man in a minute and be out of here." Sarah pulled another roll of bright orange surveyors flagging from her jacket pocket.

We used the blue. Let's keep marking the search grid fifty square feet at a time as we search. At least then we'll know he's not where we've been, and we'll know where we been."

"Keep it up," said Romero. I'll go after Sully. He's upset."

"I'm just tryin' to piss," the rancher called from the distance. "I'll be right with you."

"What about Sully's friend?" Sarah interjected. "Wouldn't it be better if we all worked together on this?"

"I'm right here." Parnell answered. "You find anything?"

"Where the hell you been?" Sarah said, observing his drenched condition.

"I fell in the creek."

"So that's what you were yelling about."

"Must have been that stink hole," Sheriff Romero said looking him over and raising his nose. "That place is no place to go swimming. The bottom's quicksand."

"I know. I just wanted to check it. I thought maybe Tom had crawled over that way."

"If this brush broke his fall enough for him to crawl that far he could walk out of here," Alonzo said. "I say we concentrate on the first hundred feet out from the base of the cliff."

"I'm yours," said Parnell. "Tell me what to do?"

"We go back and forth six feet apart and mark the area as we go." Sarah nodded in agreement.

"Sounds good to me," said Romero. You stay down wind, Parnell, until that sulfur stink blows off. I'll round up Sully and get him to join us."

Parnell and the search and rescue people went back to work.

# CHAPTER FIFTEEN

# CAT ON THE ROCKS

Catherine swung through a shaft of late afternoon sunlight and landed on a narrow ledge south of the searchers. She was on her own. No one had spotted her. Heights and rocks intrigued The Cat. She liked the sharp edge it put her on. Cat was an accomplished rock climber. She settled in the shadows on a narrow ledge where she could watch those below and not be seen herself. *Who, or what were they searching for. It had to be a who, why else the ambulance? The <u>who</u> must have fallen over the edge.* It was all strangely intriguing. Certainly the location was intriguing. The Cat had fully expected to find Parnell here. She didn't know <u>why</u> she had expected him to be here. That bothered her. *Why am I here?* That bothered her too. It had certainly bothered Wolf. He'd been nervous as a rabbit when they went to the Chevrolet dealership and she asked to try out a new 4X4, convincing them that if she liked what she drove, she would pay cash for it. It worked.

They backtracked on the same road Toad had brought them in over. So far they hadn't missed a turn. Fresh tracks and a faint trace of adobe dust hung in the still air where the sheriff and ambulance cut off the ranch road on top of the mesa. At that point, Wolf completely rebelled. He was actually frightened. There was no doubt of that in The Cat's mind. She spotted the Sheriff's pickup parked in the distance.

"Just drive me in to where that truck is and drop me off," she told him.

"You're crazy, Cat," he replied. "What kind of fucking game are you playing? You can get us both hurt. This is not a safe game. We are not on the stage."

"What's your problem?

"We got to get this car back," he hedged. "You got fuck all for cash to buy it and no use for it if you did."

"I'm using it now."

"For chasing some rag ass of a cowboy you got the hots for? I want out."

"Well get out! I can drive. You can walk back to town and turn yourself in as an accomplice to car thievery." She looked at him, her eyes burning. "But hurry up, Wolf. I need to get there and I need to get there now."

"What in the hell for?"

"I don't know!" she screamed at him. "Just move it, Wolf. Get out, or drive on. Make up your mind." There was a long moment of heated silence between them. The Cat was antsy. She didn't know what or why she was doing this either. It was just that she had no choice. She told him as much, her voice dropping to almost a whisper: "I don't know, Wolf. I just know I must get to him, and I must do it now!" She sighed, dejected and determined. "I think he's in trouble, Wolf. I am the only one that can help him."

"The cowboy?"

"Doctor Parnell Mackenzie."

\* \* \*

The sun was nesting into the western range of the Sangre de Christos . In the canyon below Catherine, darkness was already taking over. All but Parnell had started up the narrow trail. Catherine watched as Parnell fought his way back to the center of the canyon floor: back to the sulfur hot springs pool. *What's he up to?* She slid down a natural chimney in the cliff. There she left the rope hanging and slipped off quietly in the direction Parnell had taken.

\* \* \*

Sully had almost reached the crest of the rim. He was more than a few minutes behind Sheriff Romero and the medics. He was winded and exhausted. Guilt, sorrow and strain showed in his features. The big man, blowing heavily, turned to look back into the darkening depths. *Why, Tom?* He looked to the heavens. There was nothing there either. He shook his head. Prayer would do no good. It had never been his practice anyway. He continued the remaining fifty or so feet of the climb. When he reached the top Sheriff Romero was standing by his 4X4 speaking into the radio mike.

"We haven't found a sign of him, Liz."

"What did you expect?" came back the answer. "He's probably not even there."

"Where the hell did you expect him to fall, Little Sister, up?"

"No comment."

"It's all thick brush and cactus. We combed it the best we could. I don't understand what happened to the body. I know where we looked there wasn't one. We found nothing—not a sign."

"Just like the human torch, Little Brother," came Liz' voice over the radio. "I told you when you went out there." Alonzo came up behind the sheriff. He had caught most of the conversation.

"Liz, that is a damn folk tale," the sheriff replied angrily. "We weren't even born when that story became a part of Coal County's oral history. Now go back to work before I get accused of nepotism." Liz Romero's brother keyed out the mike.

"Your sister has a vivid imagination, Sheriff," Alonzo said dubiously. And she's not the only one. That crazy story's going to burst right up in flames again with Old Tom disappearing." He shook his head in wonder. "After spending the day down there, I have a few questions myself."

"Jesus, I hope not. Liz says the calls are already coming in. If we don't find him tomorrow morning we'll have a circus out here." Julio looked past Alonzo to where Sarah was untying the mountain rope from the bumper of the heavy ambulance. "Where's Sully and Parnell?" the sheriff asked her.

"Parnell? The strange guy down there?" The sheriff nodded. He's going to stay the night," Sarah said, coiling the rope. "I left him my flashlight." She gestured over toward the trail. "Sully's just breaking the rim." Sully puffed into sight a hundred yards from where they were parked.

"Poor bastard."

"Mr. Sullivan is taking it pretty hard," she said. "Who wouldn't?" Sarah tossed gear in the back of the ambulance. "Old Tom certainly disappeared, Sheriff," she said, "but I'm not sure he just <u>fell</u> over the rim."

"What you sayin'?"

"Julio," Alonzo said, turning to face the sheriff. "Sarah and I think there may be a chance Tom Sullivan never fell. "I mean we have all looked. We studied the area. We found no sign. Nothing. Nada. Period." There was a moment of silence. Sheriff Romero had not considered this possibility. *Why would Parnell and Sully story about something like this?* He thought. "You saying Parnell and Sully lied, Sarah? Sully lied about his brother's death?"

"We're not saying anything, Sheriff," Alonzo cut in. "If we are saying anything, it is only that we couldn't find the body or any sign of it having landed. It's something to consider, that's all—a seed of doubt, if you will."

Romero looked to where his friend and neighbor of five miles and many years slouched toward them. The man's face was a map of sorrow. "There is no seed of doubt there," he said. "And what would have been gained?" Alonzo shrugged.

"We'll be back in the morning, Julio," Sarah said. "It was just a thought." She looked to Sully. "Sorry we didn't find your brother, Mr. Sullivan."

"Thanks." Sully shook his head. "There is no way he could have lived through that fall. If he crawled away into some corner, he was sufferin'. Tommy has suffered enough. I hope to God he is over it now." Sully stopped and looked about the mesa from the ruins to the horizon. He turned to the sheriff. "Julio, you told me someone else had driven up. I don't see another car."

"I don't know." Julio looked about having just remembered. "Maybe they never got in this far. I only saw them at a distance."

He dismissed the thought. "You staying out here with your friend Parnell tonight, Sully?"

"No use. I tried to talk him out of it. He feels guilty. I told him it's no fault of his. This canyon is all screwed up in Tommy's mind. It was his fate to fall into it, that's all. I got to go in and call Iona's brother in California. He's the only family we got. We stay in touch. Sam comes out a couple of times each year. Tommy looks forward to his visits. Sam will want to know."

Alonzo drove a piton into a crevice on the rim. He secured the rope off to it. "We're leaving the rope for morning Sheriff," Sarah said. "We'll get an early start." She gave a cursory glance around. "I thought I left another length out here with a harness." She shrugged. "Alonzo must have packed it in." She pulled herself behind the wheel of the old Dodge. "I'm driving in. At least I'll have the wheel to hang onto." She backed around to head out. Alonzo joined her as they drove off bouncing over the rocks.

Sully heaved his bulk into his pickup. "I told Parnell it's fate," he said, slamming the door. "It is the same shit crusted fate, Julio, that followed Tommy all his life? It's not Parnell's fault. Fate, Shit. I got to call Sam.

"See you in the morning, Sully." The sheriff saluted him. "Say seven thirty, eight oclock?

"I don't see the need for a rush," the rancher said.

"I'll follow you out to the road, Sully." In the gathering haze of darkness both headed out, Sully for the empty house and Julio Romero back past his family's old homestead toward the office in town. As they passed the thick stand of pinons at the head of the canyon neither noticed the black Chevy 4X4 parked in the shadows. At the ruins, Parnell's battered pickup was the only vehicle left in sight.

# CHAPTER SIXTEEN

# IN THE DARK

In Rainbow, after Wolf and Catherine left to chase the ambulance, Kate remained on duty until noon. Her curiosity and deep concern for Parnell finally got the better of her. She called Moe. "I've got to take the afternoon off," she said. "Something's come up."

"It's Sunday, Kate," Moe groaned. She had got him out of bed. "It's my only day off."

"I'm sorry about that Moe. I should have called sooner but I didn't want to wake you." All she heard was breathing on the phone. "I guess I did anyway," she said lamely. There was another long pause. "It's important, Moe," she broke in. "Do you want me to chase out the five that are here and lock the door? I'll put up the 'Back Later' sign."

"No, Kate. I'll be there. Just hang on." She hung up.

A little before two PM Moe came in to take her place. It had been a long wait. Kate got in her battered Nissan and, after checking Parnell's room and finding he hadn't spent the night there, she headed for the Sullivan Ranch. "I got to be nuts," she said. *What the hell am I doing on the road chasing after a man that dropped me like a lead sinker in Lake Nine?* She didn't turn back.

It was an hour's drive to Sully's place. She got there at four and found no one, not even Old Tom. Kate felt a bit foolish. When they all came back from whatever they were doing what would they think of her?" There was some cold coffee on the stove. She kindled a fire, heated it up and poured a cup. It was strong. She needed something strong. She took the cup and wandered out into the yard. There were two horses in the corral. One belonged to Parnell. He seldom rode a borrowed horse. She wondered about his horse still being here. Then she realized Parnell's truck wasn't here either. Neither was Sully's. *Where the hell are they?* She finished her coffee and went back into the house where she called her mother, who was babysitting her five-year-old daughter.

"I'll be home late, Mom."

"Ya, Moe told me something came up. What is it, Girl?"

"I don't know myself, right now. I think something has happened to Parnell and I am trying to track him down. I'm out at Sully's place."

"Who's with you?"

"Nobody, Mom. I'm OK."

"Parnell's a grown man. He can take care of himself."

"That's what I'm afraid of."

"What?" Her mother was sixty-five, but she wasn't hard of hearing.

"You heard me Mom. Don't worry. I'll call you back later. Hug that girl for me." She hung up.

The Coal County phone directory was on the table in front of her. It was weighted open with the oilstone used to sharpen kitchen knives. The open page was for county offices with a line penciled under the sheriff's number. She had noted this while talking to her mother. Now she dialed that number herself. Liz, the dispatcher answered the phone.

"Liz, It's me, Kate. I'm out at Sully's ranch…"

"Did they find him?"

"Find who, Parnell?"

"No, Old Tom. Your friend, Parnell called to say old Tom had fallen into the canyon across the mesa."

"Old Tom?"

"Ya. Poor Tommy. Not much good has ever happened to that poor man. My brother went out this morning. Sarah and Alonzo followed him in the ambulance. I haven't heard a word since. Julio would call before he leaves." Liz paused—"or if they find something. There is nobody at ranch headquarters?"

"No sign of anyone."

"Probably still down in the canyon."

"Liz, I saw Julio pass the bar going wide open about ten thirty. Was he coming here?"

"Been out there all day and must be away from the radio."

*Poor Tom.* Kate thought, *but what did Parnell have to do with it?* "Is that the canyon the flaming lady dove into, Liz?"

"The human torch. Right on. I doubt if Tom had a chance for survival. I know that canyon. It's a ways to the bottom. In any case, they should have found him a long time ago."

"Can I make it up there in my car, Liz? I never been on top."

"No clearance. You might knock a hole in the oil pan. Take a pickup, if one is there, Or a horse. And when you do find them, tell that brother of mine to check in. I'm worried. They should of been back hours ago."

"I'll tell him, Liz. What's the quickest way a-horseback?

"About a quarter mile behind the house there's a trail. Steep, but a horse will have no trouble. Good Luck."

"Thanks Liz." She cradled the old earpiece in its hook, and thought a moment. *What in heaven's name could have happened? Parnell must have been with the old man.* There was no time to think further if she was going to get up there before dark. She headed for the corral and the tack room. The sky had turned a deep red, painting the edge of the rim rock in blood. *In any other circumstances it would have been beautiful.* She cinched down Parnell's saddle and adjusted the stirrup length. *Why am I being so morbid?*

In the wide Sullivan valley the old adobe headquarters was already in shadows. The deep canyon Parnell and the others were searching would be in darkness within the hour. She slid the bit into the mare's mouth and buckled the throatlatch. She had ridden Diana before. The mare was quick to move, but gentle if she knew you were in charge. Kate knew how to manage a horse. She opened and closed the corral gate behind them and swung into the saddle. In five minutes she had loped across the flat and reached the base of the steep trail. Parnell's mare seemed to know the way. Kate was glad of that. As she climbed, the red sun was at her back painting everything before her in brilliant colors. The green was almost orange. The dust she raised pushed ahead of her and her mount in a light breeze. Shafts of light blazed through it like sword thrusts spiking the earth.

The saw-toothed Sangre de Christos swallowed the red sun when Kate reached the flat of the mesa. When she reached the ruins it was nothing but twilight. She found Parnell's empty truck. There was no sign of the sheriff, Sully, or Parnell. She was too late.

"No"—*someone's coming.* A dark vehicle with only the parking lights on was moving slowly towards her. She tied Diana to Parnell's pickup and waited. Whoever it was stopped about a hundred yards from her. Kate waved. The black 4X4 looked strangely ominous. She knew no one who drove a suburban short-bed van like that. The only one in town was still in the Chevy showroom. The van flicked its bright lights into her eyes and came on directly at her.

# CHAPTER SEVENTEEN

# IN THE HEAT OF THE NIGHT

On the floor of the canyon Parnell built a small campfire on the large flat rock by the pool. He spoke to himself as he absently fed dry twigs into the blaze:

"It was me, Tommy. That fucking bird was trying to knock me off the rim, not you. You got no business being down here in the dark and cold tonight." With a sharp husking flurry of wings something flashed by Parnell's ear. He swung out wildly at what ever it was. . Instinctively he yelled out: "God damned bird. I'll kill you." Goose bumps of fear sprang up around his neck. *What the hell's that bitch doing flying in the dark?* Gathering himself together he got to his feet. The moon had yet to rise above the east rim of the canyon. He stared into the black. *Birds don't fly at night. Maybe a nighthawk—not a peregrine.* Another creature flashed by, diving erratically. Not as close but close enough. "Bats." He mouthed the word with relief. "Bats!" *The air is full of them.*

Parnell scrambled for the flashlight lying beside the fire. He cut an arc with the light and spotted a number of the flying rodents. "Where the hell you come from, bats? Where's your hole?" There was a rush or realization. "A cave—Where do you little sons-of-bitches live? Where is your cave?" Scraping the fire together so it wouldn't be inclined to spread, Parnell concentrated on the flight pattern of the leather-winged creatures. Following one after another they led him toward the west wall of the rim, the wall Old Tom had fallen from. The nearly full moon crested the east wall behind him putting the path, beaten down that afternoon, in silver cobwebbed shadows. His

214

light raised, following the erratic flight paths of these spectral creatures of the night, he ducked past the giant cedar and into the brush. Parnell hoped for the best. He wasn't alone. He was closely watched.

* * *

The Cat lay silently outside the reach of his flickering fire-light. On the cedar limb, the "loving limb", she lay, stretched over the misting sulfur spring. Even in the moon-shaded dark-ness, she felt at home here. She knew where she was. She had been here before. She was here last night. This was her fated destination, her fantasy. She rose silently, cinched up the climb-ing harness about her trim waist and followed Doctor Macken-zie. The rope was no longer over her shoulder. It was hanging from a ledge where she left it. In the dark she doubted if Parnell would spot it. He was headed slowly in that direction. *What is he up to, studying the bats?* The Cat would find out.

* * *

If it were close to dawn the bats would be more likely to be heading for the cave to hang from whatever minute crags they called home. But they were coming out to hunt, not returning to their cozy habitat. Parnell had seen them exit Carlsbad Caverns in black clouds: hundreds of thousands of them. At the caverns, their guano, bat shit as it were, or is, was harvested by the ton to enrich gardens around the world. This population here was nowhere near that dense but there were enough of the blind, silent radar carriers in the night air to give him hope. They didn't like the beam of the flashlight. On being confronted by the light they turned back. One by one he followed their flight toward the west face. When he lost track of them he stopped and stood silently until he heard the beat of their leather wings splitting the air above him. Waiting, Parnell got the uneasy feeling the bats were not the only ones being followed. Twice he thought he heard sounds behind him.

It was impossible to fight through the twisted willows, cactus and alder brush without disturbing the peace of the moonlit night air. He made a false start and stopped quickly hoping to put who or whatever following him off guard. There was a rustle of movement. Something was definitely back there. It might be nothing more than a porcupine—a coon, maybe? It was not a large animal: a dear or bear. Either of those two would be going in the opposite direction to avoid him. A coyote?

If it were a lion, a mountain cat stalking him, that was a different story. There would be no noise until the final scream, meant to paralyze her prey in the split instant before the strike of death. But a big cat, a mountain lion, would have been driven out of the area by this afternoon's human activity. It had to be a small animal—if it was anything but his imagination. He settled for a coon, or a coyote with a curious nose, nothing more. It never occurred to Parnell that it might be a person. There was no other person but Tom in the canyon, and if Old Tom were still clinging to life, he would not be out here wandering about. Porcupines moved slowly and traveled at night. They feared nothing. Armed as they were, they didn't have to. Parnell pushed his troubled thoughts aside and moved on.

* * *

It was a cat behind him; close behind him. Catherine waited until Parnell's light flashed back on. She realized now that he was following the bats, searching for their cave, a cave she was vaguely familiar with. Why? She didn't know. The puzzle of her life was what had drawn her to this location—to this precise spot of wilderness. All of her life she had been fascinated by rocks and fissures in them—cracks and caves. Her interest in mountain climbing had surfaced in the Italian Alps. In the late nineteen forties, touring Europe with a New York dance company, their promoter left them in the lurch in Northern Italy. It was a lurch she became all too familiar with over the course of her theatrical career. Members of the abandoned group had gone their various ways. Catherine took a job waiting tables in the

Italian Alps. To keep her body in dancing shape, and her sex life fulfilled, she started accompanying the resort guide on his rock climbing tours. She became fascinated with the challenge and was soon challenging him to new heights of daring. The older man, to impress his eighteen-year-old protégé, pushed himself beyond his ability.

That act of bravado nearly dragged Catherine to her death as well. When the handsome Hans Mangino lost his grip. Freefalling head first, the slack rope twisted about his neck. When he came to the end of it the sudden force of his weight jerked Catherine from her precarious perch. The two of them were now swinging, strung together, alone in outer space. Her cries raised no response from the surrounding mountains, or from the inert Mangino.

Realizing the weight dragging her down was a dead weight; she cut it free. Hanging there, truly alone, Cat watched the body settle through the rare atmosphere in silence. Nor was there a sound when it struck the distant rocks below. Free now of the added baggage, she managed to reach the narrow ledge thirty meters above. From there, spider-like, she crept to relative safety and made her descent. Back at the mountain lodge, she gathered her belongings and what cash she had accumulated, and fled.

The young Cat made her way across the border to Nice, France. There she secured a job aboard a French liner and worked her way back to New York City. In Manhattan her looks, talent, luck and determination won her a position in the chorus lineup of a summer stock company in northern New England. Unperturbed by the recent loss of Hans, she spent what little free time she had climbing the more challenging faces of the White Mountains. It was that summer she discovered the lure of caves. Spelunking became a passion almost as strong as her drive to perform on stage.

It was a time of free love and creativity. Child bearing and marriage had no part in it for Catherine. Her drive was to create her own image and position. It was a long climb from the little town in Oklahoma, where she was orphaned, and her first stage performance at a burgeoning theatre in Oklahoma City. Her road was paved with determination and—fate. By the time Catherine was thirty she had her own company. By the summer of 1969 she had come full circle. She was on the verge of losing that company. She had been there before, but this was the lowest she had ever slipped. She couldn't bring herself to face up to it. Right now Catherine was in the grip of something larger than her present life: something dangerous, unknown and all encompassing. She had no control over her impulses.

Wolf had slipped in and out of her career a number of times. As a conductor in one of the early companies she had toured with he had been instrumental in advancing her from the chorus line to understudy to the lead. When the aging Hollywood lead developed a minor throat infection, The Cat stepped in. The star spent the night in her posh hotel room. When she didn't respond to calls in the morning, the producer ordered the hotel authorities to open the room. The star was found dead and the room ransacked. Robbery was the obvious motive, but an underlying feeling in the company implicated Catherine who had so much to gain. Wolf came to her rescue, claiming The Cat, (as she became know following this fiasco) had spent the night in his bed. Catherine was innocent of that particular immoral misdemeanor, but she accepted the escape route. In her heart, she wondered where Wolf had been that night? She made a decision to live with the question, as well as occasionally accepting Wolf's sexual advances.

She kept her dark thoughts hidden under a pillow of personal greed. She never broached the question of the star's death to the fiddle player. But she learned Wolf enjoyed a sadistic/masochistic life style. The Cat took advantage of the later. She enjoyed helping him suffer. They made a good team.

Catherine took over the lead in the show. The producer loved her and she went on—into his bed as well.. She left Wolf behind and formed her own company. But Wolf was not to be discarded easily. When her fledgling company began to founder Wolf appeared on the doorstep. He had a way with numbers, both musical and financial. He managed the dollar end of the business, Catherine, the artistic end. It worked until The Cat demanded more and more control. At bottom, however, she needed him as much as he needed her. They both kept their secrets.

This time, lost in the wilderness, she didn't seem to care. Wolf was angry and frustrated. She knew he could be dangerous. This time Cat ignored him. That fueled his anger above all else. Had she pushed him too far? She knew the look in his eyes when he drove away. She also thought it weird that somehow, Wolf was involved in what she was going through now: that he, Wolf was a part of this green, wet spot in the wilderness.

Parnell was the main attraction. Something desperate was happening. Some skeleton was rising to the surface of their lives. She hoped Wolf had returned to Rainbow and turned the car in. But in her heart she knew differently. Wolf would be around for the kill. She must watch for him and be ready to defend herself, and Parnell if the need arise.

* * *

Reaching the base of the cliff where they had searched that afternoon, the bats led Parnell south past the rope Sarah had left tucked into a crevice in the rock face. They led him past the bright surveyor's flagging that marked the extreme southern edge of their search. He kept going. Parnell was on to something. In his excitement he paid little attention to his back trail. Behind him, Catherine stopped at the rope Sarah had left. On an impulse she took hold of the half-inch nylon and pulled herself up, hand over hand, to the overhang. There, she placed her feet against the vertical face and leaned out in the security of her harness to catch her breath. She could see Parnell's flashlight cutting the darkness below as he followed his leather-winged leaders.

Something moved in the shadows above her. She paused. Perhaps she had imagined it. It could have been a trick of the vague moonlight or a wisp of the mist rising from the pool below. The temperature had dropped considerably. As the night air cooled, the mist grew thicker. Satisfied with this assumption, yet cautious, she swung off to the south toward a natural chimney crevasse in the rock face. Once in the chimney she braced her back against one side and her feet against the other. Slowly, she worked her way up.

Below her Parnell directed the fading beam of his flashlight into the air. Then the light disappeared. Catherine continued her climb until she came to a horizontal ledge. There she picked up the coil of rope she had left before the afternoon light faded. She sat quietly, letting her instinctive mind form a plan. Something, someone, was directing her; showing her the way. ... *To where?* She gave herself over completely to whatever power it was. She welcomed it. *Lead on.* Catherine had nowhere to go now but where she was led. *What will be will be—and so be it.* The Cat wouldn't have to wait long.

* * *

Parnell felt a rush of cool air flash past him with the sound of unfledged wings. Bats blasted from what appeared to be solid rock. They brushed against him, seeming to erupt from the branches of a gnarled live cedar rooted to the rock itself. Parnell swung the shaft of light after them, then back to the tree. Behind it was a slice of darkness; the narrow entrance to the cave, to their home. *The bat castle.* He had found what he was looking for. Dropping to his knees he crawled through the lower limbs. Ahead he could sense the open space, the cramped entrance fetid with the scent of guano. The small opening was polished smooth with years of their passage. In the fading beam of his flashlight he worked his way through.

Parnell pulled himself along on his belly. Inside, the opening expanded. He felt the damp around him. There was now room for him to get to his feet and move stooped over at the waist. The passageway continued into the rock. Within the first fifteen feet he could stand almost erect. Beneath his feet the dust was soft as velvet. Chilled by fear and the unnatural damp, he studied the cave floor. Something had been recently dragged, or had crawled along this dark route. Parnell knew he was on the right trail. Shivering, hoping the batteries would hold up long enough he moved on.

\* \* \*

Above him in the clear night air Catherine struggled silently searching out scarce foot and hand holds in the ancient volcanic flow. From a precarious unbalanced position she made a loop at one end of the nylon and threw her coiled rope around a jagged pinnacle twenty feet beyond. It caught. She tested it for strength. *There is only one sure test.* She took a deep breath and swung off into dark space

\* \* \*

In the depths beneath her, Parnell discovered a larger chamber. Against the far wall lay the gray ash remains of a fire. Beside it was a stack of dust-covered firewood. A bat flashed past him. Instinctively Parnell swung at it with the dying flashlight. The night-blind creature cut up along the blackened smoke trail on the cave wall and out of sight. Parnell stood staring up the twisted route the bat had taken. *The back door. The smoke hole.* There was a rustling sound behind him. He turned quickly.

Parnell Mackenzie had found what he came looking for. In the dim beam of the fading light Tomas Sullivan was blinking his tearing eyes back at him.

"Tom," Parnell cried. "For Christ sake, Tom!" The batteries gave out. He slid the switch to off hoping they might regenerate somewhat. He had misplaced the old Zippo he always carried. He cursed and searched for a match. Parnell wasn't a smoker. It took a while, and the wooden matches were still damp from his afternoon dip. He felt the sulfur tip crumbled off when he tried to strike it with his thumbnail.

\* \* \*

Catherine settled precariously on a narrow outcropping. A bat swooped up between her legs, upsetting her equilibrium. Then came Parnell's voice: "Hang on Tom. Hang on." Regaining her balance, she fed rope down the opening the bat emerged from. The Cat was finding her direction.

\* \* \*

Parnell's dead flashlight lay in the fine dust. He could hear the old man breathing. Tom Sullivan was definitely, if unbelievingly, alive. Parnell found a crumpled book of safety matches Sarah had left him when she gave him the flashlight. There were two left.

"Hang on, Tom. Hang on," Parnell spoke the words quietly. In the dark he scraped together scraps of kindling and firewood. "Let me get the fire going. We'll have more light." He struck the first match. It lit up like a sunrise of hope. Flowers of flame blossomed amidst the tinder-dry kindling. The small fire grew quickly, spangling the walls with reflected light. "We'll get you warm, Tom. We'll get you out of here."

"I found her." Old Tom's voice croaked behind him. "She was in the dark. I told her I'd come back."

Parnell, engrossed in getting the fire going, knelt and blew on the flame. "Found who, Tom?" He mumbled. "Who'd you find?"

"Katrina," Tom whispered hoarsely. "I found Katrina. She was waiting for me." Parnell stopped cold in the firelight. Tom continued his voice weak and dry. "How could I have left her? How could I?" Parnell turned slowly. In the flickering light his eyes widened in astonishment.

"Good God…"

Old Tom lay, his head and shoulders propped against the wall. The old man's arms were entwined in the skeletal remains of his first and only love. *It must be her?* The blackened remains of Katrina's charred costume still enshrouded her. *It had to be.* "Good God, Christ and the Virgin." Parnell spoke the words in awe. They were words he seldom used. Parnell looked closer. Across the old man's blood crusted chest lay an antique 30-30 carbine. *It got to be the one he brought with him as a boy,* Parnell thought. *Young Tommy must have found Katrina's body, with what life there was in it—if any -- and dragged her in here.*

"I brought her here to keep her safe." The old man cuddled closer into the rack of bones. "She's still alive," he said with reverence. "The fiddle player—he landed on the rocks. He was meant to die."

"Tom, I got to get you to a doctor," Parnell said with urgency. He took a step toward the old man.

At the mention of the word "doctor" the old man showed sudden life. He struggled to a sitting position and brought the rifle to bear on Parnell. Old Tom was no longer friendly. He was in a hostile past, with murderous intent.

"We knew that you'd come back, Doctor Mackenzie." He spit the words out angrily. "We knew!" The old 30-30 saddle gun was held steady. Parnell kept his place.

"What you talking about, Tommy?"

"I left the gun so she could protect herself when you came back," Tom croaked, his eyes blazing fanatically in the firelight. "We knew you'd come back."

"What you talking about, Tom?" Parnell repeated. "You need help, Tom." Parnell reached out for the rifle. "Give me that damn thing, Tom." But Old Tom jerked it aside and drew back the hammer. Parnell instinctively backed off. "Listen to me, Tom. We got to get you to a doctor."

"Doctor?"

Parnell realized now, "doctor" was the wrong word to use. Old Tom jacked a fresh shell into the chamber of the rusted carbine. Parnell noted that the action moved smoothly, too smoothly for comfort.

"Doctor? Doctor?" Tom cried. "You're the one who killed her. You killed Katrina. We both loved her, but you killed her. You are the one to be killed now."

\* \* \*

Behind Parnell Catherine landed on a shelf eight feet above the cave floor. Smoke from the fire filtering up past her blurred her vision. As the heat rose the draft became more intense and the fire brighter. The Cat couldn't tell who Parnell was talking to, but she heard him pleading:

"Tommy, listen. You're delirious. You don't know what you're saying. I'm no doctor. I'm Parnell, Jack Parnell Mackenzie. I'm a friend of your brother, Sully." Parnell desperately tried to pump reason into the old man's disturbed mind. "I'm your friend, Tom." He was making no headway. In frustration, he repeated the words. "I'm your friend, Tom."

Tom was not influenced by Parnell's rhetoric. He held the rifle steady.

Catherine, swinging clear of the fire dropped silently to the cave floor. Her smoke-tear stained eyes cleared slightly. She could now make out the old man with the carbine. *Who is he?* She wondered. What is his role? *Why is he threatening Parnell?* She stopped short and looked around at the blackened cave walls. Realization flooded over her. *I know this place. I am meant to be here. I was here—I am here.* Her memory was sharply jarred but she was helpless, immovable, in the hypnotizing hands of fate. Parnell, yet unaware of her presence, stepped toward Old Tom.

"That 30-30 is an antique, Tom," he argued. "It's older than you are. Even if it were loaded it wouldn't fire." Parnell was trying to convince himself of this as much as he was trying to convince Tom. He cried in frustration: "Tom, you left the fucking thing here in nineteen-0- five, almost sixty four years ago." He took a step forward.

Old Tom thumbed back the rusted hammer from the first notch of the safe setting to full cock. There was a solid "click" as it made ready to fire. Parnell could see the old man's finger curled snuggly around the trigger. Parnell held his ground. "Tom, for your brother's sake, for my sake—hell for your sake, think clearly, if only for a moment. I have got to get you out of here."

Parnell started a slow move to the right side of Old Tom and his pile of bones. The rifle was kept trained on him. The thirty caliber O-ring of the muzzle followed Parnell like the death's head of a rattlesnake. Tom's eyes never wavered. The rusted carbine was steady in his old hands. Protecting the skeletal remains of his love, Tom Sullivan was definitely prepared to kill.

The cave was narrow where the old man lay against the wall. There was no getting behind him. Parnell eased back to his former position with the firelight behind him hoping it would blind Tom to some extent. He would have to try another tactic.

"Your brother will be worried if we don't get you home, Tom. You don't want to upset Sully, do you?" Parnell noted that the stress of movement was taking its toll. Tom's eyes had narrowed to slits. The rifle in his hands started to slump down. The hard lines in Old Tom's face relaxed. Parnell inched to the side out of a possible line of fire. His attention riveted on the old man, he waited for a greater show of weakness; the moment he could wrest the rifle free.

\* \* \*

Catherine, trying to get a clearer picture of who Parnell talked to, wiped at the smoke induced tears. Her focus blurred. It twisted into a vision of a Young Tommy Sullivan, rising from a bed of wild flowers. He came toward her carrying a fresh bouquet. The adolescent boy was smiling and terribly in love. Catherine's fate-driven quest was fulfilled. She knew now why she had been drawn here. It all came together. "Tom , Tommy," she said softly, lovingly. Catherine moved toward her apparition.

Startled by the words, Parnell backed suddenly to the wall and stared in wonder. "Cat," he cried in an unbelieving whisper. Still in her dream, she paid him no mind. Catherine's attention was all on her awakened vision of Young Tommy.

She called to him again. "Tommy," and stepped forward in the firelight.

Old Tom sensed movement. There was a shadow between him and the flickering light. Thinking the move hostile he swung the old rifle up to Catherine and squeezed the trigger.

In horror, Parnell heard the hammer fall and the firing pin driven home into the soft copper cap at the heel of the brass casing. The ancient black powder mushroomed. There was no time to move. Parnell watched as in a marvel of slow motion, flash, flame and smoke belched from the rusty barrel of Young Tommy's saddle gun: on its crest rode the deadly sphere of lead. Old Tom dropped the rifle and fell back into Katrina, his sweet nest of bones.

Catherine took the bullet in her chest. Nothing was in slow motion now. The force of the blow hurled her back into the flames, throwing the cave into momentary darkness. Then her long flowing hair went up like a torch.

Parnell broke from his trance. He kicked the rifle away from Old Tom and slapped at the flames raging through The Cat's hair and clothes, as he dragged Catherine from the fire. Gently he brushed the remaining strands of the singed auburn hair from her face. He stroked her delicate neck feeling for a pulse. Catherine opened her eyes.

"Why, Catherine?" Parnell spoke softly. "Why? You can't leave me now. I've been looking for you all my life. I love you, Catherine." He stroked her face and held her to him. "I found you."

Catherine tried to speak. Her eyes showed the true feeling for Parnell. At the same time they begged forgiveness. Reaching up, she touched his face tenderly. Parnell pressed her fingers to his lips.

"How do I love thee? Let me name the ways." Catherine mouthed the words Elizabeth Barret Browning spoke years before in her poem for Robert. Catherine didn't answer the question.

# CHAPTER EIGHTEEN

# WOLF'S REVENGE

Kate watched with curiosity as the strange dark van, with oversize tires and blinding bright lights rolled ominously toward her. She stood her ground by the ruins beside Parnell's mare. When it came to a stop ten feet from her, the brights still on, she still couldn't see through the dark shaded windows. For a long time, no one cracked the door. It was frightening. No one she knew drove a car like this.

The big Chevy was between her and the edge of the drop off. The driver finally shut the engine down and set the brakes. It was a full minute more before he pushed open the left hand door and stepped out. Kate had not moved. It reminded her of a scene out of some old gangster movie. The driver pushed the door shut with a heavy solid click, and stepped forward, looking at her over the hood. Dark glasses, black leather jacket and a squashed down black leather cap with a bill.

Kate instinctively stepped behind Diana where she was not so exposed. *This is stupid. Parnell has got to be here somewhere. —His truck is here.* She wondered if the key was in it? Should she make a run for it? *This is bullshit,* she thought. *The man in black isn't holding a sub machine gun.* Not one she could see. *Maybe he has a pistol with a silencer.* She waved foolishly. Then she recognized him. He was the fiddle player, the guy she had served two Bloody Marys this morning. He had been with that Catherine, the great bitch from Enid. *What the hell is he doing out here? And where in Hell is the great bitch from Enid?* Or was she still in the blackened car. When would the curtain go up?

The man stepped around the car and came toward her. He wasn't smiling. He looked like he needed something more important than a Bloody Mary. "Hi," she said. Someone had to say something.

"What are you doing here?" Wolf said quietly. "Trying to play the guardian angel again?"

"What are you doing here, is more to the point," she answered, holding her ground. "I don't think this is your kind of country."

"I'll make myself some space here, lady."

"Where's your friend? She afraid to get out of the car?"

"She's down in the bottom with your cowboy. I came back to pick her up when she's finished with him. Were you planning to join them?" There was a flicker of sadistic amusement on Wolf's thin lips. Kate did not like it.

"An old man fell over the edge of that cliff. I am here to help Parnell look for him, if that means anything to you." The lingering trace of evening light disappeared behind the western Rockies. The blush of red dimmed to shades of black. Any shadows now were cast by the pale moon rising over Tinaja. "I was just going to call to Parnell," Kate said. "I doubt if there is anyone with him. The sheriff left some time ago."

"I watched him go."

*What the hell is this guy doing with sun glasses on in the dark?* Kate thought. She started boldly past the man in black, keeping her eyes concentrated on the rim line of the canyon outlined in the moonlight. Kate moved boldly toward it. She was a step past the man in black when she felt him grip her right arm from behind.

"One man down and one to go. You, young lady, are not warning anyone."

Kate started to scream, but it never came out. She didn't know what stopped it. Her world was suddenly much blacker than it had been. She felt nothing. Wolf dropped the tire iron he had hit her with. He took the stiff leather Mexican lariat from Parnell's saddle and wrapped it around Kate's body a number of times before he cinched it down.

"I'm sorry you were here, but I guess it makes little difference how many bodies they find stacked up at the bottom tomorrow." He ripped a strip of cotton off her blouse to make a gag, in the off chance she came to. He had hit her awfully hard. She was bleeding badly. *A concussion at the least,* he thought. That thought didn't trouble him. Coolly, he dragged the body behind the south wall of the ruins. "Don't move," he said. "I doubt if you'll suffer." I only killed once before, and that was a woman too—and for Catherine, as well. When that bitch never returned to play the lead, Catherine filled her shoes—and my bed. The Cat played the role much better anyway."

The moon was now completely exposed. She lay on the stark plug that formed Tinaja's peak. Begrudgingly she lifted slowly into the clear sky. In an hour one would be able to see in the bottom of the canyon. High on the rim rock, Wolf, determined to fulfill his destiny. He watched the flickering of the small campfire Parnell had left burning by the sulfur pool below. From somewhere in the dim past, he recognized the flame's reflected glitter in that pool. He would find his way down. In this life, he would not be the one to take the fall. He would live. Wolf was pleased. He crossed to Parnell's horse. He tied up the reins and slapped the mare sharply on the rump. Diana headed back to Sully's ranch headquarters.

\* \* \*

In the dim light of the dying fire in the bat cave Catherine looked over Parnell's shoulder. Something was wrong. Wolf, barely visible, crouched on the shelf above. Her sight fading with her life, Catherine had no breath to speak a warning. Gathering her remaining strength she shook her head vigorously willing Wolf to hold. He did. He always did as she told him. While there was life in the lady he had followed for so long, he would not cross her—even now.

Wolf had landed on the shelf seconds before the shot was fired. There was nothing he could have done to stop it. The Cat was dead, or would be shortly. He would let her have her last moment. There was no rush. He would get his own back, his black revenge, when the move was sure. *The God-Damned doctor/cowboy would not get away with the final moment this time. He would pay dearly.* Parnell's death would fill the void of many guilty years the Romanian fiddle player had suffered. Parnell Mackenzie would not get away this time. The watcher stepped into deeper shadows. The maestro was in control of the strings.

Parnell lifted Catherine in his arms. "I know now, Cat." Catherine nodded, her eyes flooding her face with years of cruel understanding. "Forgive me," he whispered." She tried again to speak, but no words come. Her ravaged lungs produced nothing but a rose froth of fading life. Parnell kissed her face, her eyes. His tears washed down over her.

Wolf crept forward. The emotion witnessed below was too much for him. He was driven to act. Parnell, an easy mark, was completely vulnerable. Wolf took the rope in hand and prepared to swing down.

"It's done Katrina!" Old Toms voice shattered the moment. Wolf held, startled. Parnell whirled around. Catherine, still in his arms, shuddered and went completely limp in her moment of death. "I did it!" Tom cried out. "Just like you always said I could. I did it right this time. I am the only one now. The only one you have to dance for." The dying old man's voice grew weaker. "Dance, Katrina, Dance," young Tommy sighed, —for me—forever." He turned in and buried his face in the remnants of Katrina's dust. *Tom Sullivan, old and young, as one,* Parnell realized. *Old Tom Sullivan is now at rest. Young Tommy Sullivan is asleep. God rest him.*

They were both gone.

Tenderly, Parnell laid Catherine beside the body of Old Tom and the ghost dancer of his first true love—his Katrina—Parnell's Katrina—Cat—and—Catherine.

Kneeling beside them, Parnell spoke quietly. "Its come full circle, Cat. I guess we all belong together." Wolf held back into the shadows. Parnell stood with bowed head. "I'll come back for you—." He thought a moment. *Can I? May I?* Wolf listened as the dim gray of pre-dawn filtered down the chimney. It had been a long night.

"Perhaps, my love, I can," Parnell whispered, "In my stupidity, in my blindness, in our blindness, past and present, we destroyed a dream. But worse than that, through our ignorance we destroyed love and a boy who loved. Our biggest sin was that, Katrina. Here, in the darkness, it is all brought to a violent resting place.

"No," he spoke his mind softly. "I won't come back. No one will. This is the place you belong, Tommy, Catherine, Katrina. Whoever? Violence breeds a vengeful peace, but a lasting one. So be it. Rest in the arms of that peace. You have earned it."

\* \* \*

Parnell scraped the scattered coals of the fire together. Thin smoke rose into the gray light of the chimney hole. Parnell looked up. The fire wouldn't last long enough to draw attention to it.

\* \* \*

Wolf was no longer standing there. The rope Parnell never saw was gone. Parnell didn't think to question how Catherine got down into the cave. It was meant to be. He picked up the flashlight and in its dim rebirth of light took a last look at the bodies at rest. He reached down and touched Catherine one last time. Unconsciously picking up Tommy's old saddle gun, he made his way toward the lower cave entrance. It was all behind him now—It was once again behind him.

\* \* \*

When, thirty minutes later, Parnell crested the rim rock, the black 4X4 was nowhere in evidence. Parnell walked wearily to the ruins and leaned the old rifle against the sagging doorframe. He didn't step inside the empty walls, or look beyond.

231

Why had he brought the saddle gun? It made no sense. Musing on his past life, *or lives as it were, or was—or is,* he wandered back to the rim, to the spot where young Tommy had taken the dive—Where he himself had lost his footing and dropped to the narrow ledge ten feet below. Why had he not fallen to his death as the bird had planned? *The bird had planned it? Who knows? Someone had. It just hadn't worked out that way—at least not yet.* That thought gave him cold chills. Had he beaten fate?

Parnell didn't believe in God. How could any man of reason believe in God—in any god. Throughout his troubled life he had been forced to live with a belief in fate. The example of the past few days was proof enough of that. Fate had drawn him into Delmonico's Diner in Trinidad where Kate had turned his head back to the town of Rainbow. —Fate? Kate?

Kate, Catherine, Katrina? Were they all one? Kate had introduced him to Sully. Was Kate a valid member of the trinity? Or was she just an innocent tool? And what of the bird? The peregrine? As if in answer to his question, Parnell saw the falcon drop off of Tinaja's rocky peak. He watched her grow in size and reality as she soared toward the ruins she knew so well.

At the east rim of the canyon she stooped into its depth and skimmed the misting green slime of the pool. *Why don't you come for me, bird?* Parnell knew she had seen him. She could have circled around and, off guard as he was, hit him from behind. "Bird, you could have drilled me with your silver talons and sent me over the edge," he said aloud. *Why not?* He watched her in her silent beauty. She circled the pool and came to rest on the topmost bough of the big cedar tree. *Bird, what are you waiting for? What are you watching now?*

"You are as beautiful as The Cat—as Katrina, bird, certainly as graceful." He said his thought quietly. "If I thought I could hit you with Tom's old rifle, I'd put you at rest too. Your vigilance is over. There is no one else but me." Parnell studied the falcon for a long beat. *Why, bird? Will you try to finish it?* "Not with me, you won't. I'm the last and I am out of here. It's all behind me now. It's over!" He heard the falcon cry from her perch at the top of the cedar. Parnell sighed wearily and turned back to his truck. But it wasn't over.

# CHAPTER NINETEEN

# THE FINAL Chapter

"Shit." Parnell said .

Wolf, a look of desperate despair about him, stood in the door of the ruins. The nylon rope was about his shoulders. He held Tom's old rifle pointed at Parnell. Parnell heard the quiet but distinct click as he cocked it ready to fire.

"This is the end, Doctor Cowboy," Wolf said bitterly. "The music's over. We both lost. I guess this is what it's all about—." Holding the old 30-30 steady, Wolf started slowly toward Parnell, balanced on the mesa's tooth-sharp edge by Tommy's hiding rock. "Life is pretty damn cheap for a dancing cowboy."

"I'm not blind, fiddle man," Parnell answered quietly. He didn't move. He had no place to go. Forward was into the blast of Old Toms rifle, which he knew was capable of working. Backward was out of the question. "I guess your guess is as good as mine. But what we lived, took place before any of us were born—<u>into this life</u>." Parnell paused a moment, thinking, not about escape but the hopeless lack of that path. It was meant to be. Sully and the sheriff wouldn't be here for another hour. There was no escape. Parnell's only chance was to keep talking—to humor Wolf.

"The big mistake I made was coming home," he said, thinking of the past months in Rainbow. "I loved her, but who was I to own her, let alone be angered by her claim of freedom? Who were you, fiddle man? My mind went dry trying to remember who your were—until I saw you there, with young Tommy, by the fireplace."

Wolf kept closing the distance.

"It's not our fight, fiddle man," Parnell said quietly. "Put the gun down. We're pawns in some ridiculous game played by— damned if I know—? It's some dream-power we couldn't comprehend, but now we understand too clearly." Wolf was mentally unmoved. He kept coming.

"You killed her, doctor," he said quietly vicious. "Twice you killed her."

"You're crazy, Wolf. Think. This is impossible." Parnell was getting a bit desperate.

"I was there both times."

"Both times?" *That's a stupid remark.*

"Katrina and Catherine. —One and the same. Your macho jealousy killed Katrina. Young Tom's bullet was meant as reprisal for Katrina's death. Once again the truth was sidestepped, Doctor. You caused Catherine's death as sure as if you had fired this rifle yourself," Wolf cried triumphantly, justifying his actions. Wolf raised Tommy's 30-30 and sighted down the barrel. At a distance of ten feet Parnell watched Wolf's wild, unwavering eye framed in the splayed buckhorn sights. The rusting bead above the muzzle was centered in his pale blue iris.

Something clicked in Parnell's mind. It was a flash of hope. *Tom never levered out the spent shell after he fired at Catherine. I kicked the rifle from his hands. He had no time.* Parnell's mind was churning. He tried to hide his relief, a small enough ray of hope. If he were correct in his thinking. *I know I didn't jack in a new round. Why would I?* He kept talking.

"I don't know a God damned thing about the first time, Maestro. I'm not responsible for mistakes committed in a previous life—if such it was. Jesus Christ, Wolf, if nothing else, can't we learn from the past?" Wolf moved closer as Parnell talked. "Can't even a small slice of civilization benefit from our mistakes?"

Wolf's blank pale face twisted into a sarcastic grin. "Has the human element ever learned?" he said. Wolf held his ground, the muzzle of the rifle steady, now three feet from Parnell's chest. The crest of the rim rock was one step at Parnell's back. "Civilization recycles itself regularly but learns nothing from the gross blunders we continue to make in her name. Justice must prevail. Doctor Mackenzie, you killed her—you killed her twice."

Parnell couldn't argue with Wolf's logic concerning civilization, but continuing the conversation was better than the alternative. Wolf may possibly have loaded the chamber with a fresh round. *Do I take a chance?* He opted to keep talking. "Perhaps I learned." He said. "Who knows? I have been searching blindly for years for some lost cause—love, whatever. When I found Catherine, I knew I was close to an answer. I just didn't know the question. Neither did The Cat—or you. Jealously can spark absurdity. Look at the two of us. Fiddle man; look what jealousy is doing to you now? In mind and heart you are no better than the crazed husband who killed his wife and blew you, or your counterpart, over this edge in 1905. That man was as immoral and as insane as you are."

"You admit it!" Wolf cried, his thin lips trembling.

"I admit I know nothing but shadows of the past and the crazy story I heard from Old Tom; a story that turned my mind inside-out. That old man had been out of his mind for most of his life because of what happened—because of what we did to him—because of us. Tommy was out of his mind when he killed Catherine this morning. You, the three of us were here then as we are now. We drove that boy insane. We ruined Tom Sullivan's life, Fiddle Man."

"You. You killed Katrina!" Wolf cried. You ruined the boy's life. Don't blame me."

"We all ruined his life," Parnell cried. Parnell paused to consider the questions and the answers he had searched for, and now found. "We all ruined his life, Wolf, and so be it. And we all were drawn back here to pay for our sins in that previous life." Parnell looked past the fiddle player at the ruins. Smoke rose again from the ashes. "Will we ever suffer enough? I doubt it. Me, or whoever I was at the time, I may have loved Katrina; Catherine, call her as you will. I killed her. You killed her. We both killed her in our time. Didn't we?"

Wolf could not meet Parnell's accusing stare. He made no reply. Grasping at hope, Parnell went on: "But Wolf, Tommy

Sullivan was the one who paid with his life. He paid daily for years of his life. He paid with his youth day after day. We stole his hope and his trust. We ripped love from his heart, a much crueler fate than the simple death you suffered, that Katrina suffered and I as the original Dr. Parnell Mackenzie, went on to suffer for three drug addicted years after this place exploded in that night of madness, 1905. Now Tommy has killed Catherine. Who is to blame, Wolf?"

Parnell was talking for his life, but for once, believing what he was saying. "Tommy pulled the trigger, fiddle man, but we all loaded the gun."

"I was there," Wolf cried, thrusting the murdering rifle forward.

Parnell tried again to remember if Old Tom had ejected the spent cartridge. Had he done so? Was the chamber empty? If so, the hammer would fall on an empty chamber.

Parnell should never have taken the time to think. Wolf used the moment to answer the question. He ejected the empty shell. There was no more debate. The spent, green, molded, empty brass casing flew through the air and another took its place in the chamber. Parnell knew he had missed his chance. His heart sank.

"I was there!" Wolf cried again, tears of rage now streaming down his face. "I was too late to save her, but I saw it all. Tom's bullet was meant for you. Justice was not done."

"What has justice got to do with this Wolf? This is not a stage. The effects here are real."

Wolf jabbed the barrel of the rifle into Parnell's chest. "One step back in time, Cowboy."

"One step back and I'm over the edge with the rest of the players?"

"That's the plan, Doctor Cowboy."

Parnell made a grab for the rifle. If nothing else he might be able to drag the crazy fiddle player over the edge with him. Wolf read his move. He skipped out of reach just in time. "I didn't come this far to fail," he snarled.

"I'm not going to leave you a clean trail," Parnell cried. "You'll have to shoot. You'll be wanted for murder, Fiddle man. This is 1969, not 1905. You won't get away with it."

"Like you did, Doctor?" Wolf grinned triumphantly. "I'll take the chance." Calmly, Wolf pulled the trigger.

The hammer fell.

Nothing happened.

A misfire.

Parnell didn't give the fiddle man a chance to try a second time. He flew at him. Knocking the barrel of the rifle aside, he brought Wolf to the rocky ground with a jarring crash. Wolf Zimmerman fought like the mad man he was. The insanity of the moment pumped his adrenaline to the PSI extremity. Parnell was also desperate.

Neither was a trained fighter, but each man was fighting for his life. They employed thumbs, fingers, fists. Any low blow that presented an opportunity was used to whatever advantage. In a lucky slam for Wolf, Parnell's head crashed back against the sharp point of Tommy's hiding rock, knocking him senseless. Parnell's world spun out of control. When it steadied, the fiddle man stood over him with a fifty-pound boulder raised above his head.

On the periphery of Parnell's sight, someone stood in the background. Blood and dirt caked across a face he barely recognized. *Kate? What was she doing here?* She dragged a length of braded rope behind her.

Wolf saw her too, and turned distracted.

There was no time for Parnell Mackenzie to fantasize about a mythical savior. He rolled clear and grabbed Young Tom's saddle gun, knocked aside in the opening round. In one instinctive motion Parnell swung it up, cocked the hammer and pulled the trigger. The second blow of the firing pin on the seventy-year old copper cap struck fire. Wolf took the sphere of ancient lead under the chin. The blow threw him backward over the edge. He was dead before he took the plunge.

Parnell lay exhausted for some minutes. Then something touched his forehead. Something cool and soft. *The hand of a ghost,* he thought, eyes closed in the wonder of still being alive. *There have been too many ghosts of late.* Someone was trying to take the rifle from him. He jerked it back and opened his eyes.

"Kate?

"It's me."

"What happened?" His eyes focused on her bloody face and tangled hair. "For Christ sake, Kate. Did you come through Hell to get here?"

"With the fiddle player's help, yes. That son-of-a-bitch deserved to die, Parnell. Thank you for ending his plans. And what of you? You look like Hell, or one who has been there recently."

"I've been there, Kate. I hope I'm back."

"I'm no angel, Parnell. But I am here for you, if you want me. But no more dreams, OK?"

"Help me up, Kate, and keep me there. You are an angel, a live one. Forgive me for my sins of the past."

"With reservations, I'll forgive you, Parnell Mackenzie— with reservations."

"Sweet lady, you don't know the half of what you are saying."

\* \* \*

With Kate's help, and using Tommy's rifle as a crutch, Parnell pulled himself to his feet. He looked down into the canyon. "It's over, Kate. I hope it's over."

In the shadows of the depths the falcon swooped across the green pond and investigated the fiddle player's body. It had struck on the pinnacle of rock rising above the trampled brush. The fiddle man didn't move. The peregrine circled the body. Satisfied, she sailed over the green pool and settled once more in the topmost branches of the great cedar tree. There, she waited.

Parnell looked at the rifle in his hands and back at the peregrine. He knew the thought crossing his mind was a foolish one. Even if the next cartridge lined up in the old 30-30 and did fire, it was not meant for the bird.

"I'd probably miss anyway," he said aloud. The big peregrine, perhaps not totally trusting fate, lifted off the cedar limb
and rose quickly to a safe height. Parnell watched her. When she
was a dark spot in the first shaft of morning sunlight, he grabbed
the rusty rifle barrel with both hands and spun around, gathering
momentum like a discus thrower in ancient Greece. Once up to
speed, he let go. Young Tommy's rifle hurtled into space.

From the falcon's point of view the saddle gun spun in slow
motion out over the canyon until it splashed into the green slime
at the edge of the pool and sank into oblivion. Parnell, standing
silent on the canyon rim, watched the distant ripples settle. He
looked back into the sky. The bird was gone.

"It's over, Kate" he said quietly. "It's done. It's finished. And
I better get to hell out of here. There is not a judge or jury in the
country that will believe this shit."

"I don't know all of what you are saying, Parnell. I don't
understand, but I'm going with you."

"No Kate. Forgiving me is more than enough for you to
suffer. I need to get you to the emergency ward at the hospital.
That wound needs attention." She looked back at him in silence.

"Come." He led her to his battered Chevy and started the
engine. "Thanks to you, Kate, if I keep moving I'm free, at least
free of the past."

"What of your horse? Don't you want to pick up Diana?"

"I think Diana is owed to the Sullivan family—what is left
of that family. I borrowed her from them years ago. It's a payback. I wish all my debts were as easily paid. May this life be
the final scene."

As they passed the thick pinions they spotted the black
Chevy van parked in the shadows. The Sheriff would find it.

"I'm going with you, Parnell Mackenzie," Kate said with
quiet determination. "You have put me through too much shit to
leave me this far behind."

Parnell's hands clutched the wheel in silence.

"You heard me Parnell. Don't leave me at the hospital."

The old Chevy pickup grew small in the New Mexican dust.

At the ruins something flashed close across the frame of vision. The peregrine falcon, at ninety miles per hour, quickly overtook Parnell and Kate. She settled securely on the headache rack above the cab and stared through hooded eyes, into time and space ahead.

## The End

Tinaja, New Mexico 23/APR./2010
La Veta Colorado, 1/31/2013

CPSIA information can be obtained at www.ICGtesting.com
Printed in the USA
LVOW081046060613

337263LV00002B/452/P